I0642276

David Gilmour

Reminiscences of the Pen' Folk

Paisley Weavers of other Days. Third Edition

David Gilmour

Reminiscences of the Pen' Folk
Paisley Weavers of other Days. Third Edition

ISBN/EAN: 9783744768719

Printed in Europe, USA, Canada, Australia, Japan

Cover: Foto ©Andreas Hilbeck / pixelio.de

More available books at **www.hansebooks.com**

REMINISCENCES

OF

THE PEN' FOLK

PAISLEY WEAVERS

OF

OTHER DAYS

&c.

BY

DAVID GILMOUR

THIRD EDITION

ALEX. GARDNER

PUBLISHER TO HER MAJESTY THE QUEEN

PAISLEY; AND 12 PATERNOSTER ROW, LONDON

1889

PREFACE TO PRIVATE EDITION.

IT may be proper to explain why the distinctive name "Pen Folk" came to be given to the Christian brotherhood I have written about.

In the year 1723 the Paisley authorities resolved to remove the old Alms-House, then situate on the north side of High Street, and to rebuild a more commodious structure on the site. This was done in the following year, when there was added a Public Hall for meetings of the various Corporations, with a steeple and bell in connection with the Alms-House. The steeple, placed in the centre of the Alms-House, abutted on the pavement, and had three horologes—seen from east, south, and west; the north side being towards the hill immediately behind, it was deemed unnecessary to place one there. A stair on the east side of the steeple led to the Public Hall, and on the west side was an arched passage or "Pend"—familiarly pronounced "Pen"—the upper portion of which still remains —leading backwards from High Street to Oakshaw Hill. In 1808 both the Alms-House and the "wee" Steeple, as it had come to be called after the erection of its taller brethren of the "Cross" and "High Church," were taken down, and replaced by the property at present numbered 82 High Street.

Simultaneously with the taking down of the "wee" Steeple and Alms-House, Orr Square was laid off, by which a new passage was given to Pen Lane, and to the Baptist Meeting-house erected on the east side of it.   Paisley has long been proverbial for giving distinctive names to peculiar habits or idiosyncracies, whether of a personal, social, or religious character ; hence, nothing was more natural than that the congregation whose meeting-house was in the Pen Close should come to be known as the " Pen Folk."

I certainly had no idea that what I wrote for the *Gazette* was worth the distinction of separate publication, but on this point I have yielded to the request of certain friends who cherish a fond remembrance of the good old pioneers of the " Pen."   Never having hitherto entered openly the fraternity of authors, I allow my bantling to go forth without the name of its parent ; still I must confess to the solicitude of one who, seeing the first efforts of his child to walk alone, consoles himself with the reflection that if the babe falls, it falls into loving arms.   So, then, I commend it to the reader—

> " Besekyng hym lowly, of mercy and pité,
>   Of its rude makyng to have compashon."

PAISLEY, *June,* 1871.

PREFACE TO SECOND EDITION.

M Y Publishers tell me I must say a word or two of a private nature to the Public, by way of Preface.

Few people in the West of Scotland have not heard of the cobbler in Beith parish who, having arrived at the responsible age of seventy, finding that his education had been neglected in youth, cast aside his lapstone and awls, and took lessons in dancing. Well, my appearing as author is excusable, on the ground that the *step* is not more unwise than his. I am sure that he was not more surprised at his success, than I was at the kindly reception which the Private Edition of these Reminiscences received from those it reached. There is this difference between the cobbler and me, however—he, from seventy upwards, adopted dancing as a profession, whilst I, in all probability, will "rest on laurels won"—such as they are. Had more time been at my disposal when the Papers appeared in the *Gazette* as an obituary notice, other incidents quite as interesting would have been added; but taking the cobbler as a warning, I kept hold of my lapstone; and for the same reason I have thought it best to allow the present edition to go forth exactly as the former, with the exception of a few verbal alterations and the incorporation of some notes into the text. Whether any additions appear or not during my life-time will depend entirely on how business-matters claim my attention.

I have dedicated the re-issue to Dr. JOHN BROWN, author of *Rab and his Friends,* as a feeble expression of my gratitude to him as a writer; from whom, too, came the first note of public *heartening* to re-publish the *brochure* and to acknowledge its paternity.

DAVID GILMOUR.

PAISLEY *May,* 1873.

THE "PEN FOLK."

"At 31 Wellmeadow, Paisley, on the 31st ult., Mr. William Dickie, aged 94 years."

SUCH was the obituary notice, in the *Paisley and Renfrewshire Gazette* of January 7th, 1871, of that venerable man—the last link remaining in this country of a brave, hale-hearted band, who stood forth in defence of ecclesiastical freedom at a time when its champions were few and dissent reckoned akin to infidelity. He outlived all his compeers, and, at his great age, all worth living for, except the fulfilment of his Father's promise of the "rest that remaineth," in which he had unwavering trust.

To the younger generation of his brethren some traits of the child-like simplicity, and genuine though unconscious humility of William Dickie, might now and then become apparent; but those only who enjoyed his confidence could estimate the value of his rare truthfulness, and, under a somewhat brusque manner, the womanly tenderness of his affections. Those to whom he was not known might have readily concluded, from a casual interview, that he was ignorant, vulgar, bigoted; yet such judgment would have been beside the truth on each point. He was not an educated man; indeed, few who labour as he did for his daily bread can be reckoned educated—in the popular acceptation of the term. But few even of the educated class are so well informed; and fewer still generalise their knowledge, or trace the connection between one topic and another with such clearness and accuracy of detail, as did old William Dickie. He was plain-spoken, but never rude, never vulgar; and his apparent bigotry arose from his thorough honesty, and the directness which springs from strong loving conviction. His unassuming geniality and deep sympathy with the afflicted, and quiet open-handed liberality to the poor, will not be readily forgotten by those to whom he ministered; yet to the most intimate of his friends he seldom, if ever, complained of his own troubles, which through his long life were almost unremitting. But many who, long ago, listened to his opening prayer on First-day mornings, were often moved to tears at perceiving the undercurrent of thanksgiving for sorrows overcome. Of that prevalent piety which *seeks* a blessing, he was unobtrusive, if not deficient; but his life was a beautiful exhibition of the Christian love which yearns continually to bless others. As the door of the soul's audience-chamber opens from within outward, influx is in proportion to efflux, and the blessing received is measured by the blessing conveyed to others—so his peace was fretless and almost unclouded. We therefore discard the traditional " Peace be with him," and pray rather that his peace may be ours. His gifts as a " speaker," in his younger years, were very extraordinary— as, indeed, were those of many of his co-worshippers; and although oratory was perhaps too much undervalued, their thorough acquaintance with the subject in hand, and their highly-flavoured zeal, gave their utterances a piquancy that in finer-turned periods is altogether wanting. Whatever of eloquence of voice or tongue they possessed, was the result of sincerity and earnestness, the true basis of all real eloquence; and these were the distinguishing features of the "connection" at the time to which I refer. But "speaking," even on Lord's-day, was regarded by them as only a refreshment before the duties of the new week—(for, unlike the Jews, who *labour toward* rest, they *wrought from* it)—a week of keeping themselves unspotted from the world as became gospel Christians. This was almost the constant theme of exhortation.

The memory of the Pen Folk has now nearly died out. My late friend was the last of the generation in this hemisphere. But "when the century was in her teens," what a band they were of single-minded, energetic, "knowledgeable" men! Amongst others, Thomas Taylor and his brother John, with their genial warmth and joyous exhibition of "the promises;" James Thomson, with his gentle manner and mild voice, urging conciliatory admonitions to love the household of faith; James Craw and Archibald M'Gee, with their bundles of proofs; Sandy M'Kay, Will Gilmour, and William Dickie, snuffing heresy (as Ephraim did the east wind) from afar; and Archy Hastie, William M'Lerie, and Archibald M'Killop the souter, turning the edge of discord with their fine humour, which, where every man, ay, and every woman too, was his or her own Pope, required both wit and wisdom. Of James Craw, an old man when I was a boy, it was understood that he lived very unhappily with his wife, in consequence of her drinking habits, through which she met with a violent death. Rumour said he assisted her to fall into the river at Sneddon Bridge; but as in other respects he was a good citizen, and there being

no proof available of his complicity, the matter was allowed
to drop.   During his last illness, now nearly fifty years ago,
he requested my father, "as presiding elder," to visit him;
and I recollect being ordered to bed, in the early gloaming
of a June evening, by my mother—and sorely against my
will I went.   Not to sleep, however, it was too early for
that; and, besides, as I knew where father had gone, I
resolved to wait and learn the result.   By and by my
mother quitted her wheel, and having trimmed and lit
the lamp, sat down by the fireside to read.   After a while,
hearing father's step on the stair, I feigned sleep.   My
mother having laid down her book, I heard her approach
my bed, and I *knew* she had the lamp with her to ascertain
if I was not listening.   Satisfied that I had "fallen over,"
she tucked the bedclothes round me, drew the curtains, set
the lamp on the table, and opened the door.   As soon as
they were seated, I peered past the bed curtain, and held
my breath lest I might be discovered or miss a word of the
conversation.   To my astonishment there was utter silence
for some moments.   At length mother said,

"Hast thou seen James?"

"Yes, I have."

"Is he vera ill?'

"Vera ill, indeed—deein'."

"Deein', didst thou say?"

"Yes; he was in the dead-thraws or I left—the turn o'
the nicht 'll bring a change."

"Had ye ony talk wi' ither?"

"Deed, wife, we had talk—pleasant talk."

"What did thou say to him?"

"I tauld him, amang ither things, that he had come **to**

the honest hour, and that if there was onything on his mind
that prevented him getting comfort frae Gospel promises, it
behooved him to make confession before he appeared at the
judgment bar of the Lord."

" An' what said he?" asked my mother timidly.

" It's nane o' thy business, wife, what he said. Let us
pray."

And amidst tears and groans they prayed together, sometimes the one and sometimes the other.

It is sometimes objected that the occasional disputes and
differences that have arisen in churches governed on democratic principles are proof that democracy is unworkable,
and that church courts are indispensable. I have been a
spectator at meetings of almost every form of Presbyterian
" Church Court" held in Scotland, and my opinion is that,
whilst in these courts there have been plans to carry the
Gospel to the heathen, plans for church extension at home,
and other kindred objects, deemed of equal importance in
self-governed churches, there have been in the latter a
greater amount of true courtesy, deeper sympathy for each
other's well-being, a stronger yearning to bring souls to
Christ, and far, far less bitterness of spirit and acrimony
in party strife than were manifested in the former. Men's
ideal is generally better than their practice; but were the
objection valid, we might with equal propriety say that the
dreadful shortcomings of Christians are proof that Christianity itself is unfitted for human requirements. Democratic
government is the only one that is in harmony with a Gospel
brotherhood, because it alone recognises the Divine declara-
tions in their simplicity, " All ye are brethren," and " *One* is
your Master, even Christ." Presbytery in any form ignores

that brotherhood, because it involves a self-perpetuating order of men, to whom the laity is to some extent subservient; whilst Episcopal and Papal rule exclude the brotherhood altogether, and make the church to consist of its officials, reminding one of the regiments we formed in our boyhood, which were wholly composed of corporals, captains, and colonels. Democracy, however, is obnoxious to the great ecclesiastical trades-unions of Christendom, whose chief use in our day resembles that of custom-houses, where officers levy a tariff on the products of the earth bound heavenward, prohibit *unsound* articles, and consign them to destruction. On this subject my old friends were wont to exclaim—" Why standest thou afar off, O Lord? Why hidest thou thyself in times of trouble?"

And then the wives of the Pen! But I cannot trust myself to speak of those quiet, sensible, queen-like mothers, who, in the maturity of repose, sat during the intervals of worship in the cozy nook of the meeting-house, distributing the " promised bread" and something *till't* from their ample pocket-stores to all comers; bending at times the too general conversation to some case of pressing need in the brotherhood; now suggesting a remark that " made for peace" when discussion ran high, or appealing decisively to the law and the testimony on disputed points of doctrine or discipline;—in every circumstance evincing a love of the brethren and a knowledge and appreciation of the principles which knit them in the bonds of fellowship, yet never assuming a position that was not theirs by Nature or prescription. Such gems, thank God, may be found here and there in every church, but nowhere since have I found such a group of motherly women. The race seems to have been scattered over all the churches, perhaps to leaven the mass of womankind in general. One injunction of these mothers in Israel exercised, I believe, a more beneficial influence over their young than all the church accessories of modern times put together. It was this: the children of each family were to call every matron in the connection "Aunty." I had half-a-dozen Aunty Jeans, and as many Aunty Maries and Aunty Margarets, who were in no way related to me "according to the flesh." Those who have not experienced the benefits arising from the use of this name cannot know the humanising power it had over our young hearts, nor can they understand the influences for good it had on the minds of those to whom it was applied. Several of these matrons were childless, and hailed from other towns; and having no blood-relations in our locality, the kindly epithet made them feel part of the other families, the children of which were cherished accordingly. And there grew a stronger love between the families, such as no mere teaching can impart. More than fifty years have passed, and yet, when I meet the descendants of Aunties of the Pen Kirk, I feel the old kindly affection welling up strong within me, and I would gladly do them service. And I know that in families resi-dent for upwards of forty years in "thae weary Colonies"— one on a bleak hill-side in Nova Scotia, and two labouring at mills in Lowell—the Aunties of the Pen Kirk are still held in loving remembrance. Heaven bless their posterity everywhere!

The old meeting-house in the Pen itself has undergone many transformations since its original proprietors ceased to occupy it. At one time the followers of Robert Owen proclaimed the orphanhood of mankind within its walls;

and many a fight took place, and much fun was got, when some of the wags came and fought for the family hearth against Owen's dogma of free-love. There, too, strangely enough, the Saints of the Latter-Day advocated the same doctrine from the gospel of Joseph Smith. Again, it was the scene of some displays of singular ability when used by the Literary and Convivial Association. The late William Stewart, teacher, by his geniality and intellectual pith long sustained the vitality of the L.C.A.; but since he left Paisley for Canada, where he died, there have been in the L.C.A. no collection of men equal to him and his associates in vigour and amiability. I am afraid that all such gatherings having for a basis intellectual research and dram-drinking, are destined to corrode or wither. Since the exodus of the L.C.A., the place has seen other changes. At one time it was a dancing school; at another time there was gathered in it the nucleus of our flourishing Ragged School; and now it is used as a joiner's shop,—a trade for ever hallowed by the labours of One who had not where to lay his head.

How well I remember its original interior appearance! Against the west gable, below and between the gable windows, stood the pulpit; in front of which, and facing the passage running to the east gable, where stood the stove with a long red-hot pipe, was the precentor's desk. At either side the pulpit were the elders' seats, on a level with the others, which were so placed that all the occupants looked towards the presiding elder. The large space round the stove was filled with forms, and was set apart for social intercourse between services, and there love-feasts were eaten. I used to think these glorious times. The old people acted wisely, while enjoying themselves in their own way, in allowing us youngsters to have the run, not only of the feasts, but of the church. The only restraint experienced was when the most *unruly* boy was requested to bring a can of water, and, treated to an extra tit-bit, *told to keep the ithers a wee "quaiter."* Pawky old codgers!

Besides the regular rank and file and their families, there were the occasional hearers—wanderers; and the constant attenders, — waverers, doubters, outsiders, as they were variously named, good ordinary people for the most part, —unattached hangers on to the skirts of my old friends. Some of these I knew well. They unconsciously contributed more amusement to us young folks, and more subjects of gossip to our elders, than was healthful for either. They were types of classes existing now, as then, in society, — men whose idiosyncracies are too marked to escape observation and criticism. Of such, I remember several in particular who were refused membership; and others that would have been gladly received, but declined. One of these was Alexander Wylie, hailing from Kilbarchan. Regularly once a year for many years, on the first Sunday in March,—"Craw Sunday," as it was called, from its being then thought that on that day the crows commenced housekeeping for the year,—Sandy appeared in a front seat and made profession of his faith, with a view of being admitted, consuming therewith the time usually set apart for edification. Seeing him seldom, I cannot speak from personal knowledge of his character, but I understood him to have been a good man, and much esteemed by the connection, yet so dreadfully unsound in doctrinal matters, that several of the brethren, although they entertained him at their homes during his yearly visit, were with difficulty withheld from thrusting him out of the meeting-house. It was great fun to us young folks, who had counted the weeks, lessening as they passed, till the old man would re-appear. One memorable day, just as he was about to issue his programme, the presiding elder asked if he held the same "views" as he did the previous year; and he unfalteringly answered in the affirmative. The elder then asked the church if they were disposed to hear Mr. Wylie; and the vote being taken, the "noes" had it. Poor Wylie, taken quite aback by such a mode of procedure, suddenly collapsed; and though he continued on friendly terms with the Pen Folk, he never again applied for membership. Latterly, I believe, he adopted the doctrines of the Apostolic Catholic Church, and travelled frequently to Glasgow on Sundays for such nourishment as that body had to bestow. He was quite an Ishmaelite in tongue fence, and, it was said, "wud hae foucht wi' the win'" had it been possible; but although he continually waved his red flag and employed dreadfully hard language, he was open-handed and sweet-voiced to the poor and needy.

Another of the unattached was James Andrew—or, as he was familiarly called, big Jamie An'rew. He was one of those slovenly, loosely-clad mortals, whose habiliments appear as if made for somebody much larger than themselves. Everything he wore, from hat to shoes, was too large for him; the former was partly without brim, the latter frequently without laces; stockings without garters; kneebreeches unbuttoned; coat and vest flying in the wind. He was of cleanly habits, however, and appeared so, notwithstanding the spoonfuls of snuff he threw into his nostrils; was of huge unwieldy dimensions; and he sidled up to you, snuff-box in one hand and handkerchief in the other, in a soft, uncertain way, not unlike the manner of a young Newfoundland dog, which you are afraid is about to lay its paws on your breast and lick your face. His face beamed with good nature; he had the softest hands and voice, and mild, liquid, soft eyes, reminding one of one's mother's. To men, women, and boys he was uniformly the same genial, earnest, humble man—full of warmth and downright honesty; too honest to profess a truth of which he had the faintest doubt, and esteeming himself too unworthy to be called a Christian. He had been a sailor in his youth, which seemed to have developed in him a firm reliance on the fatherliness, and a clear poetical perception of the greatness, of God. The " connection," admiring the unsophisticated simplicity of the man, and the blamelessness of his life, would have received him with open arms, overlooking, hopefully, certain unsoundnesses in doctrine; but there was always a "lion in the way," he said, and until he got his conscience nailed under hatches he would wait. Sometimes he was much affected during the delivery of an exhortation; and when, on such occasions, any of the brethren who had perceived his eyes brimful would afterwards refer to the beauty of the remarks, expecting him to declare himself, his answer usually was, "It's no the beauty o' the truth, but the beauty o' the earnestness that pleases me; whatever doots I hae, it's very plain tae me they hae nane; it's a' as shure's death wi' them." And, with a sigh, he added, "It's very beautiful; 'deed it is." His loyalty to truth was unbounded, and his reverence for wise and good men of dog-like humility; but he had no tolerance of assumed sanctity and religious gossip—*i.e.,* the relation of personal experience or official formalism, which, he contended, were the natural enemies of true spiritual life.

John Killoch, a companion of Andrew, was also a regular visitor at the Pen, and acted as a sort of nightmare to the connection. He was a bean of a different kidney from James Andrew, yet they were for years as inseparable as light and shade. He was a little spare man, with large, rheumy, bloodshot, unsteady eyes, heavy under-jaw, and open, flabby, purposeless mouth; wore buckle-shoes, gray worsted stockings, cord kneebreeches; wine-coloured jockey-coat, buttoned to the chin; a discoloured hat, turned up behind, as if disgusted with the drab-coloured wig on which it rested. Many may yet remember the fussy little man, as he hurried along, stooping over the books of friendly societies for which he was officer; his watchchain having sundry rings, small shells, and coins attached, rattling like snakes as they bobbed from side to side. His manner was humility personified, and strangers were deceived by the seeming odour of sanctity that hung about him. He was, nevertheless, a man in whom self-esteem and self-sufficiency were abnormally developed. His " views," without crack or flaw, were perfectly sound—too sound, in fact, for even the Pen Folk, who were as resolute in excluding him as they were solicitous to admit Andrew. He had formerly been in connection, but had for some reason withdrawn. They thought him a "dour man, wi' an extraordinar' grip o' gospel truth, but withoot ony evidence o' Christian goodness." What they believed and sighed over as inscrutable decrees, Johnny gloried in as beautiful exhibitions of sovereignty. Total depravity, reprobation, and particular election—his own particularly—were leading topics in his conversation. He was, he said, not a sinner— he was a lump of sin; would not own to having broken any commandment, and of course never had occasion to repent; but, as it were, lay in Abraham's bosom all the year round, undazzled by the blaze of the noon of heaven. Had his life been as humble as it appeared to be, and as blame- less as he said it was, his opinions might have been recog- nised as the fossils of a previous theologic formation, and handled as curiosities. He had all the qualities of a fanatic, except the amiability and rectitude which not unfrequently accompany fanaticism.

What tie, then, could subsist between Andrew and Killoch that kept them such intimate friends? The answer is, Johnny conceived the noble idea of converting Andrew, who sturdily to the end denied being a lump of sin—con- tending that he was only a sinner—"a puir wan'ert bairn oot in the dark, glammerin' for my Faither's han', an' as yet hadna gotten a grip o 't. But if thou's a lump o' sin, whiles thou maun dae wrang; an' a' wrangdaeing is sin," said Andrew.

"But," answered Killoch, "thou 's aye speaking o' sin, sin, as if it werena a' cancelled, and the morality a' done by our conscript."

"Tell me, then," replied Andrew, "is thou never tempted tae dae what thy better judgment tells thee is wrang, an' hoo does thou then proceed ?"

"Weel," said Johnny, "I am; an' I hae tried a' the ways o 't; an' I fin' the best is the easiest : I yield till 't."

"Noo, ae ither question, an' I 'll hae gotten the backbane

o' the maitter. At sic times does thy conscience no gie thee a twitching?"

"Oo," quo' Johnny, "weel, I get whiles a glouf o' conscience, but I aye get twa gaups o' gratification afore han'."

"O Johnny, Johnny, tak' an auld neighbour's word for 't, thou's just as Maggie Lowe was when she kissed her image i' the looking-glass; an' I tell thee plainly, the sorra a bit o' me believes *that* tae be gospel."

What reason Andrew would have given for their intimacy I cannot imagine. They were continually wrangling on some knotty point, Johnny nervously pelting his friend with texts of Scripture, which Jamie answered with what he quietly called "scraps o' common-sense, which," he averred, "couldna be contrar' tae God's common-sense, as we have it i' the Book, if we only got a haud o 't." Thus, I recollect another occasion, when Killoch had finished an oration on the reprobation of unbelievers' infants, which brought tears raining over Andrew's honest face, which tears Johnny accepted as the fruits of conviction, but was undeceived by Jamie saying,

"Answer me this, Johnny—thou hast nae bairns; but were it tae please God tae send thee and Janet ane or twa, could thou hae the heart tae pre-damn them?"

"Does thou think that I, a Christian man, am a monster?"

"No, Johnny; only I think thou believes God Almichty tae be an awfu' ane."

And thus they went on day after day, but always parting as they had met—good friends.

Killoch, like other childless men, had wonderful theories

about the training of children. Andrew, like many who
were blessed with families, had formed beautiful maxims
on that subject by the time his boys reached manhood.
During their boyhood, however, the care of their upbringing
sat as easy on him as did his unbuttoned vest. That duty
was left to his trim, apple-cheeked wife, to whom all differences were referred, and whose decision was final. I question if care or anxiety could have availed to break them to
Killoch's yoke. Not that the lads were disobedient, indo-
lent, vicious, or wild in any way, only that the house was a
sort of liberty-hall, where each ruled himself, and others
when necessary; where all speech and action were tried by
a kind of natural justice and "scraps o' common-sense."
Even Killoch's authoritative "I tell you!" had to pass
through the fire of the youngest's wit, were that personage
so disposed. Books, then a rarer commodity than now,
were scattered over every available spot in the large kitchen,
and in great demand after the day's labour. Milton, Burns,
Shakspeare, and volumes of the *Spectator* might be found
mixed in admirable confusion with *Brown's Commentary
and Concordance*, Bunyan, Bibles, and *The Questions*. Next
to *Joshua's Wars*, Shakspeare was the book of books, however; and the attendance of the boys at the theatre in Bank
Street was more frequent than at the Pen Kirk. They were
intimate with all the players, and descanted confidently, if
not accurately, on their respective merits. But they discussed the merits of the Pen speakers with as much freedom
as they did those of Willie Johnston or Simon Byrne (the
two theatrical stars of the period), and stated very explicitly
that the "intervals" were more to their liking than "kirk
time," which, they averred, "was a' soliloquey thegither."

Latitude without restraint was permitted to all and sundry, except on the matter of personal gossip, which the mother disallowed, and when begun generally contrived to end, either by telling a story or chanting some ancient ballad. And although it was a merry, orderly, amiable group, Killoch, with uplifted hands, denounced his friend's method, or want of method, as loose and unchristian, and the boys as evidences of total depravity.

"I'm no just sure," said Andrew on one occasion, "o' ca'ing ony ane reprobate, Johnny. Thou minds that veesion Peter had o' a tooal or tablecaith let doon fu' o' a' kin's o' beasties? Weel, I whiles think it was an image o' human kin', whilk cam' first frae the Lord's haun, an' let doon frae heeven, an' I'm no clear tae ca' ony o' His handiwork common or unclean. At ony rate, my bairns are gude, honest, biddenable lads, an' that's nae lee;" and as if to conciliate Killoch, he invited wee Bobby to recite young Norval's address, which Bobby did to the evident delight of his parents, amid the cheers of his brothers, who, with book in hands, gazed admiringly. Killoch was horrified, and made for the door; but James, in an earnest, calm voice, begged him to remain and take part in the evening worship.

"Worship!" quoth Killoch, "does thou tak' the books at e'en, Jamie?"

"Oo ay," answered Andrew, "doots or no doots, we maun seek licht an' guidance—licht an' guidance."

Meantime Bobby, willing to exhibit his powers, stood with arms outstretched towards his mother, vociferating that his voice was still for war, at which Johnny made his escape. James quietly and silently took down the "books" preparatory; and then the young dramatist knelt at his

mother's knee and repeated his evening prayer. " He
liked," he said, " tae fa' asleep at the singing; it was sae
nice tae hear mither sing." Poor Bobby, after he had
grown to " Bob," fell asleep at the head of his company,
an elderly man, under the singing of musketry at the siege
of Lucknow. Killoch adjourned to the Star Inn, where he
sat till overtaken by " chaos and old night," after which the
snakes sprung their rattles during his *transverse* trot home-
wards. On such occasions his language was awfully profane ; but his worst *un*-friends admitted that he never swore
unless when under the influence of strong potations.

Mrs. Killoch was a tall, spare, grim woman, who by a
previous marriage had several children, whom she trained
to obedience under the silent system. It were easier to say
what she hated than what she loved, although her hatreds
indicated strong affection of a certain sort. Innovations,
theories, propositions, suggestions tending to disturb the
existing order of things, called forth at all times a portion
of her latent heat on the instant. She was a League-and-
Covenant Christian, held all Johnny's views on "essentials"
with intensified zeal; and, as in duty bound, hated the Pen
Kirk and all its belongings with uncompromising hostility.
Some said, however, that her daily tirades against my old
friends were only her methods of scolding Johnny, and
that, had his " walk and conversation" been squared to her
ideas of propriety, she would have fought indeed, yet ultimately yielded to their theories ; but that the excessive
leeway he continually made had turned to gall her true
womanly nature. As it was, Johnny, unless he excited her
indignation with his " fusionless abominations," had to
endure her society under enforced silence. She never

condescended to lecture him directly, and, so far as appearances went, they enjoyed much domestic peace—a little quiet, perhaps; but then, they were into years, and *severe* Christians too. It must have been much too quiet and solemn for the children, sitting for hours at a stretch on the evenings Johnny was at home, never hearing a word said except when she nudged him across the draught-board to say, by way of indicating the successive moves on her side of the game, 25 27, or when half an hour after, he responded, 13 15, and then relapsed into his choking snore.

Perhaps, because he required repose, or because he wished to conciliate his wife, he spent the evening following the visit I have related with Andrew at home; and as usual, nothing for a while was heard but the numbers of the draught-board, as from time to time another shift was made. By and by, however, Johnny began to retail, with emendations his conversation with Andrew, but without response from his caustic partner, till he told how high his friend's boys stood in their father's estimation, when she exclaimed wrathfully, "An' has Jamie An'rew the brazen audacity tae think or say his unchristened brats 'll be putten on a level wi' ma Christian bairns wi' the Almichty! My truly! but he 's fu' o' conceit, for a' his pretended humbleness—28 14. An' it 's ten o'clock. Beds." And then the youngsters crept noiselessly to their comfortable cribs, where, later in the night, when every one else was asleep, she bent over each, covering up and tucking them in with much tenderness, her usually hard features betraying a world of unspoken love—the blessings she cooingly invoked being strangely at variance with her dreadful theory of the Divine government.

The style of exhortation amongst the Pen Folk was conspicuously diversified. One brother delighted in shewing the ugliness of sin ; another in denouncing the heresy of Arminianism, which he described as an attempt " tae big hauf-gable wi' the Lord ;" a third preferred to portray the loveliness and harmony of revealed truth ; whilst others, and they were a large majority, inculcated purity of mind and life. Each member of the brotherhood, starting from the same premises, was led by his own perception of the subject to shake hands, as it were, with his brother at the opposite extreme ; but, as with the celebrated sheep's head, there was " a deal o' confused feedin'" in some of their prelections. Young as I was, there was to my mind something outrageously grotesque in the appearance of Daniel (pronounced Dawnial) Cameron, as he rose in his pew, Bible in hand, spectacles astride his nose, the end of his cutty-pipe cropping from under the pocket-flap of his waistcoat, craving attention to "a few stray remarks on a passage in Hebrews." Hebrews was "Dawnial's" decalogue and lawgiver, profound and inexhaustible. Once a month, at least, he returned to his exposition,—complex, diffuse, and sadly in want of arrangement. He was the prime favourite, nevertheless, with the boys ; for he frequently rose to make his " few stray remarks " about dismissal time ; when invariably our mothers severally handed us the door-key with strict injunctions, given in severe undertones, to "gae straucht hame, an' swee aff the kail pat, an' we'll be back gin five oors at e'en ;" and then we were free to enjoy ourselves, vaulting over the gravestones in the neighbouring churchyard, to the detriment now and then of the " kail." I am afraid we were unpromising, if not bad boys; not overburdened with reverence for our elders *qua* Elders. One of us dubbed the old man Melchisedec; and as the title was thought appropriate by the others, I ventured at dinner one day during the following week to give the nickname currency; but the horror which overspread every countenance, and the "rap" that made my ears ring for hours after, did not encourage its repetition.

Cameron was a '93 "black-neb" Democrat, and had a great fund of solid information on almost every subject then known. He was held in high esteem by the Encyclopædia Club, of which he was a member; and although he always provoked a smile from me, the Pen Folk held him in veneration for what they called his "sterling" qualities. But sterling is often applied where "rigid and unbending" would be more appropriate; and it was so in his case. He was one of those passionless men one sometimes meets with, who, never having experienced the mental conflict of resisting unsanctified appetites, had no sympathy with human weakness, and no mercy where he had the power to castigate; for, however sincere the contrition or unreserved the confession of offending brethren, Dawnial was severely "honest" in his dealing with their frailty. The wound was in every case laid open and bare, and scraped to the bone before the salve was applied, and even then there was none of *that* wasted. He could not understand how men violated principles which they had accepted as rules of life. You would have thought, from his account, that if ever he had been subject to unholy desires, they were dead and buried in obedience to the behests of "duty," and that he was at all times prepared for marching orders. And yet there was one small crevice in his armour visible to all men,

and a few boys,—its name was Vanity. In his younger
years he had been famous in his district at singlestick, had
a good tenor voice, and was unequalled for miles round
as a dancer; and although these gifts had long ago fallen
into disuse, as being evil or tending to evil, he frequently
boasted of what he had done, or could do; and from this
little weakness arose a most humorous incident in the good
man's life, in this way :—

Francis Stewart, a neighbour of his, whose wife was dead,
having occasion to leave home for a day and night, committed the oversight of his family to Daniel, who, as he sat
on his doorstep meditating at eventide, smoking his clay
pipe, was startled by the noise of music and laughter
issuing from his friend's domicile. Short time was needed
for him to stow away his black consoler, and buckle to
the rescue. "Tapping" most urgently at "the chamber
door," which was quickly opened, he was welcomed by the
youngsters, who had gathered for a reel at the invitation
of Aggie Stewart, with such evident delight that he quite
forgot the object of his mission. They placed him in the
cosiest chair, handed him Francis's pipe, gave him a mug of
homebrewed, and made him feel comfortable; and then
one of the young rascals, who knew his weakness, taunted
him with inability to compete with the lads present in
threading the mazes of a country dance. Daniel bore the
taunts for a time meekly, as became a Christian; but flesh
is flesh,. and as he eyed the sylph-like figure of Aggie
Stewart tripping a new step to the delectation of her friends,
visions of other years so obliterated the present from his
consciousness, that the Pen Kirk, the Encyclopædia Club,
and with them the experience and responsibilities of sixty

years, became as the vision of a dream; and for once, like
other men under similar circumstances, he adopted the fatal
alternative of yielding to the tempter: for, laying aside his
pipe, and adjusting his Kilmarnock cowl with great deliberation, he not only led a slip of a girl to the other end of the
apartment, and danced a reel, but having again "kissed the
tankard," actually volunteered "Jacky Tar." This was all
and more than was wanted; and as he, panting after the
exertion, wiped the perspiration from his brow, one of the
young scamps confessed his inability to compete with
Daniel, at the same time suggesting that he ought to start
as "professional." It was then old Melchis. discovered the
trap into which he had fallen, and he groaned internally at
the enormity of his sin. It was wicked of the young vaga-
bonds to disturb the old man's peace of mind, although
there was no sin, as I think, on his part. But stern old
Daniel thought otherwise; for on the following First-day
morning, he rose and made confession of his sin, adding
that henceforth he "would exercise more lenity and charity
towards those that are subject to the frailties of our common corruption." Never afterwards would he take part in
the discipline of others.

But there was an occurrence, noticeable from its fre-
quency, which to strangers must have appeared ludicrous,
but which the brethren recognised as part of the *rôle.*
William M'Lerie, from his extensive correspondence and
reading, had acquired the power to express his sentiments
with fluency, in such clear, simple, impressive language, yet
so shorn of denominational phraseology, that some of the
brethren suspected him of heresy. As often, therefore,
as he finished his "polished exhort," as brother Craw called

it, Sandy M'Kay, a theological pointer, started to his feet,
and laid down "the root of the matter" by repeating some
well-selected texts of Scripture, connecting them by pithy
remarks of his own ; but as his English was limited as well
as imperfect, he sometimes stopped abruptly, with uplifted
left hand, — the thumb and forefinger holding his next
pinch, the long middle-finger pointing ominously at William.
Sandy stood thus, frequently half-a-minute, waiting for the
proper English word, which, not coming handily, he substituted one or two Gaelic ones ; and, having primed his
nose, went on his way again,—the brethren sitting meanwhile as grave as a council of Indians. Not till after
meeting did any one notice the hiatus; *then* the big boys
would incite the little ones to *speer* at Sandy the meaning
of ——, when a rebuke from the mothers for our want
of *havens* would calm us down. The difference between
M'Lerie and his censor consisted simply in William's refinement and Sandy's fastidiousness. William, who had been
trained under Dr. Ferrier, was a quiet shrewd man, and
displayed occasional gleams of pawky humour even in his
preaching. His infirm health forbade his appearance as
a leader of the people ; but it was acknowledged that,
although his voice was unheard beyond the walls of the Pen
Kirk, his wisdom suggested and his prudence guided many
of the courses adopted to promote education and free
thought. He, too, was tainted with "Blak-neb-ism" in
politics, and in his younger years had had to abscond for a
time for having been a member of the National Convention in 1793.

Having thus spoken in somewhat equivocal terms as to
the manner of preaching amongst the Pen Folk, I think it

but just to give a short extract of the matter. The following passage from an old MS. will serve that purpose ; and I give it as I find it, without alteration, retaining even the orthography, which, in few cases, adds to its beauty. I may add, the selection is not made for its ability, but for its subject-matter. It bears date 1817 :—

" The text is, ' Where two or three is gathered together in my name, there am I in the midst of them.' This is the charter of Christian brotherhood and equality. When the Lord spoke these memorable words, He gave to every band, however small, of His followers, who might at any future time gather to worship Him, their inalienable law. He did not place their right in the keeping of any presbytery or synod ; nor did He give any control or supervision into the hands of bishop or priest whatever. The charter is Divine, and gives its duties and privileges to each gathering of worshippers without the intervention of council. It is given direct from Himself. Its grand feature is the promise of His ain presence whenever and wherever it is asked in humility and sincerity. There is nae limiting in this respect ; nothing is said to indicate what forms should be used ; gathered in my name—that's all. There is nae order that the leader of this little band was to get his authority frae any quarter. Yet the law is broad enough to include all our needments, for it conveys the Divine promise of the Redeemer's presence in all sincere worship, wi'out allusion to any other question whatever ;—gathering in His name qualifies the gathering. Do we want more ? Looking at structures that men has reared, we see great ingenuity and art, great pomp and circumstance ; and, alass, much arrogance of power and self-sufficieny. But when we look at what Christ has taucht, its simplicity, an' its beauty, an' its spirit is so childlike, we wonder that man should ever hav attempted to conceal the tenderness of the Master's order with the robes of human invention. We hav no need for legislation for our worship. The Master has given us the Law on the matter, and by it we may attain spiritual power—so rins the promise—frae God himself. And if it be, that whate'er in the name an' spirit, an' in recognition of the Lord, we get his approval, an' satisfaction of His presence therein, human athority cannot add anything of importance or utility. If there were a word of His teachings that qualified this, or a single sentence directing us for authority, in matters pertaining to matters of worship, to some gran' Sanhedrem of the Christian Body, we might well pause ; but there is not a word. No whisper from the Lord's lips can be heard to justify usurpations of those who would seek to control any band of worshippers that ever gathered in His name. The Christian priesthood is a band of brothers, each serving the Lord as the head, an' each other as those who delight to dwell in unity. Is there any one desirous of being chief? Let him be the servant of all. Those who would exercise dominion an' authority are the princes of the Gentiles.

"The errors of the past are for our instruction. We are not to hav sympathy with error, merely because of its age, nor accept any doctrine from the most learned or respected of our friends, merely because synods hav said so. We recognise no authority but God's ain word, no church law but His. We will hav kindness an' charity for all, an' receive the teachings of the Lord in preference to anything said by men."

The Pen Folk were eminently a proselytising people ; but they did so with discrimination. Then, as now, our good town had much of a village character—everybody knew everybody ; and so my old friends had no difficulty in selecting the very cream of all the churches on whom to lay their grappling-irons. Their extensive charities, too, gave them a power such as no other denomination possessed; for well-timed help and Christian sympathy will secure victory where argument falls unheeded. The beloved John on the Master's breast is a better argument than the detached ear of Malchus. Their success in this respect seems to me rather remarkable. The church, consisting of a few families, was constituted in November, 1798. WILLIAM

DICKIE was the 120th enrolled member, in August, 1802. They had no organisation to advance the cause, unless, indeed, we class under that head their mid-week meetings and love-feasts, when "desirable" folk were openly recommended as good subjects for conversion. They had no Children's Church or Sunday School, no " chasm class," no singing class, and no tea-meeting, such as are now common in all denominations: they had only the continual war of words, each one fighting single-handed, like so many Hals-o'-the-Wynd, whilst, although like the war-horse laughing at the spear, their motto was, " Let brotherly love continue." As an example of procedure in such matters, I am tempted to give the following :—

A newly-married pair having become " door-neighbours" to William Gilmour, one of the brethren, were recommended as very "desirable folk," and the duty of enlightening them was accepted by William and his wife,—he promising caution and discretion in his advances ; Archibald M'Killop remarking, with a smile, that his brother's promise of prudence always reminded him of the Irishman's assurance that he would make as little noise as possible by his pistol-shot. The campaign of conversion at last entered on, by and by little marrowless gossips ensued, friendly services without apparent cause were rendered, and a good footing being obtained, topics " of livelier interest" were finally introduced, as if by mutual consent. Afterwards came the tug of war. The new neighbours, having " covenanted " at a Branchall sacrament, were found to be tough metal, and the proselytising brother was too passionate-hearted to perform diplomatic work ; the more especially as, in this case, his antagonist resembled himself. It was Greek meeting

Greek over again. The result was that the " desirable folk" finally suspended all intercourse, and all hope of winning them over seemed lost. But in the course of events a new door opened ; and where man, strong in argument had failed, woman, with her gentle tenderness, was destined to succeed. To William's better half, who had a commendable pride in never having lost a friend or fallen out with a neighbour, the *dryness* between the families was the source of much grief. But want of perseverance was not one of her sins ; she would bide her time, not without hope, if William would only not interfere. During this state of affairs family sorrow fell heavily on the couple it had been thought desirable to attach,—trouble laid down first the husband, and then his wife ; and scarcely had they recovered when their first-born child sickened unto death ;—days and nights of disease of the body of the little one; days and nights of anxiety in the hearts of the watchers ; one day of hopeful joy, another of tearless despair ; the doctor eagerly questioned as he came and went ; his answers deepening the shadow on their hearts, as the shadow deepens on the wee burnie o' life near which the watchers gaze with bated breath. The shadow of the great abyss approaches slowly; confusion of brain supervenes ; and the mind wanders from childlike prayers to laughter with playmates. Nothing else is heard in the darkened room till "the eerie turn o' the nicht," when a great cry announced the coming of the Bridegroom, to carry the lamb in his arms in to the wedding supper. But, in all the great " multitude which no man can number," the poor mother could not, through her tears, detect the voice or the form of her little one ; and she was sorrowful exceedingly.

During all this time of bereavement and keen distress, the sorrowing self-reproach experienced by William and his warm-hearted wife was pitiable in the extreme. " Why did he provoke discord and separation by dogmatic superiority, and thus shut her out from friendly ministrations ? " was the ever-recurring though unspoken thought of her mind. Yet he knew, and felt deeply, the false step he had made. Few words passed between them, both seeming to prefer their own thoughts. The Books at night did not impart the accustomed comfort, and over all the household there reigned a *distrait* feeling. Questions were put timidly, and answered mechanically ; everything, in fact, was out of joint in the usually harmonious circle. On the day after the child's funeral, the neighbour's minister, mistaking the door, called, and took a seat, and, as might have been expected, the dead and the living was the all-engrossing topic ; individual " views " were exchanged, and differences becoming apparent, the usual battle-royal followed. The minister spoke as one having authority, dictatorially. This at any time would have been resented ; but on such an occasion, when my old friends were vexed and angry with themselves, what could he expect but plain speaking ? He rose once or twice to leave, but a stinging retort as often brought him to his seat.

" Who was he, to speak to believers in tones of a master ?"—" He was an ambassador of the Lord."

" Yes, sae are we a' ; but ye lay doon the message as gin it were your ain, an' we no your equals. Ye had better tak' your tones o' maistery to them wha acknowledge your authority. We own nae fealty to ony but the Lord,"—and more to the same purport.

As he rose for the last time, he was somewhat amazed on being grasped on an arm with both Mrs. Gilmour's hands, who, looking up earnestly into his face, said—

" Noo, dinna think us rude or angry wi' you. We hae naething but goodwill to you, as we 'd gladly shew you were you in trouble an' needin' help. Gae on your way, sir, an' speak a word o' comfort to that poor, broken-hearted, bairnless mother, for she needs it sair; an' may the Maister prosper you."

It would appear, however, that the minister had been made so thoroughly uncomfortable by the stormy interview, that he had no " word o' comfort " for the mourner. She. hungered as a dog for the crumbs to fall; but he had only stones to give her. He probed her green wound, by reminding her of God's right to take away; spoke of her infirmity and corruption for mourning over her loss; and after much to a like purport, told her that unless she had a well-grounded assurance of her own salvation, he could give her no hope of her child's acceptance with God,— as if any mother, with a mother's heart, had under such circumstances assurance of anything save her own great bereavement.

The poor woman stood aghast at the outcome of her own creed; and taking up the words of the Roman Governor to the malignant Jews, when they accused the Sinless One, she exclaimed, " Why, what evil hath he done?" and having found voice, she did what was truly human, and therefore, as I think, right—she turned at bay fiercely on the heartless man, and told him he perverted the truth. "Could I believe," said she, " that my faithlessness prevents the entrance o' my wee, sinless lamb into the Redeemer's kingdom, I

wadna ever bend a knee nor ca' him Faither again." And
he left her in anger; she, doubly bereft, lifted up her voice
and wept very bitterly. It was during this mood that Mrs.
Gilmour saw her on the bleaching-green; and, watching a
proper opportunity, went thither also, taking care, however,
to put a stripe of black crape round her white cap. Both
went and came repeatedly, doing their work without words,
—the husbands meanwhile mutually watching, from the begrimed weaving-shop windows, the progress of diplomacy
between human sorrow and Christian love. At length, in
a tremulous voice, the childless one asked—

" Wha's tu in mournin' for?"

The other, crossing to the low hedge that divided their
properties, said—

" Weel, thou widna speak tae me, an' I had nae ither way
o' shewin' my sympathy for thy loss. I ken thy grief, for
I hae lost bairns; an' oh, lass, *tho' it was their gain,* there's
nane kens a mother's grief but a mother." And (as both
women told me many years after) having first discussed the
ministerial decision, they " lay owre the hedge and took a
gude greet thegither, and had won'erfu' comfort."

These dribblings from the human fountain are cheap;
but, like stick-brimstone, invaluable as medicine occasionally. In a few weeks farther on, the " desirable folk " got
the right hand of fellowship; which, no doubt, increased our
dear old friend's comfort " won'erfu'." It must not be supposed, however, from what has been said, that the Pen Folk
were jot or tittle less logical or less heathenish than the
covenanted Kirk on the subject of infant reprobation; but
that, in states of mental depression and sorrow, human
sympathy, based on Christian love, has an influence and

power of which all dogmas and all creeds combined are, at least as they are taught, nearly destitute.

But all the victories of the " Pen " brotherhood were not won thus easily. No movement such as theirs in importance had taken place in the community since that of the Seceders, fifty years previously; and even these brethren in dissent allied themselves with the Erastian Establishment, and were in arms against the new dissenters. It was not uncommon for families to divide, and array themselves in opposite camps; discord and separation of husband and wife being of frequent occurrence. Even we youngsters were assailed by our schoolmates as " Unkerstened heathens," to which we retorted with " Priest-ridden," " Kirk-paupers," followed, sometimes, by bloody noses, and such-like theological results.

A pleasant instance of wisdom shewn by a younger portion of the opposing forces is afforded in the following episode :—

There was great consternation in the two camps, when it became known that the daughter of a " Pen " family and a son of the Establishment had " cuisten their glamour owre ither ;" and much sighing and sorrowing followed, particularly from the maid's father, who poured forth his regrets and exhortations in unmeasured streams, in order to stem the tide of backsliding. Vain, vain waste of power ! After a year of half-delirious joy, only once possible in life, the two young folks, having plighted troth, were forthwith married. In due legal time, nature " an' anither woman " (Mrs. Gibb, probably) gave them a little maid-child; and then there was a collection of ammunition by the armed neutrals, and the dread of disunion with those more immediately connected anent the christening. A few days after the advent the young father, having adjusted his *dickie* with some pride, held a consultation with his brother-in-law, on whom the question of plunging or sprinkling sat but lightly.

"Ye see," said the former, "I wish the bairn christened; but I dinna want tae fa' oot wi' my wife, an' sae I want your advice on the matter."

The brother, who had unbounded faith in his sister's wisdom, answered promptly—

"Do ye your duty, and dinna fear o' Aggie's prudence; she kens her place, for ye hae gotten the tap bird o' the nest. Let's ken hoo ye get on."

In the grey gloaming of a week later on, the young father hinted his wish to Aggie, and the following conversation took place :—

"Weel, faither, ye're the head o' the house, an' maun dae as it pleases you. Whan do you want it done?"

"Oh! when it's convenient for you,—say Sunday week."

"Convenient! it's convenient the morn, for that matter. I hae a' things ready. Sae step roun' tae yer minister-man, and arrange for the next First-day."

He rose to go, but stood playing with the door handle, and stammered, "If thou would say wha thou'd like to carry the wee lady, I'll tryste them whan I'm oot."

"Carry her! Na, na, there maun nae fremt body carry my wee queen tae the desk. I'll gang wi' you, and haun her oot frae the Session-house door, an' ye'll gie me her back when the *ceremony's* owre. We'll bide by the fire till ye skail; and that's as far as, in conscience, I can gang."

" Yes, Agnes, and farther than I expected. God bless thee."

In reporting all this to his brother-in-law, he added, " 'Od, man, when she spak' sae frankly, I felt the auld relapse come owre me, an' I took her head atween my hands and gied her a kiss. It was like our young courting-time back again." The brother-in-law, to whom the " relapse " was still a mystery, replied by a loud guffaw.

Another incident better illustrates the general character of the Pen Folk than anything else I can refer to. A husband and wife, with four children, who had become located in town, had connected themselves with the church. After a time, he and all the children were laid down in fever; and while in this helpless condition, the mother was also laid down. They were without relations, and had no friends outside the connection ; and WILLIAM DICKIE, being the church member residing nearest them, recognised it as his duty to become their nurse. He was then upwards of forty years of age, with a wife and family. He left his work and attended the family till he, too, was struck down, and he did not resume work for six months after. On his way home when taken ill, he tapped at the window of another church member, requesting him to provide in some way for the sick family's guidance. That brother immediately left work, and took his place at the bedside of the patients, where he remained till the husband's death and the widow's recovery,—over a month in all. During that time his own daughter, aged seventeen, was sick with the same complaint. Three times daily did he and his wife meet at " the yard-fit," exchanging reports whilst he took his " bite an' sup." The simple act of self-sacrifice indicated by such brotherliness is surely of more value than whole barrow-loads of dogma.

From the time he recovered from the fever alluded to (1819) till his death-trouble, WILLIAM DICKIE enjoyed unbroken health ; but when he reached his 80th year, poverty, arising from want of employment, began to press him hard, and the church had to step forward urging its aid. During '58, '59, and '60, his wants were duly attended to, but the necessity laid on him to receive their aid grieved him sorely. It would appear he kept account of all he had received; for early in 1861, having got a legacy of trifling amount left him, he called on the treasurer and paid down to the last copper all the church had given him. The treasurer, of course, refused it, and argued with him ; but had he known him better, or felt less kindly disposed, he would have saved himself the trouble. The dear old man left the money— £14 14s. 4½d.—on the desk, remarking that if "I am set in judgment on the needments of others, I maun do sae wi' clean hands."

In this connection I note a thing worth mentioning : I had a visit lately from a descendant of an old Pen family, who, I thought, needed a little help, and as I had some money furnished me for distribution, by a Pen-laddie long resident in Canada, I offered her a sovereign, saying it would help her over the winter. With tears of gratitude for the kindness, she refused it, saying she "wasna bare ;" but, poor woman, with characteristic kindness, she did not fail to tell me of two descendants of the old brotherhood who, she said, were "*real* needfu' : wad thou give them something without letting them ken whaur it cam' frae? for ye ken they're unco prood." The auld metal has a "prime tinkle."

The Pen Folk were not Baptists originally; nor were they the first Baptists in town, as is indicated by their minute-book, from which I transcribe the "history of this church."

"In the year 1796, it was first erected, on the independent plan of government. In 1797, the elder, David Wylie, and a number of the members, *adopted the doctrine of 'Believer Baptism.'* The church divided on this point, a number holding their former views. Those who adopted believers' baptism separated themselves on 4th November, 1797. They were again set in order in December, 1797,—David Wylie being chosen their pastor. It may be observed that this did not take place until due pains had been taken to see, if possible, *to connect with the Baptist Church in town.* But this was not practicable, owing to some difference in principles. The principal difference was with respect to Adam's *first* offence and its consequences. Being thus set in order, they continued in this very way until 4th November, 1798, when a difference arose amongst them respecting the principles forementioned. They again divided on this point; and David Wylie and a few others left the church and connected themselves with the other society in town.

"The church being thus left as sheep without a shepherd from November to December, they connected themselves with a church in Glasgow, of which George Begg was pastor. The church in Glasgow being fewer in number than the church in Paisley, it was agreed upon by the churches mutually that George Begg should remove to Paisley, and act there in the character of pastor. This was carried into effect in that same month of December, 1798."

The minute immediately following the above is dated April, 1799, and I copy it, because the person it refers to exercised a greater influence in Paisley as a Baptist, and for a longer period, than any of his brethren.

"The church met with fasting and prayer to choose an elder, when John Taylor was unanimously chosen,—he wishing some time to consider the matter, having some objections to solve in his own mind. The church consented, and granted time.

" Sept. 8.—John Taylor desired the church not to insist on his appointment; but the church did insist, and he consented, and 13th November was appointed a fast for the purpose of setting him apart to the office."

" Nov. 13, 1799.—The church being met with fasting and prayer, agreeable to appointment of September 8, ORDAINED John Taylor to the office of Elder."

These are not consecutive entries, however, but the intervening ones are foreign to my present purpose.

The Baptist Church alluded to in the above extract is Storie Street Church, which was formed by seven members of the Abbey Close Independents,—known as Dale's Kirk, from their having been established by Mr. David Dale, father-in-law of Mr. Robert Owen, of Socialist notoriety; whose son, the Hon. Robert Dale Owen, is—by the way— author of *Footfalls on the Boundary of Another World*, —shewing *another* turn of the mental machinery. For several years the members' roll of the " Pen " gradually enlarged, during which period they would neither "pick nor dab" with others, "because," in the words of an old Penite,* " frae the vera beginnin' the Storie Street Baptists

* Calvinism, in its most repulsive form, enthralled this good man for nearly half-a-century, concealing his originally amiable disposition under a most unpalatable crust. But men shed their theologic skin now and then, and it was so with him. After the final dispersion of the original Penites, he occasionally attended the old Methodist Chapel in George Street, where a " hive " from Storie Street then worshipped. Latterly, from age and other causes, he remained much at home. I visited him frequently during his last illness, and was pleased beyond expression to find he had completely peeled off the old hard shell. He was again like what I had known him in my boyhood,—gentle and childlike. Venturing, on one occasion, to say it was a matter of little consequence

were tainted with the heresy o' free will, contrair tae the hale tenour o' Scripture, seestu;" whereas the Pen Folk were, to state it kindly, as pure as Kilmeny in that respect. The two bodies flowed, therefore, as two streams in the community, side by side, but never commingling, till their differences had been thoroughly debated, and the basis of each was understood. Ultimately, some members of both churches again expressed a willingness to make the subject of difference one of forbearance—an amiable but short-sighted suggestion. It is not in crowds that men assimilate with each other. Crowds may live harmoniously as members of the commonwealth, where the opinions of each must be respected, but Christian union has a deeper ground than that of civil life; and so long as doctrinal soundness is preferred to personal worth, men of devout and loyal character will have to content themselves to tread the path to certainty, as they must do the "valley of the shadow" without companionship of man. The Master spake in parables to the crowd; but he *expounded* to his followers when they were alone. The wish for union was therefore

now to which side of the street he belonged—meaning the Storie Street folk, or the hive alluded to—he answered with a joyful *abandon*—

" *The street I'm travelling in, lad, has nae sides;* an' if power were given me, I would preach purity o' life mair an' purity o' doctrine less than I did."

"Are you not a little heretical," I said, "at your journey's end?"

"I kenna. Names haena the terror on me they ance had; an' since I was laid by here alane, I hae had whisperings o' the still sma' voice telling me that the footfa' o' Faiths, and their wranglings, will ne'er be heard in the Lord's kingdom, whereunto I am nearin'. An' as love cements a' differences, I 'll aiblins find the place roomier than I thocht in times by-past."

abandoned, and every one left to become free of spiritual as of ecclesiastical impediments. Personal worth and ability may sustain any cause temporarily; but if it have not in itself the elements and means of Christian progression, its decay is simply a question of time. If it contain the positive seeds of decay, or its charity is broad enough to include all the good without reference to minor points, its extinction, as a sect, will be more rapid; and I am constrained to acknowledge, maugre my deep love of its people, that the former was the position of the Pen Folk. They did not assert in words, but their treatment of Christians outside their communion said plainly, "The Temple of the Lord are WE!" No man, worthy the name, could feel a truly human love to God or man, if he thought he were saved in preference to any other man. There were some who, mistaking their ecclesiastical position for a spiritual state, slid comfortably into that dreadful fallacy; but sincere minds, with an humble estimate of themselves, and a catholic conception of the fatherliness of God, instinctively shrunk from contact with such views of His providence as were presented by them. They soon felt that the power they had wielded over others was now directed against their icy dogma of Predestined Reprobation; and their numbers slowly, gradually, but surely, were absorbed in a more humanising atmosphere. Alas! alas! the glory of the dear old Pen was now departing.

Mr. John Taylor was, as we have seen, the first elder set apart in the Pen body, and, I believe, was the first to secede, and also to enroll himself under the pastorship of Mr. Thomas Watson,—by whose energy was formed, and by whose ability was consolidated, the church in Storie

Street,—and whom he succeeded in that office. There had been "withdrawings" and "cuttings off" before ; but these were more on moral grounds, and fallings away into the naturalism of Dr. Priestley.

Cases of separation from fellowship, or "cutting off," were to me at all times alike fascinating and painful. Combining what I have seen, and know from hearsay, with what I find in the records having reference thereto, mournful pictures of brotherly love are exhibited, at war with what was believed to be Christian duty. As, for example, "Nov. 17, 1799, Francis Dunnet exhorted from John's gospel, chap. xvii., ver. 3,—' This is life eternal, that they might know thee the only true God, and Jesus Christ whom thou has sent,' in which he expressed views at variance with the church on the subject of the Godhead, saying that Jesus Christ is equal with the Father, in the same sense that Joseph was equal in the house of Pharaoh—in all things save the throne only. For this he was called to account, and admonished, when he desired time to reconsider the matter, and the 24th following was appointed therefor. Being then of the same mind, he was admonished and prayed for, and was asked if he was still of the same mind ; he answered as before ; he was then admonished and prayed for a third time, and again asked as formerly, and Francis stood up and said he felt no change in his mind." All this looks bare and formal enough ; but let the reader imagine a company of from sixty to eighty earnest men and women, chiefly of the working class, each equal to the others, every one pale and anxious, some weeping silently for what they feel must follow. For a little time after Francis in the present instance resumed his seat, there was profound quiet, as if an audible response might still be given to their prayers; then the Elder (John Taylor) rose, and by a bend of the head, asked the mind of the brethren individually on this matter. The hoarse whisper of " Separate," " separate," " separate," rose and fell as it passed up one pew and down another, getting fainter and fainter, as it receded to the circumference. The sad duty over relief was felt, and those who chose were left to weep without restraint, whilst the separated—alas! no longer a brother—went forth into the dark mid-winter day, silent and alone, " a heathen man and a publican."

During the year following (1800), there is in the records twelve cases noted of " cutting off," all connected with the point of doctrine above referred to, excepting that of Margaret Forester, who declared her conviction that " charity or love, and not faith, is the true basis of Christian unity; and that doctrinal differences ought to be borne with,"—a millennial view of things not to be tolerated in that fighting time.

Mr. Taylor was succeeded in the eldership by his brother Thomas, than whom there was no worthier nor abler man in the connection,—although at that time the Pen Folk were remarkable for ability. I asked lately of an old friend, who still " adheres " to one of the branches of the Baptists in town, if she was as well satisfied with the modern preaching in the connection as with the old exhortations? With a sigh and a shake of the head, she said, " No; I dinna ken what's in 't, but it hasna the sweet wa'gang o' the auld times." I apprehend, however, that the *wa'gang* is a thing altogether of memory, and that the present is much superior to the past. There is no doubt whatever that the privilege every member enjoyed, and in which the majority participated, of addressing the church on any particular point of doctrine, was the cause of alienating the affection of some of the old, and of crushing respect for religion in the young. It is not, perhaps, inherent in that privilege or its practice, but rather inseparable therefrom, so long as men take only a narrow view of the design of the Gospel. At anyrate, it had the effect of excluding from the church many persons who were disposed to communicate; and young people of both sexes of education and perception felt scandalised by the badly-expressed, homely language of would-be leaders.

On one occasion, at a time when there was a difference between the weaving body and manufacturers in town about a rise or a reduction in prices, a brother, who took deep interest in the quarrel, rose in church, and, basing his discourse on an appropriate text of Scripture, opened up the whole question, and concluded by denouncing the "Corks" as a pack of heartless, self-seeking heathens, without bowels of mercy. Some of the brethren were afraid his injudicious tirade would end in another *riddling* of the body; but the presiding Elder, without noticing the "confusion of the feeding," quietly gave out a paraphrase of the words, "Fret not thyself because of evil-doers." I am inclined to think the implied rebuke, and the titter which over-ran the church whilst it was being sung, were quite as reprehensible as the "exhort" itself.

Extempore speaking was the rule; speaking from notes or reading sermons the exception. My father was of the latter class. My duty was to have slips of uniform size stitched ready for his use; but as the Pen Folk felt scandalised at his "Episcopalian practice," and mother complained of the unnatural quiet at the hearth to allow his continual

scribbling, I abstracted one morning his MS., and substituted an unwritten slip, just before we left for church.　It
was customary, when he rose to address the brethren, for
some of the old, dull of ears, to move to where he stood,
and with hand behind their ears, sit open-mouthed, keppin'
the manna as it fell during the delivery of his exhortation,
and I, with mother and the youngsters, vacated our seats
to accommodate them.　To prevent suspicion, on that day
I moved in front, and in full view of his aspect, when, after
naming the text, he made the fatal discovery.　Never had I
seen such a look of blank perplexity.　He commenced,
however, without apparent trepidation, and succeeded in
occupying his usual twenty minutes.　Isobel Jamieson observed, in a whisper to Dawnial, during the interval, that
" Willie hankered awee this morning, I think, but there is
nae wonner, for he got unco near the throne whiles."　I
did not, for upwards of twenty years, tell father what I had
done ; but he then told me laughing, that my perplexed face
at the time told him plainly who was the trickster, for guilt
was written in my look ; adding, that he and mother agreed
that more good would be done me by silence than rebuke
on their part.　It was my first step in Theology.

If the present generation of Baptists in town have fewer
gifts than their predecessors, their gifts are of a higher order,
and there is more true refinement and less conceit and
exclusiveness.　The ability and the exclusiveness of the
Pen Folk were generally ascribed to the fact that, for several
years, they were drawn from the congregation of Dr. Ferrier,
which of old assumed a superiority over other bodies, and
its members gathered up, as it were, their garments to prevent defilement from other Christians when they passed.

Dr. Ferrier is said to have turned out a greater number of clever men, and qualified more lay preachers, than any other minister of the Associate body. With a laudable prudence and liberality, in order to stay the current of dissent, the doctor, by a minute¡ of session, made the doctrine of Adult Baptism a subject of forbearance; which minute, I am informed, is still in force, with what results—deponent saith not.

The tide having turned, the ebb rapidly went on till, in 1819, the members' roll of the dear old Pen Kirk having fallen to twenty-six, the colours were struck, the property sold, and the "remnant" betook themselves to less pretentious quarters, where they continued to decrease for nearly thirty years. At last they dissolved altogether; and the property they built having been mortgaged *to supply the wants of their poor*, was, like the potter's field, bought for the use of strangers; the only family remaining at the final dissolution,—that of Samuel Cameron,—having emigrated to the United States. WILLIAM DICKIE and many others had long before gone over to those ancient heretics, the Storie Street folk; for what, to those accustomed to think deeply, is heresy at one time, often becomes orthodoxy at another.

During the twenty-one years of the kirk's existence,—from 1798 till 1819,—the roll numbered 164 members. At the end of that time, the numbers were reduced as stated, to 26; 79 had withdrawn; 30 were " cut off," chiefly for heresy; 11 went abroad; and 18 died. I may as well add that 33 members remained on the roll so long as the church met in the Pen, but that 26 only were enrolled as members when the remnant met in the new place for worship at 8 Barr Street.

D

In 1854, two Paisley lads recently arrived in New York, were walking up Hudson Street on a Sunday forenoon, and had their attention arrested by the sound of praise issuing from a dwelling-house, the door of which stood open. The *wail* and the notes were familiar—had been household things at home. Their young hearts, feeling friendless and lonely in their adopted country, were open to the softening influence of the home-*sough ;* and they resolved to enter. When they did so, they found good old Samuel Cameron, with a faithfulness uncommon even amongst Baptists, holding church with the members of his own family only. After worship (and, doubtless, a short exhortation) the strangers made themselves known, and were hospitably entertained. One of the lads was afterwards laid down in sickness for several months, Samuel and his wife tending him as one of their own ; and when restored to health, they furnished him with the means to go in search of employment. It is pleasant to add that all the money was repaid. The kindness,—which could not be refunded,—is held in grateful remembrance; and thus both giver and receiver were blessed.

Samuel Cameron has since gone to join the great cloud of witnesses; and now WILLIAM DICKIE has gone too— the last of all that large-hearted band who started life with such glad appreciation of Christian privileges and duties, to whom the earth seemed so heavenly that they could have lived here for ever. But one now, and again one, dropped from the circle ; and ere mid-life was reached, the sun had lost its warmth and the earth its charms, for the majority had gone to their rest. For years this good old man wandered along the brink of the " valley of the shadow," solitary and alone, sighing over the sweet memories of his youth ; but smiling trustfully at the " oceans of mercy " that await the faithful, or it may be listening to the deep harmonies descending through the inner chamber of his spirit, where the Lord sups with His children, and they with Him. If he had any such intimation from the " chambers of imagery," we can believe that the spirit of his yearning response is expressed in the following lines :—

" I 'm kneeling at the threshold : weary, faint, and sore ;
Waiting for the dawning, for the opening of the door ;
Waiting till the Master shall bid me rise and come
To the glory of His presence, to the gladness of His home.

" A weary path I 've travelled, 'mid darkness, storm, and strife,
Bearing many a burden, struggling for my life ;
But now the morn is breaking, my toil will soon be o'er,
I 'm kneeling at the threshold, my hand is on the door.

" Methinks I hear the voices of the blessed as they stand
Singing in the sunshine of the sinless land ;
Oh would that I were with them, amid their shining throng,
Mingling in their worship, joining in their song.

" The friends that started with me have entered long ago,
One by one they left me struggling with the foe ;
Their pilgrimage was shorter, their triumph sooner won—
They wait to give me welcome when my toil is done.

" They, and other angels, now freed from care and sin,
Are standing by the portals prepared to let me in ;
O Lord, I wait thy pleasure ; thy time and way are best ;
But I 'm wasted, worn, and weary—O Father, bid me rest !"

Returning from my old friend's funeral, I fell a-thinking on all these things, and of the removal of old landmarks ; and I began to count over the names of the worthies connected with the Baptists whom I knew long ago. As they passed one after another before my mind's eye, no one loomed up in memory fresher, or with friendlier aspect, than "auld WILLIAM DICKIE," whom I had known all my life, and always as an old man. In thus musing on old friends, I did not, as *goody-good* people may think I should have done, mourn over the uncertainty and mutability of life and earthly things, and "improve the occasion" thereby, but recalled the pleasant incidents of my young life,—the sunshiny holidays I spent in a "church capacity" with these hard-headed, genial old men. My recollections of them are all happily blended with green-fields, spiritual songs, goose-berries, love-feasts, hawthorn blossoms, and a burn "whiles jawin' like a sea." My first vivid recollection of WILLIAM DICKIE is of seeing him, with *wee* Willie in hand, passing to meeting on a First-day morning, as my father and I issued from the doorway going thitherward also. We—that is, Willie and I—in new toggery of bottle-green, were put in advance, to prevent unseemly frollicking, I suppose; our fathers following in their short gray coats, with black *mool* buttons, drab kerseymere breeches, and *leggin's* of the same material, having a row of mother-of-pearls, hanging loosely on their nether limbs; our mothers, in silk brocade and scarlet cloaks, bringing up the rear. Willie and I, I remember, as the only outlet for our spare steam,—for young blood *will* keep at boiling heat,— "niffered grosets" to test their quality. Thus trying to gather up the names of my early cronies, of whom both earth and sea have some, and others are scattered in distant lands, I had reached my arm-chair, and got into a reverie; and then I fell asleep, and I dreamt a dream :—

I seemed to be sitting in the old seat in the Pen Kirk, between the two old men,—*wee* Willie having been shoved to the farther end, as usual, to prevent him and me from trafficking in fruit or penknives, as our habit was when seated together. On looking around, there were the same familiar faces seated or coming in : John Cuthbertson, with his startled-like black eyes, under a smooth dark brown wig, talking earnestly to Isobel Jamieson, in short scarlet cloak and white single-bordered cap ; and Archibald Hastie, the baxter, with his broad Roman profile and deep-set mild eyes, leans forward, whispering to Mrs. Forrester, whose husband, Peter, is talking loudly to Sandy M'Kay, two pews off. William M'Lerie has not taken his seat, but steps noiselessly up the "pass," asking kindly for each as he slips along—a pale, delicate, but cheerful man, whose looks indicate a short sojourn. Beside the pulpit stairs are James Craw, Archibald M'Ghee, and John Mulholland, conning over the subjects that have occupied their attention during the past week. Then James Thomson ascends the pulpit, and takes his seat as presiding elder. He rises presently, and in a mild voice names and reads over the opening hymn, " This is the day the Saviour rose," &c., to which " blind Robin Malcolm " leads the music with far more pith than beauty. My wonder is renewed again as to how a blind man can " find the place," and, as in the present case, read the hymn line by line. Although I am munching my gooseberries, some who enter carry large bouquets, while others shake the snow-drift from their coats (for it is a dark hazy day), yet these do not appear strange or incongruous things, but right and harmonious. From the combined smell of decayed thyme and southernwood I get drowsy, and lean myself against old WILLIAM; knowing that, had I gone fatherward, there would have been an administration of snuff; and I dreamt of being waked up by the noise of the dismissal hymn. Then there were the usual gathering into groups, and the old kindly inquiries after each other's health, emendations on the discourse, and additional proofs given. By and by, those from a distance settled down for the interval, when lunches were forthcoming from mothers' pockets, and cheery talk became general, without *much* regard to the subject or the time; for whilst these men exhibited a deeper reverence for things sacred than any other *body* of men I have since met, the First-day was only held in reverence by them, and that during Divine worship only, as a memorial of the great day on which the world's redemption was accomplished, and an empty sepulchre laid open to human gaze. I heard again the story of the journey which eight of the brethren made to Edinburgh to sign the National Convention in '93, and how, to avoid expense, each took a wallet of provender to supply his wants; of the wonders seen, and the amazement felt at the grandeur and wickedness of the great city. And, somehow, the details were mixed up with that other trip of the more daring to witness the trial of Gerald and Muir, and the recital of personal recollections of Gerald after his return from banishment; and—I was recalled to wakefulness and day-life by the not unwelcome intimation that it was tea-time. I told my dream and musings to the youngsters; but they did not appreciate, as I do, the self-denying hero-ism of these sturdy old Corinthians, who fought for the Christian people's independence of Church Courts; and so I seek a larger audience.

And now, having finished these recollections of thyself and the Christian brotherhood, of whom thou wert so worthy a member, I bid thee, dear old WILLIAM DICKIE, an affectionate farewell; thou hast exchanged much weary care and poverty for never-ending peace and joy—the riches that are without wings. And although we who laid thy old work-loom in the grave were few and of the common sort, those on the other side, who welcomed thee through the ever-open pearl-gates of the golden city, were doubtless of that innumerable company of the just made perfect, who sing the song of Moses and the Lamb. Farewell! For ever? Nay, nay! for although

> " Snags of old broken appetites torment me still,
> With pains that Death itself, I fear, will hardly kill,"

I do hope we shall meet again on the tablelands of Home; and, as heretofore,—but with clearer perceptions springing from purified hearts,—have sweet converse on the wonders of redeeming love.

> " Eyes of mine, thus hungry, gazing
> Into the great concave, blazing
> With a dazzling blueness bright,
> Ye are blind as death or night;
> Whilst my dead, their opened eyes,
>   Mute upraising, past all praising,
> Pierce into God's mysteries.
>
> " Ye, our dead, for whom we pray not,
> Unto whom wild words we say not,—
> Though we know not but ye hear,
> Though we often feel you near,—
> Go into eternal light;
>   You we stay not, and betray not
> Back into our dim half-night."

THE OTHER SIDE.

ALTHOUGH the answer is indicated in the "Pen Folk," the question, "Why, with such elements of goodness, did the Pen Brae Church fall into decay?" has been often asked of me; and as several friends have desired a more explicit explanation, I have consented to give my opinion briefly, which is my excuse for returning to the subject. What I shall say can be only in illustration of what is there said.

Every creed, whether written or unwritten, is constructed so as to be in harmony with the opinion entertained by its framers of the Divine nature and character. Where infinite Love is the fundamental idea, the creed will differ greatly from that where God is regarded primarily as of sovereign Power—where he is viewed more as a king than as a father. He is both father and king; but in the connection referred to, he was held to be king first, in that he is a respecter of persons, "choosing" here and "passing by" there, as seemeth good to him. Where such an idea of Divine providence is incorporated into the life, the result must be narrow self-sufficiency and exclusiveness. It is only while Christians think of God *theologically*, however, that he is so regarded. As a rule, their lives are governed more by the precepts of the Gospel than from formulated dogma; and hence it is that the good in Christian men sometimes drapes the deformity of their creed, and preserves it, for a time, from utter extinction. In churches that are governed by a power outside themselves, the form may exist long after the spirit of the creed has been discarded or outlived; but in small churches that are self-governed, where every member, as a king and priest, is privileged to address the church, doctrine, in some form or other, is always kept in the foreground, and held with tenacity. The danger in such cases is, that instead of recognising the universal sweep of the Gospel, they take a microscopic view of things, and magnifying their importance or perverting their meaning, each man comes to look upon his favourite topic as the all in all of revealed truth; giving offence at times, and thus dividing instead of maintaining the unity of the brotherhood.

My old friends held, in one sense, most catholic views on the subject of Christain brotherhood; but forgetting that the harmony of variety is more complete than that of uniformity, they contended that all Christian peoples of every tongue would ultimately come to see eye to eye with them. Thus, an old self-assured friend, gentle beyond ordinary in matters apart from his creed, became an object of ridicule from his exclusive spirit on that subject. Arguing on one occasion with a Seceder, as amiable and more liberal than himself, who, wearied with the continual iteration of the question, said,—

"Weel, weel, Thomas, we'll get that an' mony ither things redd up to us when we gang up by."

"Ou ay," answered Thomas, "we'll be a' Baptists there, William."

The same conceited spirit cropped up in other forms, which proved disastrous to them as a church; and the scorn with which they undervalued the worship of other Christians did them much harm in that respect. At funerals, for example, they refused to rise from their seat, as the custom in Scotland is, during the prayer then offered, if it was performed by one belonging to other connection than theirs; the reason they assigned being, that by rising they might be held as endorsing all unsound doctrine that *would* be uttered. Their exclusiveness on such occasions, and the case of Naaman the leper, when he required to kneel in the house of Rimmon, recurred to my mind lately on reading of the refusal to sanction an "orthodox" prayer at a meeting of a School Board. One is disposed to doubt that men guilty of such assumed purity were influenced by a devout spirit, as otherwise they would have accepted "the will for the deed." It is not the words, but the incense of humility, that rises to the throne of mercy.

This exclusiveness, in after years, when taken in connection with their doctrines of "personal assurance" and "reprobation," had other ramifications which wrought meikle dispeace in several families, and was the cause, latterly, of decimating the body. These two doctrines were distinctive features of the connection; and they further maintained that, when any one is once assured, no falling away from grace is possible,—saying, in effect, that having put hand to the plough, there is no such thing as looking back. Brethren expressing doubts of being "within the veil" were brought under discipline, and failing to give satisfaction they were "cut off." Tender peace-loving men and women were thus, for lack of sympathy, thrown in upon themselves, and became silent or withdrew; and in several cases where husband and wife varied, there were grievous heartburnings; while in others, prudence and mutual love prevented discord.

Clouds and constraint began to invade the most worthy of those remaining; whilst the most logical became more intolerant, harder, and less lovable. A case occurred with a husband and wife which I will state briefly, and, for convenience, will call them Peter and Martha. Like all Dissenters of that day Peter was a radical in politics, and waxed eloquent now and then in defence of liberty and equality; but he was from constitutional tendencies a strong-willed aristocrat, and exercised his family headship, not as a responsibility for which he was accountable, but as an authority that ought and must be obeyed. His assurance, therefore, had more an appearance of worldly pride than of Christian humility. If he felt the road narrow at times, it was so straight that he saw its whole length, and he went on his way rejoicing. Martha hoped that she too had entered the strait gate, but it was only a hope; she could not see as Peter saw, and did not feel as he felt; but, like her namesake of old, was " troubled about many things." Her misgivings were not diminished from the want of wise counsel and Christian sympathy of Peter, who had reached the unenviable conclusion that the acceptance of the brotherhood's form of words, and of them only, ensured salvation; it tended rather to shut the doors of the heart against all such as, for any reason, did *not* accept them. Martha prudently abstained from disturbing her family peace by dwelling on her doubts, and was docile and painstaking in all her duties as a wife; but when assailed, she was faithful to such convictions as she possessed. Hence, when discussion arose between them, the breach widened at every onset; and Peter unwisely brought her unsoundness before the church, and procured her separation from the connection.

It was remarked that when the church was about to deal with her for the last time, all the female members, with one exception, left the meeting, and when the voice to "separate" had passed, that courageous matron rose, and in tremulous voice requested that her name should also be taken from the member roll.

Another and a more enduring grief awaited poor Martha. In the evening of the same day she handed Peter the Books, as her custom had been on Sunday evenings; but he declined to worship with an unbeliever. On the following morning he, for the same reason, refused to give thanks at breakfast; and Martha, unwilling to forego that privilege, took such viands as she required to a place apart. They never broke bread together afterwards; but the gentle woman's heart was broken, and she did not survive long; the church's action and Peter's unbending orthodoxy, it was thought, threw her into a decline. The only words she was known to say having reference to his treatment of her were,—" His Judge shall be my judge, and my judge his Judge."

It was sitting before my mother on a winter day, during my father's absence at Martha's funeral, that I first heard the details of her misery—details which it can do no good to repeat. I listened till the lump in my throat grew so large that I could not contain myself; so I put my head in her lap, and clasping her knees, cried like a boy—as I was.

I learned to love Peter in after life, but I hated him then. I had only one way of shewing my dislike : I stoned his cat vigorously till I was told that "nae doot Peter's cruelty wud ha'e sma' beginnin's—strikin' puir dumb animals, or sic-like."

Peter was being "dealt with" in another way. His children, who early found separate homes for themselves, were as unloving as they had been unloved by him. When they had all scattered, and his Martha gone, himself old, poor, and living with strangers, he began to learn that in order to soften and enlarge human hearts, Infinite Love has first to break them, when necessary. That "sword" was the forerunner of a submissiveness on his part, and a peace of which till then he had been a stranger. If his manner remained hard, it was hardness of manner only. Those who knew him most intimately said his varied troubles were substantial blessings, in that they made him more like what Martha had been ; the memory of whose gentle devotedness he cherished with a fervour that delighted those who had long before "separated."

There were other cases of a similar kind occurred, but none so pitiful. The husband of the matron alluded to above attempted to do as Peter had done, whose wife without words removed her food to another table; but he rose and placed her "tea things" beside his own, saying,—

"Let us be as we've been, lass."

She with a smile replied,—

"Thy heart's a gude bit bigger than thy heid."

He withdrew from the connection shortly after.

These were, as I think, the causes why the church in question came to its end ; and as the Gospel is not a dogma but a life, such, sooner or later, will be the result to every church that recognises truth as an end, and not merely as the means of fostering that belief in the heart, which is righteousness, humility, and love.—*From the Scottish Baptist Magazine for April,* 1876.

JOTTINGS.

PARTED, NOT LOST.

I HAD a friend once, from whose varied acquirements and practical sagacity I derived much benefit for several years, and for whose kindly disposition many poor people had good cause to be grateful. He brought to the topics we frequently discussed an amount of information, keen perception, and power of illustration seldom met with in men who, like him, were engrossed in commercial pursuits. He seemed always to grasp the kernel of every subject he touched, and to perceive whatever beauty it possessed. Genial and kindly himself, he had the rare faculty of making others kind, and to feel and see as he did, that anything in creation or providence harmonised with Universal Love. By his kindly influence I was led to adopt as a principle his oft-repeated saying, that "in the sight of God angels, men, and devils, are of equal value, for that He is no respecter of persons." The only weakness I ever discovered in my friend was the pride with which he gloried in his ancestors, and even that weakness was modified by his frequent lamenting that his reverence for the dead sometimes interfered with his duty to the living. It appeared from his version, that two brothers, twins, each with a Bible under his coat, fell sword in hand in the Battle of Bothwell Brig, and that their descendants, without exception, proved worthy scions of these progenitors. My friend's father was descended from one of these brothers, and his mother from the other. In him seemed to be aggregated the varied good elements of his race, and their love of truth was in him sanctified by being changed and elevated to the love of goodness,—unconsciously, of course, for his reverence for truth, *as a means*, deepened with his years. With his years came doubts also, and questionings which disturbed his mind, as to the accuracy of the saying of his just referred to; and there arose in consequence a cloud between us, no denser at first than a summer mist, which obstructed somewhat the outflow of our old brotherliness. And when the doubts became settled convictions in his mind, the cloud so deepened in density and colour, that no ray from either side could penetrate. Knowing that his heart was bigger than his head, I would have continued our friendship, talking and strolling with him as of old, and loving him, as I still do, for his native and acquired goodness; but he would not permit this. I must either ride with him in his rickety old carriage—built on the narrow gauge—or we must part company. Well, I accepted the latter alternative. I am not going home by way of Bothwell Brig; for although many who go by that route carry unsheathed swords in their hand, and a confession of faith *in their hat*, few, I am afraid, take a Bible under their waistcoats; nor will I go knowingly in the company of any one claiming truth as his private property. And so, because I cannot agree with him, he denounces me as the enemy of God, and as such destined to perdition. And he hugs himself in his little carriage, which he has shunted on to a circular turn-table, from which he expostulates with me when business leads me his way; but his carriage has too scant accommodation to my liking, and therefore I must keep to the carriage of the broad gauge ; and so we have parted company, for he will not permit us being friends any longer. Sunlight is not the property of any one in particular, but each has his prismatic ray, and there is light for all. I cannot see why dear friends should separate because they see the same subject at different angles. Some people insist that every one should look with *their* organ of vision.

There is one thing vexes me not a little in connection with my old friend : in former years his voice was cheery and his manner blithe on all occasions, particularly when he ministered to the needy. Now these are greatly changed to the worse ; for his manner is morose and sad, his utterances come all drawling through his nasal organ, and those only who ride by the narrow gauge receive of his bounty. I have urged him again and again to rejoin our harmonious company, but his only answer has hitherto been that all who travel by the broad gauge will inevitably go over the terrible embankment. I do not believe that the passengers of any gauge will suffer because of its width, and therefore I hope to meet my old friend (whom I will not cease to love) at the union terminus, when we and others—differing from both in many respects—will receive the cheering " Well done !" of the Conductor under *whose supervision all the gauges were made,* and by whose permission a certain nameless gentleman in black *may* have raised the steam occasionally.

I think sometimes it is not my old friend who utters such awful prophecies as I have hinted above, but some streaks of the Bothwell Brig twins that fulminate through him in their old exclusive way.

E

A WORD IN SEASON.

IN taking a short cut through one of our by-streets, I pass groups of boys and girls in various states of dilapidation and dirt, and of cleanness and wholeness, romping about a school door—the sorrows of life all in the future, and, let us hope, unthought of. Of the two or three scores that I encounter there is only one has caught my special notice hitherto. From the time I first observed her she seemed too fragile to mingle in the general mirth, and stood apart content, it would appear, to look at the fun the others enjoyed ; but although she followed their movements with interest, she yawned at times as if wearied. Unlike all the others, her clothes were never soiled or crumpled ; in the afternoons, as in the mornings, she presented the same tidy, clean appearance. The blue veins shewed through the pure skin of her temples, and her large black eyes had an absent far-away look. Her dark-brown wavy hair, although neatly shaded in the centre of her brow, she sometimes attempted to turn by resetting a comb with her long delicate fingers. As she stood beside an entry one day, and just as I asked myself, "Is she too ill to attend school?" a tidy woman—evidently her mother—patted her cheek softly as she passed, and in return received a very sweet smile. Daily she stood so as I hurried along, till one day, as if worn out, she leaned on the side of the doorway ; but as I approached her to give my usual smile and nod, I saw her eyes brighten as she hurried on before me, and presently put a hand in that of a "black boy" begrimed with dirt

and smoke, and staggering from the effects of drink. Instead of accepting her proffered love he lifted his clenched
fist as if to fell her to the ground, and he certainly would
have done so had not timely aid come. An elderly gentleman, who saw the movement, caught the falling fist in his
palm ; and folding his free hand beside the other's he said,
"Eh, man, that big haun o' yours could smash mine tae
bits, an 's far owre heavy tae fa' on that wee thing's heed.
Dinna, like a gude chiel, hurt the bairn ;" and bringing his
mouth to his ear he whispered, "Ye'll no hae her lang ;
puir lassie, she's dwinin' awa". The great groosy-looking
fellow looked down on the brown head, withdrew his hand,
and lifting the child in his arms he gave her a kiss. When
marching unsteadily away, he looked round and said,
"Thank you, old Cockalorum, I'll no forget your sermon."

"Old Cockalorum" and me have become friends in our
walk to and from business since ; and in passing the entry
together a week later we saw the little girl again, in company this time with her mother, who, addressing my friend,
said, "Jamie bade me tell you he's a Good Templar, sir,
an' I needna say hoo much I'm obleeged tae you." He
returned her smile, lifted his hat, bowed his somewhat bent
body, and then we passed on in silence. I noticed that his
spectacles and his nose troubled him a good deal during the
remainder of our walk that morning. I see "Jamie" and
his wife walking together now and then in evenings, and I
observe she wears a black gown. I miss the wee lassie
with the brown hair, and conclude that she has gone Home.

REMINISCENCES

OF

PAISLEY WEAVERS.

PREFACE.

THE sketches of "PAISLEY WEAVERS" were written for the purpose of recording some of the old methods of our local industry, and of odd traits of character of men and women whom I knew in my early youth. They appeared in the *Glasgow Weekly Herald* from October 3, 1874, till January 21, following, and, as I thought, served my purpose; but when the last chapter was in type the publishers of that paper received a letter from the Rev. Thomas Wilson, Stoughton (Mass.), which, with the repeated desire of many friends, induced me to give them a more permanent form.

The letter runs thus :—

"A stray copy of the *Glasgow Weekly Herald* of November 7, 1874, has recently come into my possession, in which I have more than a transient interest. I have been greatly interested in its perusal; but what specially made it attractive to me was the first article entitled 'PAISLEY WEAVERS OF OTHER DAYS,' which had reference to my honoured father and mother, Mr. Claud Wilson and his wife Peggy Downie.

"Such an unexpected description of them was quite startling. It was like a voice from the dead; for they each, at the ripe age of 83, have passed on some years ago to the other and better land. It was with quite a thrill I read the admirable portrayal of their character.

I think the writer—whom I would be glad to know, to thank him for the unexpected pleasure which he has thus imparted—has succeeded wonderfully in reproducing the social habits and mental traits of one whom he knew long ago as his father's friend.

" The son of that friend from across the Atlantic would tender to him heart-felt thanks for the truthful and interesting way in which he has delineated their characters and perpetuated their memories in his brief sketch."

There is necessarily an appearance of egotism in personal narrative; but to avoid as far as possible that ill-favoured feature, I have introduced my parents under assumed names; and in order not to give offence I have adopted the same course in the case of (so called) James M'Lean and his wife, with some of whose relatives I am on terms of intimacy. To have written in the second person might have led to its being supposed that the narrative was fictitious, which I regard as more objectionable than the form adopted.

A new Edition of "PEN' FOLK" being called for, it has been deemed advisable to add that tractate to the volume, which is sent forth in the belief of its being not unwelcome to such as take an interest in the manners and customs of bygone times.

PAISLEY, *May*, 1876.

PAISLEY WEAVERS OF OTHER DAYS.

CHAPTER I.

I T is singular how the merest trifle will sometimes disturb
the current of one's thought, and, as it were, obliterate
for the moment all cognisance of the present; carrying us
on the airy wings of imagination to distant lands, to times
that are past, and to men and incidents that have slum-
bered in some long unused recess of the memory. When
the mind resumes its everyday functions one is haunted
with the suspicion that everything of the past still lives
as vitally as ever. So, at least, I felt on a late occasion:—

I was sitting at my desk pondering in thought about
"Sufficient unto the day," when from behind me two soft
fingers were laid across my eyes, and on the instant I was
transported back beyond fifty years, and to a certain street
corner, where I met with the cronies of that time, in whose
company I visited the "dookets," and examined our "fan-
tails" and "tumblers." Then, as a voice whispered
"Guess," I, with the same facility, returned to 1874,
wondering who of all I knew in old times had taken me
unaware in this fashion. No one for many years had
dared on such an undignifying liberty. I went back again
to the dear old corner ("Naeplace," we called it) where
we used to congregate at gloamings, and I recollected that
of the dozen boys then so full of life and health, and of

hope in the future, only four remained on the hither side, and only myself in our good old town. He from Canada, thought I, has just gone back—it cannot be *he*. Is it the soldier stipendiary magistrate from New Zealand? Not likely. Then it must be "James Buchan," I said. "Jamie Buchan it is," was the reply of my captor, who, turning me square round, bestowed one of his old hugs; and sure enough there he stood, with the same Scotch terrier-like face, shaggy, confiding, sly but trusty. James Buchan! His name and presence called up such a crowd of old memories, that it is difficult knowing to which I ought to give precedence.

As he was overcome by my "good guessing," I had to allow him time to recover, which he did by blowing his nose, and performing sundry other little matters that I do not require to name. We did not get far beyond a few preliminaries at our first interview, but even these were prolific of old, old memories. One of my first questions was, "And how is Mary?"

"Eh, man, she'll be right glad you guessed sae weel! There she is," was his answer, as he laid before me the carte-de-visite of a douce-looking, comely dame, of middle age, well rounded, and evidently in good keeping.

"What a change!" I said after examination.

"There's a note for you on its back," he replied; and on turning the card I found these words—

"I am not a bit older, and *feel* younger than I did thirty years ago,—Mary Watt Buchan." I felt gratified by her attention, although it was what I might have expected. We were intimate from childhood.

Mary Watt, when a wee, wee lassie, told me confidingly

that she "thocht Jamie Buchan the nicest laddie o' a' the laddies she kent;" and when James became a young man, he hinted in his *thieveless* way that I might introduce him to her. I, as a matter of course, did so, and within a year thereafter they were married. Our paths lay apart for several years after that event, during which time I saw little of them; but it so happened after a while that I was employed in a warehouse to which he wove, when I learnt that Mary had lost health, and that little hope was entertained of her recovery. Doctor Macfarlane, of Glasgow, recommended rest, nourishment, and change of air; adding that, were it possible to give her a voyage to, and a short residence in, Canada, she might regain strength. "It's puir encouragement ye gie me," Mary had said; to which his cheering reply was, that he found in his experience, that hothouse plants like her, when carefully nursed, lived longer than such as he. The ambitious young couple were disheartened at the honest verdict; for James told me in a shaky voice, with a forced smile, that on their way home he "*waled* for saft stanes" on which to rest now and then, and that Mary wept silently at the dreary prospect before them.

I got these items of information one day whilst James stood in the service-box, and I was surprised to find him take such a gloomy view of his condition; for he had considerable stamina and resources on ordinary occasions formerly.

"And what," I asked, "do you intend?"

"What would you recommend?" was his rather con-temptuously-expressed reply, I thought.

"Emigrate at once." I said, "You have something at

your credit here," pointing to the books; "you have your furniture—sell it; your 'stroke' will bring a good price for your loom : the proceeds will take you over, and leave a few pounds on your arrival. If you think of returning when Mary's health is restored, I will find you a loom and work ; think on what I say."

I had other and longer talks with them at their house; and in a month after arrangements were being made to sail for Canada.

The influences which come from outside the family hearth, surrounding and controlling us more or less for a time, are various ; but being often antagonistic, they frequently neutralise each other ; whilst those of home leave more permanent results. The *kelson*, the vertebræ of character, so to speak, is laid down at home ; and whether the constitutional tendencies be good or bad, home influences will, as a rule, fan them into activity. What is ordinarily called education can do much to enlighten and expand the intellect, but the leading out, the marshalling and training of the good, and the repression of the evil, in the affections, is essentially home-work—work that cannot be delegated to others by good parents, without danger or detriment to the young. It is because I feel, after the lapse of many, many years, the effects of my early home life, and because the relation of some of its leading incidents may be of use and amusement to others, that I have determined to throw them into readable form.

The nearer we can go to our early years the brighter gleams do we get of their innocency, and of the "heaven that lies about us in our childhood," for the guardians of the little ones always look heavenward. If my readers participate to any extent in the delight with which I relate the enjoyments or the griefs of my boyhood, their time will not be altogether misspent. But first of all I give them this warning—if they dislike old-fashioned people, or anti-quated modes of expression, bickerings anent "essentials," or innocent mirth, or to spend half an hour in a kitchen with a sanded floor,—let them pause; for my story will consist of gatherings of such people in such a place, and such or such like will be their talk. Before I favour them with the *entree* to these select people, however, they will have to spend half an hour with weavers on their looms, as belonging to the outer court of my life.

It is less, I think, from reciprocated personal affection than for the sake of old associations that James and I remain friends. I met him and his father, Henry Buchan, at the house of William Thomson, and often heard them argue in a *lown* way some knotty points of Christian doctrine. Henry was, for certain reasons that will appear as I proceed, a rather disturbing element to William and his wife. His views, unlike William's, were, as that friend thought, very undefined, and seemed to vary with his mood; but I found in after years they were generally in advance of his time, which may be the reason why William was under the provoking necessity to discover new arguments at every visit. Henry's quiet, slow, uncertain delivery was tantalising to such as "were perfectly sure they were richt," and therefore it surprised no one who knew William to hear him pronounce Henry "a daumert body, wha cudna be said to hae ony settled belief or guid-ing principle whatever, but was aye jouking roon corners gripin' at new notions; he has unco little stability—and then he gangs to nae kirk. I kenna hoo I hae sic patience wi' him, whan he tavers at een here." When this petulant mood was indulged, there was usually a passage-at-*arms* between William and his wife. She had a high esteem for Henry, because of his transparent sincerity, and for the way he had " bent the hard lines of his early life."

" Canny, gudeman, canny," I have heard her say, at such times soothingly. " Whar can ye fin' a man wi' an evener walk, or a deeper sense o' his ain shortcomin' ? or wha amang a' we ken is ane wi' an opener hawn to the needfu', whether it be yerbs for their ailments or meat for their body ? It's true he disna frequent a kirk, mair's the pity; but an' there werena a body worshippin' o' thy way o' thinkin' in the burgh, lad, I doot me thou wad hing owre the fire just like Henry Buchan. Dinna be owre hard on' the auld man ; keep min' o' his up-bringin' ; he ne'er kent what a mother's love or a father's smile is ; nor did he ever ken onything but onkin'ness frae the crew his lot was cast in wi'. The won'er to me is that he ever grew to man's estate, let-a-be bein' a byordinar' good man."

As Henry Buchan will frequently be referred to in the course of this narrative, I will here allude to his " upbring-ing," so that my readers may have some idea of the man.

Henry was found in the roadway when about six years of age, unable to give any account of himself further than what his name was, and that his father and mother were there—pointing to Gleniffer braes, then under a covering of snow. No one offered to shelter the little waif till after nightfall, when a disreputable man, named Matthew Brown, volunteered to give the poor thing house-room till his " payrints cast up." But as the boy was never inquired after, he remained there. Brown's family consisted of his wife and a boy, also named Matthew. Father and son were weavers —ostensibly, but thieves by constitutional tendency and practice. They were Irish too, and in many ways their character contrasted unfavourably with other Irish families in the locality, in consequence of which every boy was instructed to avoid them. Matthew the younger therefore became the bedfellow and only playmate of Henry, and so they came to be fast boy-friends, although differing widely in disposition and manner. Henry, a slender, quiet, silent boy, fair, with blue eyes, spent much of his leisure time poring over what books or newspapers he could lay hands on, and was unconsciously laying up materials of thought by odds and ends of knowledge; whilst Matthew was a strong muscular, boisterous boy, ready, like his father, with a saucy word or a blow, of which Henry got a full share; but fair spoken when not contradicted, and ready also to do a kindness or to fight in defence of the weak if need were. As years passed and the blows predominated over the kindness, we may suppose the friendship to have become less warm. At the end of Henry's apprenticeship, he betook himself to other lodgings, the neighbours remarking that he had a scared look, and that young Matthew thereafter fell into idle, if not evil ways. There was a time, indeed, when he appeared to settle down to honest work, his heart having been smit by the personal charms of an Irish Scotch Presbyterian. To the astonishment of those in the secret of his character, Rosalinda M'Dermot returned his love, and immediately after their marriage, with true womanly faith, set her heart and life to the task of rescuing him from his native mire.   With this end in view, she returned to the Roman Catholic fold, to which he belonged, and during the early years of their wedded life, led him occasionally to confession.   For a while Matthew became a favourite with his former unfriends, who congratulated him on his improvement.   But acquired habits, if unaccompanied by contrition, become as chaff in the wind of natural disposition when it sweeps over the soul; and so, although Mrs. Brown made it known that Matthew "said a mouthful of prayers in the mornings," it was notorious that their home comforts were not diminished by his increased idle habits, and that depredations of which he was suspected multiplied in number.   She gave no sign, however, and uttered no reproach, but bore her cross meekly, bending somewhat, and failing rapidly under her burden.   But though he, breaking from her influence, sank gradually lower, she did not fall with him, but maintained her integrity and an untainted reputation.   Ultimately Matthew was brought before the Justiciary Court at Glasgow for robbing the Nethercraigs Bleachfield; and it was said that, had it not been for the exculpatory evidence furnished by Henry Buchan, he would have been "justifit."   He was banished for life.

Whether it was that Mrs. Brown had failed in the great purpose of her life, and therefore had lost faith in the prayers of the Church and of confession, or that she felt comfortless in that communion on general grounds, I am not informed; but it is certain that after Matthew's banishment she returned to her Protestant faith.

I remember her as an old woman, tall and spare, in a short grey duffle cloak, the hood of which formed a large cavity before her face; the dark lines round her eyes frequently reddened from weeping, her grey hair straggling over her withered face, which in colour resembled unbleached linen. She visited my mother now and then with a letter from Matthew to read, and always had a volume of Flaval under her arm, which she said was "gran fat meat." Once when, as a mark of respect for her sorrow, and poverty, and goodness, my mother called her Linda, the poor creature burst into tears, and begged her not to do so again, as it reminded her of her dear, misguided man. Her name, like her personal beauty, which in youth was said to have been considerable, had faded long before my day. I knew her only as " Rosie Broon."

Henry Buchan being from an unknown stock, it was prophesied that his family would turn out ill, and *their* upbringing was watched by certain gossips accordingly. When any hints of that nature were given in the presence of Mrs. Thomson, she silenced the detractors by saying she "didna see hoo his bairns could be waur than ithers, seein' that the hale race o' man was totally corrupt, and un'er the curse o' Adam's transgression." The story of Henry's boyhood was old long before my day; and although I often heard the minute details of his early hardships, and of the means he adopted to obtain a plain English education, I cannot hope to reproduce in words the early impressions left on my mind of respect, amounting to veneration, for his patient, steady, plodding determination. His boys were models of obedience, but were not exempt from the mischiefs incident to their years; and his wife, unassuming as she was, was guided by very clear preceptions of right and wrong. An incident to which I was witness will better

F

illustrate the tone of her mind than anything I could say. It was the following:—Jamie and I were amusing ourselves near their door one afternoon, when his mother called him to go a message; and I went with him to a small grocer's a few doors west. I did not know the nature of his errand, which he gave into her hand on the door-step, where she had stood during our absence. We had scarcely resumed our game when she laid her hand on his arm, and asked where he had gone for the change.

"Granny Polson's," answered he.

"Did she coont it?"

"No; she had it in a paper as you got it."

"There's a mistak; there's nine haufcroons in the paper; rin awa up wi' that ane," handing him a halfcrown piece.

"Will ye no keep it?" said an impulsive urchin at our side. She looked round on him with a serious face, and said—

"Na, na, bairn, there's a day comin' whan a' the haufcroons will be coonted; an' that ane's no mine. Rin awa, Jamie, wi't."

I will introduce her formally by and by.

Henry himself was a gentle accessible man; and as our weaving shop was occupied with plain weavers, whilst his had work requiring drawboys, I was a frequent visitor after school-hours, and enjoyed the unusual *stir* and noise. I am not likely to forget doing so; it was there I committed my first great blunder, which consisted of forming the resolution to leave school and become a drawboy—a fatal mistake, which I had reason to regret for years after.

It was not long till I carried my point, and entered on

my labours—against much good advice. I found, when it was too late, that I had made a very terrible mistake. But there was no help for it; I was too self-willed to confess myself wrong, and too proud to complain of what was the common lot of boys so employed.

CHAPTER II.

BEFORE my readers can understand the extent of my grievance, it will be necessary to say a few words respecting the daily life of the working men of my boyhood, although the changes in our manners, and mental outcome consequent upon improving our once famous shawl trade, have been so great that it will be difficult for any one not connected with the locality to appreciate the difference between then and now. Nor will it be an easy matter for even the younger portion of those engaged in it to realise the difference between their condition and that of those who lived fifty odd years ago. Those who, like me, endured the drudgery and harsh treatment common to drawboys will certainly not sigh for the return of the "good old times." It was a time of suffering—to some from necessity; to others, stupidly enough, from choice; though, indeed, the demand for the labour of the young being often in excess of the supply, it was difficult for any boy to escape.

Previous to 1818, when the shawl branch of our local industry was in its infancy, so to speak, both weavers and their boy-helps must have had comparatively easy lives; but onward for many years, so long, indeed, as the weavers remained masters—for latterly the boys ruled *them* —things assumed a very different aspect. As the shawl trade waxed, the trade in silk gauze and other fine fabrics

waned; and the manners and general bearing of those
engaged appeared to me then, and still appear to my
mind, as different as the goods they manipulated. At'
the date just named the inhabitants numbered 34,800; of
whom there were from 6000 to 7000 weavers, and of these
not fewer than from 4000 to 5000 required the assistance
of a drawboy. Now, when the population has reached
50,000, the weaving body is reduced to 1750, only 750
of whom are on the electors' roll, and there is not one
drawboy in town. New industries, steam-power, and the
Jacquard machine have all contributed to the changed
character of the people—in some respects for the better,
and in others for the worse.

In old times, every weaver, being his own master, came
and went at his convenience; when he took a day's pleasure
—fishing, curling, bowling, or berrying, as the case happened—he made up work for it before or after, as pleased
him; the loom was his own property, and he was an-
swerable to his employer only. The introduction of the
Jacquard has changed that condition of the weaver entirely.
With only 1750 looms in town, there are not, I presume,
over 750 owners of looms, all the other hands being but
"journeymen," who are not responsible to the manufacturers, but only to the master weaver. With the loss of
social standing, the old spirit of independence and much
of the greedy intellectual research have vanished; what
these have been replaced by I will leave others to name
and designate. Hand-loom weaving factories have no
doubt done much to destroy that peculiar individuality
of character for which the class was noted, when the town
was one huge weaving factory of master weavers, and the

well-being and comfort of the whole population were directly or indirectly dependent on the produce of the "shuttle e'e." The picture had its shade as well as its sun, however. When trade failed, which from its fancy nature and other causes it did frequently, want and its accompanying wail were all but universal; it was only the provident that escaped destitution. Many of these having saved some money were induced to feu a piece of ground, and had a house built for themselves, which, from ever-recurring stagnations in trade, fell into the hands of the superior. At this day not one of whole streets of houses built from the savings of weavers remain in the possession of the original feuars or their descendants.

From April to September the usual working hours were from six in the morning till dusk; during the other months of the year we began at the same early hour, and toiled on till ten, eleven, and sometimes twelve at night. In the weeks preceding the New-Year and May and August fairs it was common to work one night and two days without cessation, in order that one or two days' relaxation might be had during these holiday seasons.

The "drawboy's" duty was to "chap up" his master in the morning; if at any time he was half-an-hour late in doing so, he had to take a "cuff" when his master did arrive. In the interval of his coming the boy dusted the lay and temples, and cleaned and oiled the spindles. If a drop or two of oil chanced to fall on the yarn or cloth, he took a kick in addition with what philosophy he was possessed of. I have seen boys so treated, times without number, and what never failed to astonish me was, that long before breakfast hour the master and boy were singing some favourite song together.

But all masters were not alike severe. I had one—the only one of the six working together—who never punished his boy; but, on the contrary, he spoke to him and treated him in every way as his equal; recommended some particular song as beautiful, repeated scraps of poetry, or told some interesting tale which awakened a thirst to drink at the fountains he indicated. I got the cream of Scott, Hogg, and Galt in this way before I had heard of their existence. When everything failed to recall my interest and attention, "Tak a jink for five minutes" he would say; and on my return we started a song, and everything went on to our mutual contentment.

Singing was a never failing solace to many weavers and boys then, and it is, I believe, still practised by many in town. In one of the shops where I wrought, one of the men was particularly famous as a singer in after years. He wrought at a web, I remember, of soft organzine, which material, if not carefully handled when being "dressed," is liable to "plait," and thereby causes the loss of one or perhaps two days to get it into working order again. At times when it was being dressed, the weaver alluded to having adjusted his "pace-cords" and set up his rods, took his fan in hand, which he waved gently, and with his free hand touched the hardening warp lightly, now and then, till the danger was past, when he would burst out rapturously with "My Nannie's awa," carolling beautifully, but quite unconscious that all his mates had stopped work to listen. On one occasion when the web went wrong, I saw him lay down his head on his yarn beam and sob like a vexed child. His wife, too, when she heard of the mishap, came with tears in her eyes, and laid her hand tenderly on his neck; the wee, delicate, humpback lassie they had adopted was at her side looking up wonderingly. She, poor thing, had to wade barefoot through the snow another week or more in consequence of the "plaiting." It was understood to be on her account they were so grieved; certainly it was for her sake the other hands lent assistance so cheerfully to repair the web. The weaver in question led the praise to a church in town, and afterwards became a teacher of music, and maintained a good position while he remained in the locality.

After he left he paid us a professional visit once in a while. Twelve years later I heard him sing the same songs he had sung when I was a boy, and was delighted to listen to the old natural " wood-notes wild," and when other five and twenty years had rolled past, I heard him again: when he ascended the platform, it was as if he had been stowed away in some hermetically-sealed box, with the identical black trousers, white vest, blue coat with metal buttons, and massive gold watch-chain, that he wore on the former occasion. I met him on the day following, and had some pleasant talk about his shopmates of the old time, of whom he had lost sight, and of the changes that had taken place in styles and texture of the trade, which led us to refer to the old sub-stantial "trimmings" with their hard and soft organzine warps—material quite out of use with us at the time. I recalled the day on which his web "plaited," and he appeared to shudder as he answered—" Eh, man ! it was an awfu' day that, an' an awfu' time a' ways."

His adopted daughter, whom he loved so well, had been dead some years I learned, so that "My Nannie's awa" would have a deeper significance to him than it had formerly.

Besides our ordinary duty during the long day I have noted, the Saturday afternoons, which were said to be our own, were occupied in preparing for the work of the coming week. First, we had to sweep the loom-stead, going under the treadles, where lodged rotten dressing, damp ravellings, spider webs, snails, and other abominations; then there were bridles to mend, isinglass to melt to dress the simple, and brushes to wash. Now and then we were sent to the weavers' wright to get the drivers tipt, after which we were sent to the mistress for our wage. But here again we were caught, and sent to bring one, or perhaps two "gang" of water from a well two or three streets off. Lucky we thought ourselves, if there were not a crowd before us, in which case we might be detained till dusk; our only hope left being that the well would run dry. So it went on, week after week, for months and years—a cheerless grind, with little variation, except an unmerciful punishment for the merest trifle. Who can wonder that boys. under such unbroken toil and hard treatment, became exasperated and quarrelsome? Some of them made their escape by running off to sea, and in various other ways. I was more fortunate than many boys in that respect, and less so in others. For if my masters were less severe, they were generally of the regular, sober class, who tied me more to work. I can account for many of the boys submitting to their fate only from the fact that other unrecognised influences were at work restraining them, and which I will here refer to.

It was the custom of many parents, when hiring their

children, to stipulate with the master that the boy or girl would be made to read a chapter of the New Testament at some hour every day. Some parents—mine among them—were so tenacious on that condition that its omission cancelled the contract. And although few boys esteemed the reading a pleasant duty, we all felt it, I believe, a relief from the hard, monotonous work; and the words, although unheeded, had a soothing effect on most. Many of the passages we then repeated come back now, I have no doubt, to the memory of others as they do to mine. Some of the masters disliked these readings more than the boys did, which they shewed by never interrupting work while the boy was so engaged; and these were often of the church-going class. Others, again—the kindest in other respects—heard the chapter sitting on their looms, and let the boy enjoy himself when the "dressing was in." I had one master of the latter sort, a young harum-scarum, and a poet in a way, who preferred portions of Isaiah or Revelation, which he pronounced "gran', man." Next to his loom was one of the sober sort, but cruel and exacting towards his boy. He took "the books" at both ends of the day, except when he indulged in a day's drinking, which was not often. He had no family of his own, and took his revenge on Providence therefor, by horsewhipping his drawboy. The boy told me years after that the yellow wales on his back still testified against him. He added with a smile, that the one redeeming feature in his character was that he drank at times, giving his boy time to prosecute the art of bridle-making. That weaver is identified in my memory with an incident that is not likely to be forgotten. For some carelessness he thrashed his boy so severely one day, that a shopmate leaped from his loom, snatched the whip from his hand, and applied it to his back and head with such force as made the shop ring with his cries and laughter of the other hands. How we boys blessed that man ! and how we mimicked the other when safe beyond hearing ! The boy's defender was not beautiful, or even comely, to look upon; he was a low-browed, long-jawed, broad-chinned man, whose vicious mouth, when open, shewed a straggling row of tusks ; he swore like a Turk, drank frequently, and fought when in drink; but when sober was kindly, even tender-hearted to the weak; he chaffed his boy when he got careless, but was never known to punish him. What he had done in the poor boy's interest was not calculated to promote his obedience; and as he refused to give up his bridle-making, unless the others did so likewise, which we refused to do, he unhooked his cords, put on his jacket, and left. As I had a few minutes' leisure, I accompanied him part of his way home, and heard him bless Jock Lamont for his interference, whilst he laughed hysterically at the recollection of his master's screams under his flagellation. I daresay some boys required correction at times, but the punishment inflicted was almost always in excess of the carelessness—almost the only fault of which we were guilty. The indignity was to me more painful than the blows. I never had to submit to punishment at home, and every kick or cuff I received at my work made me, for the time, hard and obstinate.

But the sorrows and the anger of the young are intermittent; even in shops notorious for hard masters, mirth alternated with the bitter cup. I recollect a shop in which the boys were tightly held where one of the weavers was

what we called a "character"—of which our town was,
I think, prolific long ago; and as mimicry was a never-
failing source of enjoyment, he was daily made the subject
of imitation by some boy. He was a Highlander—a tall,
muscular man—and being as "het as pepper," he furnished
us with additional items to the programme, on which account he became a favourite. He had considerable difficulty in speaking intelligible English, and the most uncouth
manner of pitching his shuttles, bending back at every shot
as if afraid of being struck, grinning viciously the while,
and brought his lay home with a force better adapted to
the stroke-oar in a boat race than to a well-trimmed loom.
We gave imitations—in his absence, of course, for his hand
was large and heavy—and for doing so were gowled at by
some weaver, whose gowl was imitated in reply, which
intensified the fun, in which other weavers joined. The
favourite imitation was of some drawboy going on to his
loom when he was absent. In this case one boy cried
in Rory's fashion on another boy, in broken English, and
proceeded to work "owre the draught," growling at the
boy in the best Gaelic he could make. The weavers,
although pretending wrath, enjoyed the sport as heartily
as the boys. It must have been on the principle that
stolen waters are sweet, that we persisted in occupying
some loom at every opportunity, for it was strictly
prohibited, and punished severely; yet, in defiance of
authority, scarcely a day passed without its being done.
It had results of which we knew nothing at the time.
Sometimes we broke a *bridle*, or a *cord*, or *yarn*, a *simple*
came. down, or a *tail* cast the *whorl*—all which, to avoid
reproof or a "skelp," we had to repair. Those of my

readers who are not conversant with the terms I have italicised cannot imagine the amount of insight we thus obtained, or the familiarity our mimic weaving gave us with the uses of the various parts of a loom. I believe I could not have kept the position I held afterwards without the germs of knowledge conveyed to my mind by indulging in that forbidden sport. I never was a weaver, but, excepting the mechanical operation of throwing the shuttle, I learnt to understand and do almost everything about a loom as well as most weavers can do now-a-days.

CHAPTER III

A S I have frequently referred to bridle-making, it may be as well that I explain what it means. During the greater part of the first twenty years of this century, the figured goods manufactured in town were of the simplest description, a large proportion of the fabrics having only one cover-colour, and few had more than three. The patterns were then "read on" in the weaving shop to the simple attached to the tail of the harness, and generally speaking, the "lifts" were formed into "lashes" by the weaver. When the whole pattern was thus finished, two strong upright cords of three strands each, called "gut cords," were placed ten or twelve inches apart, and as far distant from and in front of the simple. These had what were called long heads kenched loosely round them, having a knot at their end. On each head was kenched firmly a lash, a head being taken from each gut cord alternately, when there was only one cover or colour in the pattern; but when more than one, the left hand gut cord was set apart for the second and third colour, the first or leading colour being confined to the right hand one, and was then and ever since called the first lash. When the lashes were kenched, there was a bridling cord attached to each head, ten or twelve inches apart, so that the first and last and all intermediate lashes were connected by this "running bridle," as it was called. As

patterns came to be more complicated by having an increased number of colours, as many as three or four gut
cords were used; but before this had taken place, flower-
lashing had become an important branch of industry in
connection with our local manufacture, and the patterns,
instead of being read on in the weaving shop, were given
to the weavers on the simple, headed and bridled, ready
to attach to the harness-tail. But as patterns became
more and more elaborate, having from six to nine colours
or shades of colour, the running bridle and double files
of gut cords were found to be too complicated, and in
efficient withal. By a simple contrivance of the late Mr.
John Roxburgh, the "cross bridle" was introduced, and
the gut cords reduced to two. Cross bridles stretched
from right to left, and were knotted at about one and a
half inches apart, as often as there were colours in the
pattern. On each knot a "short head" was kenched,
to each of which was kenched a lash, as in the running
bridle. The head next the boy's right hand contained
the first lash, and had its own colour as all the others
had. The cross bridles were made and headed by drawboys at their spare time; but as the employment gave
them an interest outside their proper work, it was the
cause of much heart-burning between man and boy; and
my readers will understand that one very important feature
in a good master was that he allowed his boy to bring his
bridles to the loom-side; and another feature not less in
value in the estimation of the boy was, that his master
drank a day or two occasionally, because from sixpence
to ninepence a day to the boy was involved in such conduct. Sometimes the boy lent him a shilling or more

when funds were low and thirst was strong; but such men were not considered respectable, and they were generally members of some drinking "core," of which there were one or more in each of the districts of the town. Some of their schemes to "raise the wind" were even more disreputable than borrowing, and others were not without a certain grim humour. As I am on the subject, I will give two instances of such conduct that are well authenticated.

The late Mr. John Clark (of J. & J. Clark) often felt grieved, on passing to his works at Seedhills, to witness the cruel treatment inflicted on a lame, ulcerated, starved horse; and on one occasion he saw two or three well-known members of a drinking core walk deliberately from Bank Street to the door of a spirit shop at which the animal stood, and "lowse" it from the cart, and trot it round by Mill Street to Whitehead's Tanwork, where they sold it for what they could get. Prosecution was threatened, to avoid which Mr. Clark paid the damages demanded—— "Because," said he, "it was a pity to see the honest chiels bothered for putting the poor beast out of pain."

The other case is not less characteristic. The funds of the same core were exhausted on a day in winter that Dr. M—— had a dinner-party, and in order to replenish the coffer, they contrived to render one of their number helplessly drunk, and after nightfall carried him in a large bag to the doctor's door, and offered him as a subject. Dr. M—— being engaged, could not examine his purchase at the moment, but handed them the key of an outhouse and a one pound note to account. Some hours later, when his company had left, he took key and candle, and

went to examine his bargain. He looked over the floor
for the bag in vain; and was rather startled at hearing
sounds in a back corner of the cellar, and cried out—

"Who's there?"

"It's me, doctor."

"You," bringing the candle to his face. "An' what
the *deevel* are you doin' here?"

"Faith! I'm wantin' oot—it's a cauld place," and he
made for the door.

I do not know if the doctor was tipsy when he entered,
but it is certain, his wife said, that he was quite sober
when he came back. The pranks of the several cores
that were in town gave the weavers in general a bad reputation, which they did not deserve.

My aversion to my work intensified with my experience,
and every time I saw a boy punished determined me to
quit it; in the meantime, my dislike of the work was in
part transferred to the boys, because they were content to
toil on, and therefore I avoided them as much as I could.
Their hard work and harder usage, no doubt, made them
turbulent and reckless of what they said and did; and
their number being legion, made them a terror to quiet
people. During all hours of the day some of them were
on the streets, and at meal-hours there were swarms everywhere scampering through their games or mischiefs. Rude,
loud, and daring for the most part, they were ready for fun
of any sort, or for fighting, if need were; and, like their
masters, cruel to the weak and defenceless; yet, as far as
ever I saw, gentle and deferential in an uncouth way to
the girls. The garb of almost every boy was of fustian,
corduroy, or velveteen, and blue worsted bonnet. In

G

summer all went barefoot; in winter time they wore strong comfortable stockings, and shoes that were a continual source of complaint, of which I will speak by and by.

After the boy left of whom I have spoken, the weavers combined to exclude bridle-making from the shop; and my web being out, I was told that I would be engaged only on condition that I threw it up. I was only too glad of an excuse to leave, and refused. Like other patriots, I was awarded a hearty vote of thanks, and a waving of bonnets at street corners, for a week after.

My anxiety to get a new master was more apparent than real. When one came in my way I became very particular respecting his web, his habits, and temper. I was so engaged one day with an idle weaver, whose grim, solemn face did not please me in the least, and was heard to decline his offer by a pleasant-looking youngish woman, having a child in arms, who asked if I wanted "a gude master, wha had a nice licht stroke?" The little one made overtures of friendship to me, and instead of answering the mother I returned the salute of the child, who put forth its arms and almost fell into mine. I was caught; but thought that what I had to say could be said at any time, and so without making answer, I, with the child in my arms, accompanied the woman. On reaching the shop we found her husband, who took the "shute" bag and money from her, while I sauntered round examining the surroundings, which I concluded were about the right thing.

As that was my last shop, my last master, and in every way a very pleasant time of my boyhood, I will devote a few lines to the several oddities in connection with it.

The name of my new master was Sandy Reid, a young man of great muscular power and endurance. Before his marriage he was a member of the "King Street Core," notorious over the town for their quarrelsome disposition, and disreputable alike for their drunken habits, and the pleasure they took in witnessing and engaging in the brutalities of the prize ring. Some of the men continued to be members after marriage; but Sandy, on giving the core the customary marriage "booze," announced his secession, and although some of his cronies sneered at his resolution, they took care to do so in private, for he was known to be dangerous at fisticuffs. He kept his word too, although he did not refuse to spend an afternoon once in a while at quoits, or in throwing bullets on "the toll road-side" with them, and spending an hour on such occasion in Mrs. Rowand's "public," called the Linn. That he might avoid their society, he seldom went to the warehouse, but sent his wife instead. Full of health and animal spirits, all his likings were in exertion—working hard during six days, and walking from twenty to thirty miles on Sundays, to the grief and "black disgrace" of Lizzy, who would greatly have preferred seeing him guard the plate, like his father, at the church door. Sandy was wonderfully tickled at that proposition, and never failed to laugh loudly. At the same time he put his arm round her waist, and kissed away her forebodings.

I was the only boy in the shop, the other hands being plain silk weavers. Reid was a silk weaver also; but he wove a sewed bord and sprig with sewing frame, and required a boy. The others, who were elderly men, wrought a "turkey gauze," a rainbow and a gossamer. The tene-

ment in which we worked had been built to hold six
looms, but was too short to admit of more than four of
the stretch these occupants had. The joisting and floor
overhead formed the ceiling of the shop, so that what
was said in the one place was heard in the other. Reid's
loom was directly under Lizzy's wheel, and he and she
occasionally carried on a conversation from where they
sat; privacy during the day was beyond their reach. The
portions of the shop not occupied by looms, and also all
the window-sills, were filled with verbenas, roses, and other
flowering or sweet-scented plants, with the combined odours
of which the place was saturated. The front door was
kept closed, and the long garden behind, with its fruit
trees, bushes, flower beds, and bee-skeps was a really
pleasant retreat to me at times. Mrs Reid was my only
bug-a-boo. She was a kind, well-meaning woman, whom
I would not willingly have offended, but was constantly
under the fear of doing so, by laughing at her. On the
day Sandy took a game at quoits she required my presence
upstairs to read my chapter to her; and she discovered,
she said, that although I had "a gude smattering o' Bible
knowledge," I was wofully ignorant of certain doctrinals
which she said were essential to be known and believed.
These she expounded at such enormous length and with
such prolixity that I never could catch her drift. On
everyday subjects—subjects relating to right and wrong—
she possessed not only a *roug* of common sense, but a
keenness of perception that few women were equal to, and
fewer still, it is to be hoped, have such an awkward mode
of expressing their thoughts. She appeared never to pay
any attention whatever to her breathing, but spoke on,

on, and on, without pause or modulation of voice, till she had not a particle of breath to emit. The end of every breathful of words came away in stutterings and sputterings; and in recovering breath she sent forth a sound not unlike, as I thought, that of a child under whooping-cough. When she had "crowed," away she went again with renewed vigour. I never was present when she argued or was excited, if I could avoid it, so afraid was I to offend her. I dare say I perplexed the good woman at times by my ineptness to apprehend her explanations of Christian doctrines, when the fact was, I paid more attention to her manner than her words. On one occasion she asked me if I "kent ony o' the questions," and on my answering "Some," she said,

"Whilk o' them?"

"The chief end o' man," I said.

"Ony mae?"

"Yes; what? what is the chief end of God?"

"Gude be gracious tae us a' callan whae'er heard o' that question its no i' the book what pits sic a query i' thy heed bide still bairn awee Tamas Jardine come awa up an' speak tae me will ye man gude bless me whatna droll callan dinna stan' there an' laugh at me or I'll brain thee."

What boy could resist laughing at such a torrent of words, uttered without break or change in tone? I could not, and was very glad to escape with Thomas Jardine, who came up, but did not remain long, as will be seen.

Jardine was one of the plain weavers I have referred to He belonged originally to Dumbarton, from whence he joined the army in his youth, and after twenty-two years' campaigning, settled in our town with a good-service pension.

Short in stature and somewhat corpulent, he had a comfortable appearance.   Unlike weavers in general, who paid little
attention to the demands of the stomach, or to personal
cleanliness, Thomas lived generously, and he continued
his soldier habit of shaving and washing daily.   He never
wore slippers, as others did, at their work, but always
appeared in creaking shoes, brushed and shining.   His
stockings, of the finest wool, were fastened under his
knee-breeches of worsted cord, such as horse-dealers wore.
His short blue coat with metal buttons was nearly concealed
by a spacious white linen apron, tied round his arm-pits.
On his head was a huge otter-skin cap, the peak of which
hung down behind, like that of a sou'-wester; and whilst
working he carried a white bone slay-hook between his
teeth, ready to enter broken yarn.   He never could have
been a comely looking man, his face being seamed over
with pox-pitting; added to which, there was an ugly sabre
cut crossing from the left eye to the right side of his chin.
Altogether his appearance was grim and fierce; but his
uniformly open, gentle manner to myself prevented him
becoming the terror to me he was to his shopmates.
He was always ready to exchange a little chaffing with
them, in doing which his quaint humour gave him the
advantage; and when in a talkative mood, his subjects
were a curious medley of battlefields, theology, and Tory
politics.   Although he had a hard metallic tongue when
roused, he never used unbecoming language, unless taken
by surprise, and the only objectionable word he was liable,
perhaps from long habit, to utter, was " Oh, demit !" or
"demit, sir !"   When in compliance with Mrs. Reid's
call he came up, that good woman opened with—

" Did ye ever in your life hear o' sic a question he was sayin' the chief en' o' man an'"—and so on she went in the words I have given. Thomas, with his habitual good breeding, stood silent, till she had exhausted her breath, and then said—

" Oh, demit, Mrs. Reid, you mustn't ask such questions at the boy; his father won't stand it, you know; will take him away if you do. Let him read his piece to us below when Sandy's away—we like it, you know. If you wish to hear, listen, or come down, he belongs below. Demit, why do you laugh, chit?"

I was thenceforward relieved of going to Mrs. Reid when Sandy was quoiting, as Thomas, with military regularity, assumed the duty of " hearkener."

CHAPTER IV.

JARDINE, on pension day and at other uncertain times, returned, but not often, somewhat elevated with liquor, lamenting the " de-generacy" of the age, and propounding schemes for the " re-demption" of man; after which he seated himself on a high stool in the middle of the shop, and commenced denouncing James Fleming, another of the shopmates, for some real or imaginary delinquency, by which he kept the shop and the houses above ringing with laughter. The story he related had just so much truth for a basis as irritated Fleming, who had not a vestige of humour, and who stuttered with rage at the romance that provoked such mirth. When Fleming approached the white heat, Thomas quietly withdrew, and immediately after he might be seen with his head under the pump in the garden. In a little while he appeared in his large cap, white apron, and with slay-hook between his teeth, proceeding to his loom, where he remained grim and silent for the rest of the day.

On a day following one of these tasting days, I was reading the nineteenth chapter of John's gospel, which I frequently selected when I had the choice, because I had read it so often that I could repeat it without using my book and work at my bridles at the same time. All the looms were stopped, as usual, while I recited, and Jardine was standing before the fire, bent forward towards me, intently listening.

David Wilson, the other shopmate, passing where he stood, said—

"Ye seem tae like that, Thomas ?"

"Like it ? no, demit, I don't; but I see it all, as plainly as ever I saw battlefield, and it makes my blood rise. Poor soul! not a finger lifted in defence of Him! All ruffians! The world was not worthy of Him; poor soul, poor soul."

Fleming, as if eager to repay the chaff of yesterday, hissed in his ear—"Tak' tent, Jardine, or ye'll be losing ony head ye ever had."

Thomas had fairly broken down, however, and for a minute kept his hands over his face; but recovering himself, he looked up with mournful eyes at Fleming, and with a sob and a sigh said—

"The wonder is that any one keeps his head. Look at it, sir; in a battlefield we lose now and win another day. Some fall, some live on, and the stake for the soldier is life, more or less; for the King, God bless him, it may be a province or his kingdom; but this, sir, relates to eternity—that's the stake here. Lose my head? demit, sir, and a creditable thing, too, to lose in such a cause. Don't interfere in the matter, Fleming; stick to Cobbett."

Jardine's strong religious convictions, like streams of water, were strengthened by their boundaries being confined. He could not find any society of Christians holding his peculiar opinions of the brotherhood "having all things in common;" and therefore, whilst agreeing with the so-called orthodox on other points—points that are considered of greater importance—he stood aloof from all. Liberal on one subject, he was narrow and exclusive on all else, whether relating to theology or politics. Perhaps his

procedure in this matter was the result of his condition
as a solitary man.   He had, for one thing, no family
ties to lift him out of himself; and then his hard life as
a soldier must have weakened his sympathies, which his
isolation as a bachelor tended to enfeeble still more.   Kind
he could be, and was, where material aid was required;
but he had no tenderness, nor could he understand its
meaning, except in a poetical sense.   With less dogmatism
and more affection and desire to appreciate the difficulties
of others, he might have controlled the turbulence of his
mates in no small degree, of whom he was the tacitly
acknowledged leader; but as he made dogma and life
exchangeable terms, he only restrained their Republicanism
with his highhanded Toryism, whilst he loosened their hold
of matters of greater value.   What to him was freedom, to
them was licence.   Fleming, through his influence, and
from his own innate obtuseness in such matters, came to
confound the practice of Christians with Christian principle,
and then to discard the latter as unworthy of his regard,
and embrace what he called the "Deistical line."   Fleming's
forte was politics in general, and Cobbett's *Register* in particular.   I question if he had faith in anything that was
not in harmony with Cobbett; and he expressed himself
in the same plain, terse, outspoken way as that writer.
It was not till years after that I discovered where he had
culled the fierce epithets in which he declaimed.   He
was of low stature.   The most noticeable feature in his
appearance was that there was no visible dividing line
between his body and his head.   It was as if his backbone ran up into his head, making him stiff-necked looking.
In other respects he had a *wersh*, unsatisfied look.

Whatever wild oats David Wilson may have had in youth were all sown long ago. In personal appearance he was the cleanest I ever had seen; yet somehow he gave one the impression that he paid little attention to his person. Let the reader imagine a man rather above average height, spare and sinewy, with broad open forehead wrinkled like a rig-and-fur stocking, clear black eyes, and dark grizzly hair, dressed in drab knee breeches unbuttoned at the knees, gray stockings and slippers, bleached linen apron and shirt to match, without neck-tie, and sleeves turned up to his elbows, and he will have some idea of the outward man. He was a fair specimen of the old class of silk weavers, the reflected glory of whose sturdy independence, wide range of information, and general intelligence has rendered all our handloom weavers famous ever since—in over-credulous minds. He was less confined than the others in the subjects he discussed, being a well-read man to whom any subject was welcome. What he did not know he was not ashamed to learn. Where he found any man assuming a knowledge he did not possess, Wilson was not slow to expose the pretension. Besides his plain, outspoken manner and pawky humour, which frequently led him to say more, and say it with greater severity, than he intended, he was modest and unassuming, and never quite satisfied with the knowledge he possessed, being haunted with the suspicion that higher knowledge was attainable. With Jardine he discussed theology; with Fleming, politics—these being their respective specialties. Jardine's curt, sharp phrases, kept Wilson within reasonable bounds in his replies, whose thoughts, like those of Fleming, seemed to be located on the tip of his tongue, which, once agoing, went on for ten, and sometimes fifteen minutes without pause. Fleming spoke choice English—a rare accomplishment with his class— which it was pleasant to hear; and being a political authority in his district, he was imperious and dictatorial in manner. When he was about to propound some new "Cobbettical nostrum," as Jardine called it, he prefaced the speech with "I tell you most distinctly," and he said this so repeatedly, that "Most distinctly" came to be his by-name. Wilson, on the other hand, spoke the broadest of broad Scotch. His speech usually began with, "Whether thou speaks sense or no is of'en vera questionable, Fleming, but there can be nae doot aboot thy fine style o' language;" and he finished invariably with, "Noo, Jamie, come awa wi' a wheen o' thy distinctlys."

Wilson, it would appear, had been too carefully nurtured and admonished in his youth; his father being so strict an observer of Sunday that every natural impulse of his children were repressed from morn till night of that day. The consequence was that as the boys reached manhood they took their revenge by disregarding its legitimate authority altogether. David had gone so far even as to renounce allegiance to Christianity itself for a while. But the remains of his childhood's innocency, which had been inseminated through his mother's love, saved him, he said, from utter godlessness; and he sustained less injury from his disbelief than by his father's enforced sanctification of Sunday. So long as I knew him he never *sweetened* on that subject, but continued to treat Sabbatarians with reprehensible severity or ironical respect. He had no reverence for professing Christians, whether elders or ministers, from whom we had visits occasionally. Of the former class were neighbouring weavers, who came for information about new cordings; when disquisitions took place as to the best mode of arranging them. Frequently the topic merged into politics and religion, and then the stream of talk flowed on for an hour or more without pause, giving me leisure to peg away at my bridles. At other times we were visited by a clergyman to talk with Thomas Jardine about bees and tulip-roots, when ecclesiastical and kindred subjects were discussed; and as these were Mrs. Reid's own private pastures, that earnest woman came down, with her child in arms, and took part in the fray. As the minister did not understand her peculiar mode of adjusting the balance of supply and demand of her breath, his nervous starts at her crowing were a source of amusement to Wilson, who contrived to give her opportunity to speak. Wilson's antecedents were known to the clergyman, and during one of his visits he lamented that he had never connected with any church, which put Wilson on his defence. Wilson met him with banter rather than argument, and, with much else of a like nature, said—

" It 's no' the like o' me you kirk folk want amang you; am no' gude enoch; I dinna think mysel' a saunt, an' it 's the saunted kin' ye prefer; although I canna see hoo they need your help. Sinners maun a' hae a gude opinion o' theirsels afore ye 'll admit them, onless they can haun in a gowpen o' siller, an' than ye speer nae questions; it 's just wauk up, ladies an' gentlemen, the yett 's open for *you*,

'And ye shall dine by the glassy sea,
Aneath the shade o' the evergreen tree.' "

Jardine, who, although a rough, eccentric man, deprecated anything approaching to irreverence or personal disrespect, came from his loom, where he had listened with interest, and taking the slay-hook from between his lips, and pointing it at Wilson, said to the minister—

"I hope you won't identify me with his profane buffoonery? I despise it, you know, and all his damnable heresy. He gets ruder, too, as he gets older. Why, sir, he laughs at the good tidings I give him, you know."

The visitor replied that he was truly sorry that David spoke with such rudeness, "and, as you say, he gives expression to damnable heresy."

"Ecod," cried Wilson, "the twa corbies are clawin' ither's back. Let me tell you, sir, that if I seem disrespectfu' I dinna mean 't. I whiles speak as I think, an' whiles as I feel; sae dinna misjudge me. As for my heresy, an' its being damnable, that's anither story. Langsyne professors were ca'ed hypocrites, an' vipers, an' a generation o' serpents; an' the misbelievers an' onbelievers were tawld calmly that they erred, no kenin' better. Noo, we're damned for what the Maister said is only an error. But I'll put it tae you in anither way. The hale o' us here present believe that mercy is a law o' God. We a' believe in mercy—the mercy that draps frae His ain throne, saftenin' every heart it touches, makin' the maist mercifu' likest God himsel'. We a' believe that. But, sir, if you or me is onmercifu' in oor life, will oor belief lead us tae His richt haun or oor cruelty tae His left? Tell me that, if ye please."

"Well," answered his reverence, "that, you must allow, is an extreme case."

" Extreme? oo, aye, it's a wee extreme atweel. But isna damnation a vera extreme affair? Od, man, I won'er ye dinna use your thinkin' faculty mair on maiters o' this kin', an' no just talk buff an' nonsense b' rote like."

" Oh, demit, hold your tongue, Wilson," Jardine cried out. " Come away, sir, and I will shew you the new tulip I spoke of, you know."

After they left for the garden Mrs. Reid went forward to Wilson and said, " Gif I micht advise you as ye advised him Dauvet use yer ain thinkin' faculty an' spin fewer lang speeches an' listen mair tae what yer ain conscience says things micht come richter."

" Thank thee, Lizzy; thou means weel, I daur say ; but if thou only kent what conscience says whiles, thou 'd har'ly recommend keepin' company wi't."

" Ah but haurken till't Dauvet it's no pleasant but it's ay true haud on till't He sen's a swurd first but peace 'll come gif ye heed it's whispers whisht bairn whisht ' There wuz a wee wife had wee pickle tow an''"—and she went away singing, leaving Wilson and me together.

The *Glasgow Chronicle* came to the shop three times weekly, and all the looms were stopped when it was being read and its leaders discussed. Sandy Reid, being more inclined to outdoor sports than to reading, I was deputed to perform that duty for him when his reading day came round. He at such times adjourned to the " Linn " I have referred to, much to the sorrow of his highspirited wife, but to my profit in bridle-making. On one of these sederunts he engaged in a wrestling match and sprained one of his ankles, which rendered him unable to work for I do not know how many weeks. I made the ₁discovery during

the first week of his injury, that I earned as much at the
bridles as I got for drawing; and no one can imagine my joy
at the discovery.   Not till after I had received the proceeds
of my work did I fully realise the fact.   Pleasant though
my position was in that quiet shop, I was glad of the opportunity to leave it.   My first step, therefore, was to acquaint
Mrs. Reid of my intention, and offered to relinquish my
week's wage, in consideration of having earned it otherwise.
My offer was refused, but she took me in her arms and
showered on me a whole breathful of benedictions.   My
next move was to agree with the flower-lasher to work
for him only, provided he employed me before he gave
drawboys work; and as this was arranged at once, I visited
his place daily with and for work, and had opportunities of
picking up a knowledge of the very simple operation of
flower-lashing, so that in a month I was promoted to a
frame.   This lifted me into the position of bread-winner—
not yet into my teens.   In the meantime I was Emancipate!
Free !!   But I was not elated at my release; on the contrary, I felt rather like one who, having undergone the
punishment of a crime of which he had repented, is quieted,
sobered, sedate.

CHAPTER V.

IN my riper years I often recurred to the prudence and tact with which my mother anticipated any expression of my sorrow, by suggesting a certain line of conduct under circumstances which she *supposed* might turn up. If she shewed less exuberance than Mrs. Reid when I announced my deliverance, the sparkle of her eye was to me far more satisfactory. I was not aware till long after my release that any one knew of my unhappiness. But I was given to understand that, although my tongue refused to complain during my waking hours, my grievances were all babbled forth in my dreams, of which she took note; and hence her hints, advice, and warnings, being well-timed, were of use, not only at the time, but they left a strong impression on my mind that she watched over me with a wisdom that startled me now and then with its apparent witchery. My readers will, I think, perceive that although I had some real sorrows to mourn over, I still had a court of appeal, in whose judgment I could trust—a bosom on which I could rest, whose sympathy was not less, but more real, because it did not find expression in words.

I now recur with something akin to the old exuberant delight to the pleasant evenings in the harmonious circle at home, in which she was supreme, and can recall to memory the very tones of her gentle voice, the wise saws with which her talk abounded, her deep abhorrence of

H

meanness, injustice, and unkindness; her tolerance of every variety of opinion, and the distinction she drew between sins of weakness and " engrained wickedness."

Besides the everyday home life common to every household, there were occasions that bulked large in the mind of us youngsters, and which do not appear smaller to me at this hour. These were of two kinds : one was when the leading matrons in the church, or connection, as it was called, came to spend an afternoon, to arrange for a love feast if the time was winter, or an excursion to the country—a pic-nic it would be called now—if summer. The enjoyment of these gatherings to us was prospective; business meetings they were for the most part, at which there was little *fun* till near parting time, when a few husbands came to learn results, and to take their help-meets home. The other kind of home-gathering which I specially desire to describe, was of a very different sort, inasmuch as it was of yearly occurrence, and consisted of friends belonging to different churches, or to no church, and was of a purely social character. My father, for more than twenty years laid in " a mart " in November, and the great event of the year came off thereafter.

For the information of my young readers, I may as well say, in a word or two, what a " mart " is.

In the times I am speaking about—and long before— it was the custom of " bien " families to buy and kill and " salt down " a cow for their winter use. Men with large families, or having 'prentices boarded in their house, re-quired a whole cow; others, with a more limited demand, went shares for one with some intimate friend. The cow was usually bought young, and put to grass for a season, and brought home and slaughtered at Martinmas—and hence was called the "mart."

I was privileged on one occasion, which will be referred to by and by, to assist in bringing home the "coo;" and because I inflicted more pain on a tender part with a switch than was necessary, I was compelled to witness, after the death, the bruise caused thereby under the skin. I felt long after as if my *mind* had been bruised by the incidents of that evening, when the weaving shop was converted into a place of horrors, and the apparent cruelty was mixed up with another incident not less repugnant to my sense of propriety, but which, I learned afterwards, took place annually.

Soon after my beautiful cow had been prostrated, I was led to where it lay; where I found my mother standing with a small tub in her hand. She was speaking to my father, who did not seem at first to relish what she said.

"Tuts, man, although thee an' me thinks 't wrang tae eat bluid, there's a needfu' family in the gait-en' thinks 't nae sin; is 't no a pity tae let it gang tae waste?"

"Kepit, then, kepit," was his rather hasty reply. When that was done, she said—

"Thoo maun gie me something tae pit it in, lad," and by and by he threw a lot of skins into another tub, saying,

"Will that please thee?"

"Na!" was the answer, "they 'll be unco puir pudding athoot something mair than bluid in them; gie me a piece suet, an' bena scrimpit in thy giein'." He cut a "whang," and cast it into the tub, then catching her round the neck he gave her a hearty kiss, and amidst the laughter of those present, said,

"Noo, dinna thoo be scrimpit wi' the meal, lass, the girnal's fu'."

I was accustomed to see scores of people kissing on Sundays during worship, but kissing in a weaving shop over a dead cow had the effect of destroying in my mind all idea of kissing being of Divine ordinance in worship.

Of the many gatherings we had at Martinmas, I am not conscious of being present at more than six or seven; and what I will relate of these from memory and old notes may not be stated in the order of their occurrence, but as they turn up in my memory, tarnished somewhat, it may be, as old things are apt to become for want of air.

I can well remember many of the onsets that took place between the narrow and the broad, or liberal-minded, at these social meetings, when bitter retorts were bandied from one to another, and oil was as deftly thrown on the rising waters by mother's pawky humour. In doctrinal matters it was generally understood that her tendencies were heretical, one of her cherished beliefs being that goodness was true wisdom, no matter what doctrinal garb it assumed. One of her very dear friends had no doubt whatever regarding her heresy, who was nevertheless welcomed with the same "kiss of love," as heartily as the others who were less censorious. As I intend introducing the most noteworthy of the friends who came to "pree the mart"—that is, to dine, take tea, and spend the long winter afternoon and evening—I may as well begin with the old lady I here refer to.

Her name was Mrs. Henry, but she was better known by her maiden name of Christina, or rather Kirst—a very particular Christian and Baptist of the hardshell order,

who gloried in apostolic plainness and uniformity of be-
haviour, speech, and dress. I cannot recollect of seeing
her without a short scarlet cloak, which was always without
other crease than was caused by its having been carefully
folded. Under its hood, lined with quilted black silk, was
a clear starched linen cap, with lace edging on its single
border; a substantial, coloured gown printed with what
was known as the birslt-pea pattern, nearly covering her
white worsted stockings, and strong leather shoes, tied
with *firrating.* She never wore ear-rings or finger-rings,
and had no ringlets of hair concealing her earnest haffets.
Methodical in all things and at all times, she doffs her
cloak on entering, and after the "salutation" folds it with
deliberate care and hands it to mother. Then from her
pocket comes the seam or knitting wires. Looking round
the apartment, she nods to each one present whilst passing
to the low nursing chair, hoping "ye are a' in ordinar."
A woman of few words, except when Christian life or
doctrine were the topics, and even then they were well
chosen and pointed; she detested personalities and gossip—
never had street news to repeat, but was full to overflowing
with "precepts," precepts being very much beloved by her.
She spent one hour three times a week reading the *Glasgow
Chronicle* to her husband, Hugh Henry, whose large, soft
untidy appearance was as noticeable as that of his prim,
metallic-tongued wife. She occupied the arm-chair at the
head of the table at home, and said grace at meals, whilst
Hugh squatted wherever he could find room among their
turbulent boys. It was said that before asking the blessing,
she placed the sugar mug in her lap, spreading her long,
thin fingers over it during her lengthened "Say awa;"

and that if any daring urchin tried to abstract a quern while her eyes were closed, a finger and thumb caught the intruder, and by a "nip" produced a yell and general titter—without disturbance to the devotion, however. It was only when she was absent that she ceased to rule; Hugh, who never accompanied her, was her deputy on such occasions.

Mrs. Henry and I never succeeded in keeping on friendly terms. I rejected her proffered kiss when she came; and long before she left, mine, I feel sure, would have been refused by her. Not content with controlling the most minute details of her own house, she assumed the censorship of those of her friends by advice, reprimand, or admonition—in satisfaction to her conscience. Had her interference been confined to the "Christian walk" of her peers, none but the subjects could have complained; but when she illustrated how I ought to hang my cap on its peg, I had nothing left but open rebellion, or to raise a laugh at her expense by a little mimicry of her manner.

Besides other grievances, I had one in especial against her. She had a relation located in Kilmarnock, a shoe-maker—the wonderfullest man for honesty, Godfearing, moderate charges, and strong shoes that ever was known. He supplied all *her* children, herself, and Hugh; and she became his unpaid agent by sending him orders from several families in the connection. Ours was one of these, and so she came now and again for our "mezzurs"—the measure being a straight stick notched at the sizes wanted. What are now known as right and left shoes did not then get any encouragement from her friends, and such articles

she was known to abominate. The shoes made by the
" honest" man were of the kind called " straucht shoon "—
i.e., fitting either of the feet equally well or ill. They were of
the coarsest, hardest description, and a most uncomfortable
wear, against which I was at all times in a state of chronic
revolt, and she knew it. At every visit for the notched
stick there was a dispute between Kirst and mother, because
the latter would not furnish mezzurs for my sisters' shoes;
and it was a source of quiet amusement to father to witness
Kirst's attempts to overrule mother in purely domestic
affairs.

" Na," mother would say, " I 'll no hae my lassie bairns
wawblin like deuks in sic like; an' were I in thy place,
Kirst, I 'd dress thy lassies in vera different fashion—trig,
clean-shin'd things they wad be, an' they were shod like
their age, instead of heavy slobberin' shoon that wear the
stockings aff their legs, an' get them by-names besides."

" By-names ! Whatna by-name hae they gotten, can thou
tell me ?"

" Weel, tae save daurnin', I reckon, thou has sewed bits
o' leather on the heels o' their stockin's, an' I hear they 're
ca'd ' leather heels.' It may save thee wark, but there can
be unco little comfort or self-respec' tae the wearer."

Economy and simplicity in dress, manner, and life were
the weakness and strength of Mrs. Henry's character.
Foiled she might be in many houses on different points,
but she returned to the charge with undiminished vigour;
for no argument was ever strong enough to convince her.
Her honesty of purpose and her large almsgivings gave her
a warm corner in all her friends' hearts, however much they
differed from her. Some of these were economical, that

they might accumulate : she saved that she might scatter to the needy. Well read in many subjects, she was particularly so in her Bible, with portions of which much of her talk was interlarded. She was, in fine, a living edition of Paul's Epistles, done up in kip leather and birslt pea-cloth. There was very little love lost between Mrs. Henry and me.

It appeared that although Mrs. Henry was argument proof, she quailed before the ridicule of by-names. Her daughter Nell, shortly after the visit I have recorded, caught me at a street corner by laying her hand on my shoulder. With the other hand she turned up the sole of one of her shoes, and looking with glad eyes into mine, said, " Richts an' lefts; I ken wha I 've to thank for them." Then, with a one, two, three hop, she joined the band of gilkies she had left to make the announcement.

Beside the low chair occupied by Mrs. Henry, and about the same height, there was placed a queer-looking chest, which, except on the annual occasion, lay in the lumber-room above—a seaman's chest, broad at bottom and narrow at top. It was full of cannel coal, to assist the lamp hanging from the roof above the mantlepiece; its presence always appeared to my mind as necessary at "Martimas" as the "coo." Where it came from originally, or where it went afterwards, has ever been to me a mystery. There was another article of equal importance that became visible on the same day only. That was a small-headed hammer with a long heft, such as is used in breaking road-metal, which, to save the burnished fire-irons from tarnish, was used to "break up" the chunks of coal in the grate. It, too, has gone the way of all hammers. Two persons could have sat with comfort on the chest, but it was occupied by Henry Buchan alone, whom, I think, if a precept could have been found to hate, Mrs. Henry would have hated heartily; but as there was none, she just "couldna thole him." Henry came with a book in each hand and one or two in his pockets, all which he placed on the chest beside him, ready for reference when required. He spoke slowly, and with great deliberation, and as, perhaps, he *thought* slowly, he found a passage to express his mind with more readiness than his tongue. I came to know, years after, that the books he consulted were, among others, Law, Behmen, Sweden-borg, and Fenelon.

Henry Buchan was a quiet, unobtrusive man, who never tried to lead conversation, but was ready to bend it to the subjects he loved best, and to give a cheerful assent where he could do so. He had a large fund of humour, and a ready appreciation of it in others; also much sound know-ledge, "jumblt up," Mrs. Gillespie said, "wi' ootlandish views o' Christian doctrine." It was known to every one of the company that he never went to church. When oppor-tunity offered, he was apt to ask awkward questions and to draw disturbing inferences. It was hinted, too, that he had caused Mrs. Thomson and Andrew Cochran to lift their theologic anchor, as it was their custom to assist him with arguments when several voices were raised against him. On the other hand, it was acknowledged that his boys were models of order, obedience, and good manners—more dis-posed, like him, to spend an hour on a book than at games proper to their years; and that men of learning with whom he corresponded, and who visited him occasionally, had pronounced him fitted for a much higher position than the one he occupied. Another feature which told greatly in his favour was, that he never spoke boastfully of the friendship of these men; but he will speak for himself by and by, which will save me further trouble just now.

Mrs. Buchan, Letitia, or Lily Soutar, the last being the name she was better known by, was a clean-skinned, fresh-looking, round, cheery woman, somewhat above average height, with reddish hair in abundance falling down on her cheeks; large hazel eyes, which wore an apprehensive expression; small sensitive mouth; lips thin and pale, that quivered with excitement as she sat cracking her finger-joints when Henry was in the thick of an argument. I cannot recollect seeing her without at least one child in arms, and oftener than once she came to "pree the mart" with two, and then Peggy Downie's services were in requisition till Lily "sortet hersel'." Lily had on three occasions presented Henry with twins, who, being all alive, destroyed the pan-pipe appearance of the family. "The extraordinary mercies," as Henry called them, so confused him when work was scarce and stocks low, that he had to count the porridge luggies before he could realise the extent of his responsibility.

On one occasion, memorable from its occurring while a snow-storm was raging, Mrs. Buchan came late, after the repast, and when the company had settled down to social talk. Under her large cloak, which was covered with snow, she closely hugged two little ones, and sank in a chair, crying bitterly. Several pairs of willing hands relieved her of her outer garment and burdens; and as 'mother thought it was a family sorrow, she led Henry

and his wife to the nearest room, from whence we heard
such words as "What a scud!" "Dear, dear," "Noo,
Lily, dry thy face, an' say naething aboot it just yet."
Whispering followed, followed by a sobbing laugh from
her. It was not till the company rose to sing "Lord,
dismiss us with thy blessing," &c., that the cause of her
grief was known. Henry told her that "noo we are
partin', thou maun tell that story, Lily. It'll cost thee
a cry, nae doot, lass; but we're mair the better o' weepin'
wi' them that weep, than in dancin' tae their pipin'." And
truly she cried—cried before and during the recital of her
story, and cried in company with more than one man and
woman after. The incident is a painful one; but was not
without its use, from the talk it called forth, and which is
worth preserving. I will repeat the story first, partly in
Mrs. Buchan's words, which came in jerks, and as it
were in bits, and partly in those of another.

"I wud abeen here in time, but I gaed roon tae speer
hoo Mary Swan's son was, an' I was taiglt. For whan
I gaed there things were a' in confusion; mae than ae
bairn was greetin', an' naebody heedin' them; an' the head
o' the hoose was stan'in haudin' on tae the chair back,
takin' note o' naething, dazt-like; an' Mary hersel' stood
mair fierce than ord'nar' even. Grippin' an arm o' Doctor
Thamson, wha wi' his hat in 's han' stood as white as
his sark; an' wi' the head hingin' owre the bed lay the
puir misguidet laddie stark deid. Mary, wha was wild
wi' anger, shook her nieve i' the doctor's face, an' was
saying', as I gaed in, 'If ye couldna save my bairn, ye
surely can pray wi' them he's ta'en frae;' an' a' the big
gowly man said, 'God pity you, Mrs. Swan, and me too—

we all need His help;' an' pressin's hat owre his heid, een left.us a' stanin', Mary kin' o' helpless-like. Sae I put the bairns doon heeds and thraws in the cradle, an'. put-to my han' to red-up things an' help. In a wee while I sat doon beside auld Andrew, an' drew Mary doon aside me, an'-an we spak wi' ither."

" Thou needna mourn owre what thou canna men' Lily," Mrs. Henry said, in her sharp, self-assured manner. " The decrees of God are His eternal purpose according to the council of His will, whereby, for His own glory, He hath foreordained whatsoever comes to pass. He has a covenant with the elect only."

" I declare !" cried Peggy Downie, "if she's no quotin' the question-book ! I thocht thou didna fa' in wi't, Kirst ?"

" Naither do I—although I think it's an excellent summary o' Christian truth," was the reply ; to which Peggy answered—

"The ne'er o' me thinks sae ; I'll never believe the Lord ordeens ony ane tae the ill place."

" I tell thee what it is, Kirst, my Henry there has a garret-room tae let, and the rent ot's five-and-therty shillings a year ; but we'll no let it tae ony man wi' a character sic as thou gies the Almichty, no for a ransom o' five-an'-therty pounds sterling. He wad be an ill neebor, wha I wadna hae hingin' aboot the close-mooth at meal-times. An' that's my min' in plain terms, Kirst," Mrs. Buchan said between her sobs.

"I wadna hae used the same language that Lily has done," said her husband ; " but I question if I could hae expresst the same opinion in as forcible words."

Mrs. Buchan trembled with suppressed emotion while

Henry spoke these words in his usual slow way, her nostrils dilating and her eyes swimming. Mary Cameron, ever gentle, put a hand on her arm, and said beseechingly,

"Did thou no pray wi' them, Lily?"

"Weel, Mary, it couldna be ca'd prayin', for I sabbit amaist a' the time. But, Mary Swan, she brav'd it oot by-ord'nar', braver than her gudeman, wha didna believe like that his laddie cou'd be deid. He took nae notice o' things till ance Mary gaed tae a press for a dram; an' my certie he looket fierce then. He gied her a shuve, an' turned the key in the lock, an' tell't her he thocht they had had owre muckle dramin', and that there wud be nae mair wi' his gudewill."

The company all stood while the conversation just recorded took place; and as Mrs. Henry had been worsted in the encounter, father requested her to pronounce the benediction, a duty to which she was supposed to be partial, after which the parting kiss was exchanged, by which all remaining· bitterness was believed to be extinguished.

On the following day, Doctor Thomson called and desired mother to visit and try what she could do by way of consoling the Swans, and gave some details of the young man's illness. He had fallen into evil courses, and ended in an attack of *delirium tremens*. The doctor from the first had grave doubts of his ultimate recovery, but acted as if he had none—visited him regularly and often. On the day before, in the morning, he left an opiate, and called repeatedly to watch its effects, and up till mid-day had some faint hopes that he would "weather it." "At my last visit I found the parents sitting at the bed-side; on a table stood the glass containing the dregs of my prescription.   I saw at a glance that the end was coming, and was coming fast.

"When the lad saw me he started up in bed, drained the glass, and waved it round his head with 'hip, hip, hurrah!' twice repeated; then he cast it through a pane of the window, and fell back dead.   The poor mother wanted me to pray with her; but, God knows, I'm not a praying man."

CHAPTER VI

NOT the least important of our guests at the Martinmas dinner were a couple from the far west end of the town, where, by industry and economy, they had saved as much money as bought or built the house which they occupied. They were known to their friends as "Sarah and Jeems." I never, even at this distance of time, hear the name of Gillespie applied to a person that is unknown to me, but there rises before my mind's eye a dainty small-sized man, with a broad, clean shaven chin, whose face appears as if so dusted over with flour that it is difficult to say where his thin white hair and the halo of his innocent expression meet. He invariably wears a jockey-tailed, bottle-green coat with metal buttons, black knee-breeches, white small-ribbed worsted stockings, and substantial creaking shoes with silver buckles. One hand is in a breeches-pocket, enjoying itself restlessly among the small change there. The thumb of the other hand is thrust into the arm-hole of his parti-coloured vest, and its fingers beat a tune lightly on the edge of his shirt ruffles —the only ostentatious-looking item about his person. His hat is set well back on his head, which allows him a good outlook through his silver-mounted spectacles, and —there he goes down street, smiling calmly as he hums a psalm tune—at peace with himself and with all the world— a man who, never having pierced through the rind of his being, has never subjected himself to introspection; so well cared for that he is without wants; so well provided for that he is without ambition; whose creed is so rounded and complete that he has no misgivings, no doubts. It is sufficient for him that he lives; Sarah, the evangelical, whose delight is divided between hoarding the produce of his shuttles, beholding him decorated for church and market-place, and splitting theological windlestraes with any one daring to express an opinion at variance with hers; she is wife, husband, deacon, and high priest to him and all his belongings; guiding him in all things pertaining to time and eternity. No one ever spoke of them as "James Gillespie and his wife," but "Sarah Troup an' 'er man" was a common form of expression.

Had their connubial relations been reversed, it would have been more in accordance with our idea of the fitness of things; for then Sarah, as husband, would have dominated the household, and the session, perhaps, as became a self-willed opinionative man; whilst Jeems, as matron, with his thin, low voice, and gentle sympathies, might have modified in no small degree the angularities and wordy extravagancies of the husband. This is purely hypothetical, however; and I must speak of the worthy old pair as I knew them. One thing is certain: Had the love of rule been as strong in him as it was in her, or as weak in her as in James, things would not have flowed so smoothly, peacefully, and prosperously with them. If he was weak, Sarah was strong; and his facile disposition fed her strength, till, in the most natural way, "the key o' the bawbee drawer" was transferred to her keeping, and the family revenue controlled by her alone.

Sarah was an undersized woman, and she appeared shorter than she really was, in consequence of the curve about her shoulders—caused, it was said, by her eagerness to "hain and gather," and her innate pugnacity of soul. James had the face of a woman, his features being small, smooth, and tender; Sarah that of a man, hers being large and strongly marked. Her whole bearing gave one the impression of strength; her very homely face was freckled and pox-pitted, and her dark gray eyes seemed to look into and through you; whereas, when he noticed you, it was with such benignancy that you felt you were beloved.

The couple were seldom seen together, except on Sunday, going to or returning from Dr. Ferrier's church, and on occasions when on tea-drinking excursions at some friend's house, where Sarah hoisted her red flag as opportunity offered. Her ordinary everyday dress consisted of a lace-trimmed "mutch," a buff-coloured neckerchief, having a narrow border of black, the corners fastened before and behind by the bands of her chequered apron, a lilac-printed gown, white stockings, and prunella slippers. With one arm laid across her stomach, on a finger of the hand of which *skinkled* her marriage ring, the hand grasping the door key, the bowl of which hung over her thumb; with the other arm swaying backward and forward, keeping time with the swig of her gown, she stepped along with fearless look, not without a certain dignity, notwithstanding her small dimensions. At visiting times, however, and at church, Sarah dressed in very different fashion. If her Baptist friend, Mrs. Henry, whom she met and fought (yet loved sincerely) at our house, gloried in apostolic plainness, and quoted Scripture in justification therefor, Sarah was not

I

less proud to ornament her person with figured silks, finger-rings, ear-rings, ringlets of black hair half-concealing her face, coloured silk stockings, and shoes of the newest cut. She, too, was guided by apostolic teaching, she said; and sometimes poked fun at Kirst by contending that when St. Paul speaks against female ornamentation, he must be understood as addressing spinsters of hopeless condition, but not the young in the bloom of womanhood, and far less married women, whose primary duty it is to make home beautiful and pleasant to the husband, by keeping her person as lovely and lovable after as before marriage. Kirst was puritanic through and through, whilst Sarah was more of a Jacobite—in a poetical sense—with a strong love of whatever she thought beautiful or true. Although she was an object of terror to certain disputants, whom she had the good fortune to meet wherever she went, no one disliked her; and we youngsters hailed her visits with delight, because of the quaint old tales of '45, which she had learnt from her father, who took part in the troubles of that time, of which we never tired hearing, and of the dear years 1799 and 1800, in which she suffered. Whatever she was to her older friends, she was ever genial and sympathetic to us in our mighty small troubles; but, excepting Mrs. Henry, so indeed were all the female friends of our mother.

Mrs. Henry had no humour, nor had she any appreciation of it in others. She never smiled at Sarah's witticisms, nor did that polemic ever succeed in diverting her attention from the subject in dispute. No matter how many turn-ings she took, or how fierce her voice, or contemptuous her epithets, Mrs. Henry was impassive—always the same quiet, cool, watchful woman. *Her* voice never varied in tone, and her manner was so calm during Sarah's strongest proofs, uttered in loud excited voice, that a smile passed over every face except their own, as, threading her needle, she suggested to Sarah to " compose hersel'." But under this smooth exterior she was vigilant and lynx-eyed to the defects of her friend's positions. Of all our female visitors she alone was dauntless and unruffled under Sarah's choicest invectives; yet, when not engaged in theologic fence, they were loving as Christians ought to be. For under Kirst's icy manner, and when not defending her " essentials," there was, the friends said, a wonderful amount of true human sympathy. And as Sarah believed this, she lamented that " Kirst had been dippit in frostet water; she used to be a blythe wee thing, but she 's unco changt."

When the two women last named took possession of the arena, the male portion of the company were silent, and exchanged snuff-mulls occasionally. At one trial of strength Sarah's gentle " man " was so scandalised at the uncouth treatment of her self-contained friend, that he remonstrated in his mild way on Sarah's want of courtesy; and I well remember the general groan of dissatisfaction when she retorted, " It'll no be ill tae ken whatna side thou 'll stan' on when the Lord's battle 's fochten, Jeems." At another time Mrs. Thomson interposed a soothing word, and received a similar reply; but, unlike James, she returned to the charge. The subject was church organisation; and although she was Baptist by adoption, she was by descent a seceder, and had a strong loving remembrance of early friendships and associations, which to her were of deeper importance than any mere form of " constitution." I re-

collect her bringing quite a storm down by saying, in reply
to Sarah, that "forms o' kirk government were the fashions
o' generations, just as ribbons an' gown-prints are the fashion
o' weeks an' months; a' the difference is, their season's
langer. Ae form stan's like an oak, the ither fades like a
saugh, tho' growin' side by side. Some like oor way, Sarah,
some like thine; ithers fin mair comfort under Prelacy, and
thoosan's, like ships bedit amang san', can get peace only
frae the Pape o' Rome; but a' forms maun be left ahint us
when we gae hame—Gude grant we a' won there." These
words seemed to take the breath from both Sarah and
Kirst, who became allies at once; the former denouncing
Katherine as "neither fish nor flesh," the latter sneering at
her want of assurance. They, although differing on organisation, were agreed that there was no salvation without the
form of sound words, and that Prelacy and Popery alike
were at best only true in part. She, on the other hand,
maintained that Infinite Wisdom had "num'erless ways an'
means o' workin' His will; an' if half a truth sair'd the en'
o' bringin' an' keepin' men in the acknowledgment an'
practice o' Gospel precepts, it's better for *them* maybe than
what ithers think is wholly true. But wha amang us kens
a' the oots an' ins o' ony truth?"

"Hear till her!" exclaimed Sarah. "Isna the precious
doctrine o' justification by faith a hale truth? an' isn't it
absolutely true?"

"I'se no affirm that, Sarah," answered Katherine, "but I
ken this is true o' thee as it's o' me:—Oor dishes are no
big enough tae haud onything that is absolutely true. We
can only gie room for bits o' things. Yesterday I had ae
glimpse o' a truth, an' I hae anither the day. Dootless I'll

get anither the morn, Sarah; ilk ane's absolute till a new
ane is gi'en me. ⸺ Whiles there's nae absolute certainty for
lang an' weary; whiles I tint it a' thegether.   Sae the
darkness gaes on ; but I ken it's only a gloom that'll
pass awa whan the comfort comes o' doin' my duty.   There
can be naething absolute tae us wha are dependent for the
vera breath we draw."

" I confess," sighed Kirst, " I dinna un'erstan' what thou
means wi' thy glimpses an' glooms.   For my pairt, I lean
on the word o' promise He has gi'en to His Church, which
is His chosen people."

" The Church *is* his chosen people," Katherine replied,
" and yet I, wha belang till 't, am beset wi' hankerings,
whilk he chooses to lead me by.   But in a braider an' better
sense, a' the hale race o' man are His chosen ; only, His
ootgangin' is regulate by the capacities o' them wha ha'ena
the licht o' the Gospel.   Nor do I think that a' Gospel truth
is wi' us, or, indeed, wi' ony connection whatever.   As for
forms o' government, I whiles won'er if there werena as
muckle ill-bluid as principle amang them wha seceded
frae the Establishment.   I ken there wur a hantle mair
pride than humility wi' us wha cam' frae *them*—mair than
was guid for us."

" Haud thy tongue, Katherine," said Kirst incisively,
" we a' ken thoo's a Seceder, oo-dyed, but it'll tak' mair water
than thou has to spare tae cool the ardour o' thy brethren,
or stay the progress o' oor principles."

" I haud the principles as tichtly as need be, Kirst ; an'
if I'm prood o' my seceding forbears, I hae nae less satisfaction in being a Baptist.   Yet wherein do they differ
except on the formalities o' baptism an' the constitution o'

the body? I think we hae the richt o't on baith pints; but naebody will ever gar me believe that the difference warrantet separation. William there kens, for I tauld him my views ere we left the brae folk, that it was wrang to coontinance division; but that nae-theless for peace-sake an' for example tae the bairns, I'd gang whar he gaed. Yet am I to contend that whae'er differs frae me on sic sma' matters are in the gall o' bitterness an' bond o' iniquity? I trow no! Speakin' frae my ain experience, an' mezzured by my means o' grace, I hae faun short o' duty far mair than some o' them thou wud hae me contend wi'."

"Noo," said Lily Soutar, "I wuz just waiting till thou wud come roon' to that word again, Katrine. Thou may wan'er whar thou likes in thy expositions, but I aye ken they en' in duty. It does nae gude to be remindet that a' doctrine that's worth ca'in', points the finger at some evil to be avoidet or some gude to be done."

"Warks again, Lily!" said Kirst; and "Warks, warks!" echoed Sarah contemptuously.

"I declare," exclaimed Lily, "you twa are aye chowin' the beans an' swallowin' the ladle! What's the use o' ony doctrine without warks? An' isna the requirin' o' fruits the hale burden o' the message? Ae precept says, 'Do this,' anither says, 'Thou shalt not;' ane threatens death, the ither gies the promise o' life. I canna see hoo we can do without warks."

"Without warks," was the dictatorial reply, "we lose the comfort, wi' them we hae the comfort, but we never lose the confidence o' faith, whether wi' warks or withoot them. Aye, there's nae merit in warks; nane ava."

"Weel," answered gentle Mary Cuthbertson, "I wad

rather hae the comfort than the confidence. It's a fearfu' thing pride; and the pride o' never havin' fa'n maun be a dreadfu' fa'."

Here Peggy Downie, with her keen perception, said, "Thou's weavin' wi' an extra shuttle, Kirst, when thou speaks o' merit. Naither Katherine nor Lily claims merit, am sure. Nane o' us think o' merit when drawin' oor breath, whilk's as muckle His gift as grace is."

"I want," said Sarah, "tae gae back to a subjec'. Arna' Christians favoured aboon a' ithers wi' the word o' truth?"

"Ay, an 'sponsible for the use they mak' o't," Peggy answered. "It's sma' favour, I trow, to be made its libraureans, an' we, like the Jews in auld times, dinna do the duties o' oor trust. What's tae come o' us though we *hae* faith, if we lay by the Book, as we do oor sillar-spoons, in a box, and only use it at orra times, like this present? We may amaist as weel want it."

"I'm clear," said Kirst, "that some o' us will hae tae lay by oor novices when we gae tae the holy city, for naething oot o' harmony can exist there. We are tauld that the heicht o't an' the breadth o't are equal; sae there maun be unity in essentials."

"Yes, an' in a' things charity," Katherine replied; "but what we were speakin' o' are no essentials, for baith baptism an' the constitution o' the body belang tae the ooter coort, which was left unmezzuret."

"Ay, an' then," added Peggy, "there's a roun' dozen o' yetts tae gae in by."

"Trouth, Kirst," said Sarah with a sneer, "there seems

an unco divergence o' opinion amang you ; ane hardly kens
what ye wad be ettlin' at, every ane has a new novice o' her
ain."

"'Tweel," sighed Kirst, " I maun confess that the principles hing unco loosely aboot some o' us ; an' what savours
waur than a', they are aye pleadin' for warks, than which
I think naething is mair abominable."

" Did thy life no gainsay thy profession, Kirst," Lily said,
" I wad think that remark o' thine a wee ill-natured.
Brawly thou kens it's no whaur we gang tae worship,
or what we profess to believe, that 'll sair us when oor
reckonin 's ca'd an' oor tawlents are countet ; but, have we
gi'en the cup an' the bit tae the wayfarer in the Maister's
name, an' stay'd the tongue o' slander in ithers by frown or
rebuke whan necessar' ? "

When temper began to mingle with precept and principle,
and a breach of harmony became imminent, as in the argument just noted, my mother " raxt " a hymn-book, saying,
"We will now sing one or two verses" of a hymn, which
she named, and told me to read.   As I had shewn some
aptitude for music, I was privileged to raise the melody.
Every one appeared to know all the hymns without book.
I must have been over-vain, I fear, of my musical powers,
for I once offered to lead the praise at church ; but I never
repeated the offer, as I was given to understand by Archibald M'Fee that no one but members of the brotherhood
were allowed to contribute any assistance in worship ; and
he added, for my comfort, I suppose, that although I was
the child of believing parents, I lay in the same state of
rebellion as the heathen, until I made open profession of

my faith. As I had a comfortable home and pleasant surroundings—consisting of some choice cronies, a few fan-tailed pigeons, and two or three books—the condition of the heathen did not strike me as particularly awful; but then I was dreadfully behind in my theology.

CHAPTER VII

THE present is not less a reflex of the past than the outward is of the inward; and if we would pause and
listen in reverent mood to our intuitions of futurity, which
never sleep or slumber, we shall find that with its highest
and noblest aspect are blended in harmonious tones the
purest joys of our earliest consciousness; for the childhood
that was is a type of that to which all pure delight is tending. The circumstances that called the emotions of youth
into recognition, and even the emotions themselves, may
appear most trivial, yet, like the alphabet, which is the basis
of all book-learning, we build upon and work from them
as from our stock in trade during all the years that follow;
nor can all the wisdom of the wise and prudent insure
our escape from the "Where art thou?" of our lost Eden,
or adjust our ears to the melody of the same sweet voice
calling "Mary" in the sepulchre. Just as only the virtues
of the dead live, so the troubles and griefs of early life grow
faint, and fade and die, whilst its delights shine back on us
in refracted rays. It is not till long after we have emerged
from that sunny time that we become conscious of their
tendering value; and it is only in those rare cases where
manhood is the unbroken outbirth of childhood that their
worth and importance can be duly appreciated. But come
when and as they may, it is always like soft breezes they
come, wafted through hawthorn blossoms, invigorating the

mind as with the auras of that Home for which every human heart has a quenchless craving.

. If we are driven from our youth per-force of time, we are compensated by a nearer view of home, where all are little children, and with brightening memory of the child-hood we have left. And so in memory I look back through the thicket of years with quite a boyish zest; and when thoughts of futurity mingle with those of the past, I feel as if any state of being to come would be incomplete were something akin to my early and earliest years not comprised within it. If the higher forms of animal life include the lower, surely the highest spiritual joys of heaven are but the perfected innocency of earth's little ones.

Such, at least, were my thoughts lately, as in overhauling some old letters I came on one from my friend the late Mr. Claud Wilson, Lowell (Mass.), which recalled an incident connected with our yearly gathering that must not be omitted, and which will likewise serve the purpose of introducing another pair of old friends, whose memory I delight to honour :—

I was very particularly engaged one day chaffering about the value of a pigeon I wished to buy, when I was caught by the nape of the neck, and turned faceward to my captor, who said,—

"Is the coo hame? No? Whan is 't comin'? Tell them am gettin' vera yawpish; term day's at haun; if they're no quick I'll no come, and it'll be nae denner without me."

"What's this he'll no gang tae? The dinner? Dinna heed him, he'll gang; nae fear o' us," said his wife, Peggy Downie, who joined us at the entry; " but," she added, " tell the mistress tae gie me twa days' warnin', sae I may lea a' things in order."

Peggy before marriage had been our house-servant, where and at church Claud Wilson met her, and after a while they exchanged hearts. On occasions such as I am describing, Peggy came early to lend help to prepare the feast. She was by nature and culture a servitor, and never more in the delight of her life than when ministering in some way to the pleasure or necessities of others; never out of order, or work, or good humour; always ready for any duty, and any assigned work seemed a favour conferred. At love feasts in church Peggy, under instructions, provided whatever was required; at excursions to the country she was the advanced guard, attending to the commissariat; and there, or wherever else she was, every sleepy or fractious child found in her a kindly mother-depute. A favourite with the young, she was our court of appeal, and her decisions were always accepted as just, her gifts, privately conveyed to the losing party, I daresay, increasing our sense of her wisdom.

Her husband, Claud Wilson, was a notable man with the circle in which he moved, which, I may add, comprised the majority of the weaving body. He was one of the few that lamented the drudging to which the young were subjected; and I believe he was the first in town who took measures to dispense with their services to weavers. With this end in view he introduced Cross's machine, which, from its expense, was not genera'ly adopted, although he and others led the way by using it. His leaving the country may have had some influence in its rejection, for he had great persuasive powers.

It was not as a weaver, however, that I knew Mr. Wilson, but as my father's friend and frequent visitor at home, where, as Claud or Gloud, he kept the circle on tenter-hooks by his untempered denunciations of the British aristocracy, for the iniquity of their lives and their want of Christian guidance in the "affairs of State." People who did not know him were repelled by his uncompro-mising bitterness at what he called the worn-out-ness of men who assumed the reflected glory of their ancestors as their own, and who spoke of the toiling millions as if forming no part of the human family. He had visited London, where he was employed as a weaver in Spital-fields; and he told us graphic stories of misery resulting from drunkenness and other irregularities of the weavers there. He had also been to Nova Scotia, in the hope of finding a comfortable home, and of acquiring a compe-tency for old age; but there he only found poverty in new forms, intensified by an ungenial climate; his only acqui-sitions on his return thence were budgets of tales of hard-ships, and increased venom against "the natural enemies of the workman, the fat, lazy, ignorant, conceited aristoc-racy." I thought him an orator, and was delighted to hear his long speeches, which somehow his wife always contrived to spoil. When he warmed with his subject he rose to his feet, turned this way and that way, his arms and body swaying, his voice waxing louder and louder; his terms of apparent hate became stronger and stronger, and his audience getting very much alarmed—for the times were ticklish—till Peggy emerged from the children's crib, and laying a hand on his mouth, said, " Whist, noo, Gloud, an' no wawken the weans." And then the big fellow would grasp her round the waist, whirl her round and round, and finally bestow on her a kiss, setting all the company into fits of laughter.   Bitter?   There was not a drop of bitterness in his veins : he was clever, genial, and impulsive, thoroughly in earnest, laughing sometimes at his own extravagancies, yet believing every word he uttered.   Gentle, yet stern; but being just, he gave the liberty to others he claimed for himself.   It was an unsolved problem to his most intimate friends, whether the love of innocent mirth or of mechanical innovations had the greatest control over him.   He never, I can aver, spoke on the latter subject at our great annual gathering. For months anticipation of its coming lent enchantment to *me;* and the tones in which he asked if the "coo was hame" led me to think that he longed as much as I did for the "denner."

I made stolen visits, getting a ride in a cart at times, to Drifenbeg farm to see and hear reports of "the coo," returning weary and footsore, but proud of my knowledge every time.   And then there was the day of days, when I donned my "kirk claes," and accompanied father to bring her home.   No earthly honour conferred on me *now* could evoke such a sense of unmixed delight as I experienced on that journey.   We started with an early breakfast in the grey of the morning, and we had reached the Tod Burn almost in silence, before objects became visibly distinct to me.   Then my father, who was naturally taciturn, began to make talk.   Every stile and by-road on the way was pointed out, and the place each led to named.   One led to the Glenquarry, where Sauners Muir lives; another led to Hollybush and Dykebar farms, where Watty Bowie and

John M'Nab bides; "yon on the ither side gangs to Mr. Taylor's o' Broonside ; but it's a' puir, caul', fushonless grun' roon here." When we had nearly reached the junction of roads at Grahamston tollbar, where a belting of stunted oak trees lined the field on our right, my father pushed his staff into the marshy ground beyond the low wall, and tapping on a substance that had a dull, hollow sound, said, " Does thou hear that ? "

" Yes," I answered. " What is 't ? "

" There was a man hang'd himsel' on that tree," pointing to a branch that spread over to the road, "an' they made a rude box an' buried him aneath 't. It was a custom langsyne—an 's sae still—to deny Christian burial tae folk that rushes into eternity before they 're wanted ; but it 's a barbarous custom that canna last. Naebody ever destroys life till they hae tint reason; an' as every ane is judged by their haven's, I canna believe the Lord will reckon wi' them, as wi' thee an' me; an' at ony rate we hae nae richt tae turn our back on an errin' man, wha 's mair tae be pitied an' pray'd for than blamed." And then he descanted on the wonderful gift of reason, " whilk gies us a knowledge o' oor ain evils, an' o' keepin' them un'er control ; an' o' speakin' an' actin' wissly and kin'ly tae ithers, and o' leadin' the thochtless frae evil coorses."

When we had nearly speiled the brae east of Neilston, we halted at a spring issuing from a hedge-root, and with a tin bicker we took a drink to the bread he produced. The sun had dissolved the haze that had hung over the hills to our left ; but although everything about us wore a cheerful face, I somehow felt it a very lonely road, which the occasional scream of the peesweep served to deepen. I knew that

my father was kind, and did his very best to give pleasure to
me and every one, but except on rare occasions, his subjects
wanted tenderness, and were too heavy for the young. It
was a relief, therefore, when I caught sight of a beggarman
sitting with his hat between his knees on the wayside, his
thin, white hair falling on to his shoulders. Taking two or
three hurried steps in front, I dropped what remained of my
piece into the hat. Father handed me what was left of his
portion, saying, "Hæ, laddie, thy stamach's sharper than
mine. I didna think thou was sae gleg. See that thou
dinna turn close hant when thou grows auld. Thou min's
what's said aboot the richteous turnin' away from his
richteousness? In the sins that he had sinned, in them
shall he die." As we jogged along he got into a talking
vein, sometimes of his boyhood, that was spent in the
district through which we were passing; and sometimes of
mine, that was partly in the future. This led him to speak
of my oldest brother, who was in the army, and of whose
return he entertained some doubts; if he did not return,
then I, as the next oldest man-bairn, would have to fill
father's chair in case of his death. I now think it was
unwise to speak to a mere child of such a possibility,
particularly in such an eerie place; perhaps it was because
he saw how it affected me with excitement that he proposed
a change of subject by bidding me sing some song, and he
would try a second with me. It was indeed a pleasant
change, which we both enjoyed. "The Bonnie Woods of
Craigielee," "Gloomy Winter's noo awa," and other songs
came in turn. At the end of some of the verses we stood
in silence and listened to the echoes as they rose and died
away among the great calm hills that surrounded us; and I

felt thankful that it *was* father that was my companion. It was the first time I had heard an echo, and the silence of that lonely place was oppressive. But the silence did not continue long at a time, for we sang till we came in sight of the farm-town, and kindly Mrs. Barr, hearing before she saw, came to give us welcome. The marvels of the court-yard in front of the house-place burst on my view as the most wonderfully quiet, sleepy state of things imaginable. In one place two speckled calves were drinking milk from pails ; in another a large sow, and what appeared to me fifty small pigs, sunning themselves on straw; hens and ducks every-where, and over the stable-door the head of a colt—all which I saw at one glance, for she had whisked me into her brawny arms to carry me round and shew the ferlies of that wonderful place. When we reached the kitchen there was a table furnished, but before I was allowed to partake, I had to strip off shoes and stockings, and have my feet bathed. After refreshment of *such* bannocks and *oh such* milk, father went to view the crops that had been gathered, and Robin Barr's various young cattle, leaving me with aunty to rest. Rest? ay rest! The sun was wester-ing when I was wakened up, stiff and wearied, but happy as a king ; for was not the " coo " just outside the window ?

As I was unaccustomed to long walks, it had been arranged to yoke a horse and convey us a few miles. So with that magnificent " coo " tied behind, and Robin and his wife seated in the cart with us, we came to Barrhead. Robin, I recollect, told me in his quaint way that nothing in the whole " worl' was equal to a rummel owre a rough road for sooplin' a laddie's jints." It was mainly down hill on our return, and although I was tired, the time passed

K

lightly with repeating the songs of the morning.　Father, too, gave me a lift on his shoulder going up the hill a bit west of Grahamston tollbar; and then the glory of paying the tolls and of holding the halter when in sight of home, no doubt betrayed me into forgetfulness.　But I was too tired and happy to enjoy the sunkets mother had prepared for our home-coming, and too excited to entertain any reflection, except that the "coo was hame."

CHAPTER VIII.

ANDREW COCHRAN—whose acquaintance my readers will make by and by—used to say that when he was at home plying his needle meditatively, he thought the inhabitants of our town the most unlovable and the wickedest in the world; but that when he sailed foreign, he considered them the most religious and the queerest people he ever met. And although his friends usually discounted Andrew's extreme conclusions, there can be no doubt that, apart from the religious aspect of the subject, our locality was singularly fertile in personal oddities, of whom Andrew himself was a fair specimen, and of which remnants may, here and there, yet survive the wreck of old habits and decaying industries. He belonged to the class of mind that think the past more glorious than the present, and that cannot contemplate the future without apprehension of the coming dissolution of every social tie. He was accustomed to expatiate of the time when the voice of praise and prayer might be heard daily from almost every dwelling. From all I can learn, such was really the state of matters; but it was before my day. I look back, indeed, with delight to my early youth, and feel thankful for "the nurture and admonition" I received; but prayer and praise formed a very small item of my education or training. I think the circle in which my parents moved was deficient in piety, family or household devotion being very rare, and not the rule, as with other circles. People who are fighting for a doctrinal foothold in their community are but too apt to undervalue a devout mind; and besides, when any sect of Christians are persecuted, or as " our circle " were, ostracised, they generally discard the forms and duties their opponents favour; and as the people I refer to emerged from the Seceders, who were then remarkable for piety, they followed the line I have indicated.

But if the families were without a very devout example, the deficiency was amply compensated for by other means, arising chiefly from the care and counsel of the mothers. Had they not taken in hand the training of their young, it would have fared badly, I am afraid, with their future welldoing and wellbeing. I recollect hearing one of these women say that although she did not see scripture for infant baptism, she felt the want of *some rite* whereby her bairns could be dedicated to the Saviour. They were, she said, growing up without doctrinal instruction at home, without the benefit of Sunday schools, or any other instrumentality that would strengthen in them a love of divine things; and hence it was, I believe, that she and others fell back on their own resources, to square the account as far as they could.

I do not know whether the people of the same branch of the church now are as lax in devotion as these old worthies were; but I have good grounds for knowing that the old warmth and the disposition to render personal *service*, as well as to give, continue without abatement.

In this chapter I will state the course adopted by one of these dames—not as a specimen of the whole, but of the devotedness that in one way or other was all but universal.

For this purpose I select William Thomson and his wife
Katherine Sutherland; and as their dispositions will come
out in my narrative, it is unnecessary to say anything about
them further than that they were the complement of each
other—the different hemispheres of the same brain, or, more
properly, perhaps, the different ventricles of one heart.

Like all Baptists of that day—and of this day as well, for
that matter—William was conscientiously opposed to written
creeds; and it was understood between him and his wife, to
whom the training of their children was assigned, that no
dogmatic theology was to be taught them; and as the Cate-
chism was used in Sunday schools, none of the family were
permitted to attend them. His theory, which he rigorously
insisted on, was this:—Let them read a portion of the Word
daily, and commit to memory the Lord's Prayer and the
commandments; "when they reach a ripe age they will
choose for themselves, as I did." Mrs. Thomson was
allowed every liberty within these limits; and several of
their friends smiled when they saw how near she trod the
debatable ground at times. I never could understand how
William, while denying the freedom of the will, reconciled
his view of that subject with his allowing such unrestrained
liberty to his family. He must have done so to his own
satisfaction, for he was thoroughly conscientious; but he
employed a very questionable logic on certain topics.

Sunday was esteemed the pleasantest day of the week by
their children; yet, although the parents did not recognise
that day as holier than any other, there never was any
boisterous mirth indulged in by the youngsters. If no week-
day work was done by the parents, it was not because they
thought it sinful to work, but, I believe, they abstained in

deference to what they called "the weakness of neighbours." Be that as it may, its weekly recurrence was hailed by them and their children with delight. To them, because of its memory of a happy deliverance, the story of which it was their custom to repeat in varied form of narrative to their young, that, in after years, they might estimate its value, and repeat it to their offspring in turn; to the children it was a joy, for it furnished opportunities to listen to their mother's talk of times and things long passed away. She formed them into class, when, after reading "the chapter," each got a copy-book and slate, where they made attempts at writing. Then followed oral teaching, all of which had a stronger tendency to evoke feelings of kindness and pity than to oppress the brain with nice distinctions. Her chief aim appeared to be to make her children happy, whom she never wearied with long or complicated stories, but with wonderful tact intro-duced some topic of interest, at one time relating to Bible history, at another to that of Scotland; now and again she repeated an old ballad—" Hardy Knute," " Lord Gregory," and "Andrew Lambie" being favourites. When the weather permitted, she took them to the garden, where they gathered such fruits as were in season. William usually adjourned to another apartment with his book during class time; but he enjoyed the day and the proceedings as heartily as the youngsters. The only drawback to his pleasure was the pain *his* father endured because of his son's " unholy on-gangin' on Sundays."

Theirs was " a gawn hoose." Had they been poorer, and in any way less reputable, " gangeral," or such like epithet, would have been applied to it. Whether it was its roomi-ness, its cheery warmth, or the couthie welcome of its mis-

tress, I have no means of deciding; but certain it is that,
besides the visits of friends on week-day evenings, there
were persons known and unknown went in at all hours of
the day, with or without a reason. Children went to ask what
o'clock it was, "or will ye gie me a drink"—these were troubled with the "packman's drouth," and went away with satisfied soul. Neighbours dropped in for a "han'fu' o' camovil
flow'rs, or bogbean, or a tait o' saw" for a bairn's use.
These, too, left with what they wanted, besides good advice,
which they did *not* want. Then, on certain days, beggars
went—"needfu' folk" Katherine called them—who, for
aught she knew, might be angels, and therefore were served
with much tenderness. One of these, an old man with long
white hair, known in the district from his preaching power
as "John Knox," called for alms one day, and being tired
he sat down near the door. Mrs. Thomson placed an arm-
chair opposite the fire, and bade him "come ben an' lean
doon awee." He did so, and after being refreshed by bread
and milk fell asleep. After half an hour's repose he awoke
and asked pardon for his intrusion, in language so unlike
his condition that she encouraged him to talk. Nothing
loth, John opened his budget of peculiar opinions—opinions
so much in harmony with those of his hostess, that she
touched a cord that rung a bell at her husband's loom,
whose entrance did not interrupt John's long exposition.
No one spoke till he finished his discourse, and he rose to
leave, when William, with a gratified smile, held out his
hand and said, "Shebboleth." No more was said; they
accompanied him to the door, the woman's eyes "wat
shod" as she told him outside he would be welcome whan
this gait again. But he never, as far as I know, returned.

Others went, taking the shop-en', to borrow or buy (and sometimes did not pay) reeds, rods, lays, or heddles, or to ask advice about "tweels" or "ties." When William grumbled about losing time instructing such, his better half reminded him of the law which said that "if he saved others, he couldna save himsel'," which usually reconciled him to the "fash."

I will here stand aside, for which my readers will be pleased, and give an episode, written by one of their sons, that is not without interest as a picture of old-world life in our town. He says—

" I recollect, and am not likely to forget, our first copy-line, which we wrote six times each Sunday for a while. From its continual repetition the words came to be a source of intense fun to us. But as our first copies were nearly filled with them, the time came when they were hateful to hear. They consisted of ' What is the chief end of man?' And the way we had a new line given us furnished some quiet enjoyment. This is how it was :—My sister and I were set down one day in the month of October over a tubful of potatoes to ' scraip,' preparatory for dinner, when strangers were expected. It was a bright, clear day, and the shouts and laughter of boys and girls in the roadway made our task a rather wearisome one, particularly to Annie, who was younger than I. We worked on, however, for a time, quieter than usual, and talking less, getting a word of caution from mother now and then to ' tak' care and no' waste '—not without reason, for Annie was losing patience, and in view of our slow progress, was losing temper and becoming careless. At length she cast her knife into the tub, and, rising hastily, exclaimed—' Tuts, bother, thae tawties are like the chief en' o' man, they 'll never be done;' and leaping over the tub, rushed towards the door. Mother, who heard the pettish remark, caught her up in her arms, and setting her down gently, with a kiss, on the 'creepy' she had vacated, said, 'Let us finish this job, dear, an' ye'll get a new copyline next first-day;' and then she told us of the wonderful birth in Bethlehem of Judea, of which we never wearied.

"Is a new copyline such an extraordinary affair, I wonder, to boys and girls now as it was to us then? I doubt it. Nothing seems wonderful or unexpected to the little manikins now-a-days. They are philosophers from birth. One of them explained to me lately the causes of the ebb and flow of the tides in the most nonchalant way, and the only sense of wonder he exhibited was at mine. Why, we dreamt about that line, and spoke of it in whispers in the day-time, and told of it to every one we could induce to listen.

"On the Saturday preceding what I thought so important an event, I paid a special visit to grandfather to acquaint him of my prospects. That stern old disciplinarian had not knowh of my having learned to write—he knew, indeed, that scraps of paper were used by us on Sundays, and could hardly tolerate such a breach of its sanctity; but writing or learning to write he regarded as a profanation of the day, and as such a reproach to the family name. He was a grand old man, nevertheless; and if too pharisaical on the visible forms, he was a true publican in humility. It was after sundown when I entered his Island of Patmos. The labours of the week were over, and the sanctity of the day of rest was tacitly acknowledged by the low calm tones of every voice, and general finish that pervaded the whole surroundings. Water stoups were filled and covered with towels ; pots and basins contained washed potatoes and cut vegetables; the coal bunker was heaped up, and rows of boots and shoes stood brushed for the morrow's use. Grandfather was seated on a chair placed in the centre of the floor, whilst grandmother stood before him shaving his beard. When he expressed indignant horror at what he called mother's 'unrichteous conduc',' the peacemaking old dame advised caution :—'Were I thee, William, I wadna risk disturbing family peace. Katherine has a gae sharp tongue when its lowst, for a' as quait 's she luiks, an' wunna brook dictation frae onybody.' Wiping the lather from his face, he answered with a bitterness which his strong burr *seemed* only to increase, perhaps, 'I carena altho' it wur as snell as a nor' win', I 'll gi'e her a bit o' my min', an' clear my conscience.' I went home rather crestfallen, I remember, and told mother, who, I saw, was worried on learning that a battle was inevitable. Father, I thought, was more pleased than otherwise, for he put an arm round her waist and said, 'It 's as weel to come sune 's syne, lass; keep a stoot heart ; I 'll no be ayont ear-shot; an' a little opposition, whan it canna be avoidet, tends tae strengthen oor principles.'

"Our wonder was immensely excited on Sunday afternoon when we got our new copyline, the words of which were—'What is the chief end of God?' We knew the answer to the former question, but this was such a puzzle as made me whistle to look at. When father examined our copies after a while, there passed over his face an anxious troubled look. Commending our diligence in a few encouraging words, he turned to mother and said, 'Thae new words, gudewife, savour a good deal of speculative theology, an' I thocht we understood ither on that matter ?'

'Thae are nae mair sae than the ither anes, an' thou was weel enough pleased wi' *them*, I min'. They're just the ither hauf o' the same question. A' questions, I've heard thee say, hae twa sides, a Godward an' a manward ane;' at which he smiled, and said,

'Thou wud hae made a gran' lawyer;' to which she replied,

'I'm better employed here at thy side.' She was too conscientious to violate her vow of obedience, and was content to drop a suggestion now and again, or, as in the present case, a word, and let it germinate.

"We had not been long seated in class when grandfather made his appearance, and mother rose to give him welcome, father having retired to the 'shop-en'' with his book—*Booth's Reign of Grace*, very likely. 'She was glad to see him;' hoped there was 'naething wrang oure-by; an' as this is the first time ye hae darkened my door on a first day, ye maun lean doon an' break bread wi' us before we begin tae converse.' Placing a chair for him and a table, which she furnished with the ever-ready bread and milk, we were told to go into the kitchen 'an' get a bite an' see gran'faither.' When we had ranged into our places, mother bade him 'say awa.' Laying aside his cap, he began the blessing, which lengthened into a prayer for the household, and finally extended to 'all whom Thou hast created.' The meal was a pleasant one—as impromptu meals usually are—for mother led him on by inquiring after old friends in connection with Dr. Ferrier, and spoke lovingly of old times when she was a member of his class; and then grandfather unwittingly began to talk of his earlier experiences of the church, and of the first Seceders in town. By the time she had cleared the table, he appeared to have forgotten his message. But she had no wish to avoid a conflict since war was necessary. She therefore told us to bring and shew him our copies. When we placed them before him, he adjusted his glasses for examination. He ran his eye over a page of each, turned to another, and another, and another; then, looking up, amazed like, he said, as if speaking to himself, 'What is the chief end of man?' 'Man's chief end is to glorify God, and enjoy him for ever,' three small voices answered slowly but stoutly. He was startled by our response, and closing the copies, he held out his hand to mother, and said kindly, 'I have to beg thy pardon, Katie; I have judged thee unjustly; thy end justifies thy means. May the Lord bless thy endeavours.'

"He was a fine old man, and when not speaking theologically was gentle and winning, particularly to young folks. I recollect his once challenging me to a snow battle—a regular pitched battle—to be fought 'to-morrow, if the snow keeps in order;' and we fought it, too. 'To-morrow,' when I went to see him, he and grandmother had gathered snow in the garden into two heaps, my heap having balls ready made. He threw his snow in handfuls that never reached the mark. He made me believe he was being beaten, and retreated. I followed, peppering away in great style. At last he became so overpowered with snow and laughter, that, in lifting me into his arms, we fell on the snow. He rose, and taking me on his back, carried me inside, where we found Dr. Ferrier sitting at the back-jamb window, laughing at our onset."

With another extract from the letter I have been quoting
I will close this portion of my narrative :—

"Years after—after I had left the old home," he proceeds
to say, "I went to see my mother, whom I found alone
reading, and I asked, Can you tell what is the chief end
of God, mother? Closing on a finger the book she was
reading, she looked up with the old benignant smile on
her face, which 'years and tears had blencht,' and said,
'Sae, it has come back on thee! Yes; God's end and
design is to mak' angels o' a' the men an' women He
creates, an' He canna be thwartet.' And then we talked
about the old times, 'when a' the bairns were aboot my han'
beginnin' tae learn,' and about the love feasts in the meeting-house, and of the jaunts to the country in 'gude weather,'
and the yearly dinner, when all early friends, without distinction of creed, gathered round the board. Then, recurring to my question, she impressed on me with earnestness,
as usual, that never here nor hereafter would we cease to
learn; adding, 'Keep the channel open, therefore, by a life
o' justice; an' dinna forget that a' abidin' knowledge comes
frae the love o' justice, an' a' justice springs frae mercy an'
kin'ness.'" His concluding words are, "I would fain linger
on and say more, much more; but of what use would it be?
Rather let me uncover and bow my head in silent thanks to
God for the priceless gift of my pure-souled mother."

CHAPTER IX

ALTHOUGH I cannot believe that the friends who gathered to our annual festival were so good or so wise as my memory indicates, yet I am more disposed to regard its teaching than that of my reason as the truest reflex of the past ; and so I continue to cherish the impressions of my early life in defiance of the doubts of the present. I never was blind to the peculiarities of manner, nor to the grotesque outcome of some of these old worthies' minds, which, indeed, were the baits that generally first caught my attention, by provoking my faculty of imitation ; but that questionable practice did not diminish my love of the geniality that underlay their oddities. On the contrary, my subsequent penitence for the fun I extracted from their various singularities contributes to magnify, perhaps unduly, their intrinsic value.

Not one of these men was more highly esteemed by me, and no one presented so many points to imitate, as Samuel Cameron. He, and all that are yet to be noticed in this narrative, must be more briefly described than any of the foregoing.

A very common-looking man was Samuel, yet uncommon when better known, in that he was an exceptionally good man. His dress, common to his class, consisted, when at work, of striped waistcoat, with sleeves of fustian, and pants of drab kerseymere. When he dressed for the warehouse, or for a collection tour for the funeral society of which he was officer, he donned a short brown coat, with black cloth buttons, and a hat brown also from long service. In cold weather he wore the coat at work, but in all weathers he had over all an ample apron of green frieze, in the bib of which was placed his turkey-red handkerchief and spectacle case. His hair was thin and soft—so soft that with the faintest breath of wind, or, as I thought, when he was excited in any way, it flew hither and thither in a rather confused manner; but when in repose it lay scattered on his high, narrow forehead. Being near-sighted, he wore glasses, which appeared to give him an immense amount of trouble; for his nose being straight and slender, it was in continual motion in the effort to keep them from falling. He was spare and delicate, and the force required to work the "lay" allowed his waistcoat to droop down the left arm, so that when at work, with the movement of the shuttle hand and the lay arm, the plunges of his feet among the treadles, the spasmodic twitchings of his mouth, and the contortions of his nose, he was to me a never-failing source of observation and amusement. Even when he rose to address the brethren in church, the habitual twitching of his shoulders and the nasal motions were continued. But his sweet voice, gentle manner, and saintly life neutralised the incongruity between his appearance and his words. I did not dare to mimic him at home openly; but we often "gaed by" our first sleep from indulging in the arm or nose movements, and repeating his favourite church expressions— "Rejoise, brethren! I say, rejoise! I say again, rejoise!' The only features at rest were his eyes, which never, as far as I could see, lost their steady expression of wonder. He was a sincere believer in the doctrine of personal assurance, and was happy in his own assurance; but he was almost the only man I have ever known in whom that belief did not beget spiritual pride. In several instances I have seen that form of pride accompanied with contempt of others whose lives compared favourably with theirs. Samuel must have had self-esteem very low, as phrenologists would say. He never, as he told me twenty years later than the time I now refer to, could understand why *he*—he of all men—should have been selected for the happiness he enjoyed and the bliss he hoped for. I once hinted to him, by way of question, whether one's own feelings were a sure test on such an awfully important subject? and his reply, if not satisfactory, was definite enough—" I am beyond reasoning and question on the matter; I can only humbly and gratefully rejoise." What he called the peace of assurance was, I think, the happiness that invariably accompanies God's best gift—goodness; and this Samuel's life portrayed. If anything could have recommended his theology to my mind, his kind, pure, self-forgetfulness was eminently suited to do so.

Can you, reader, suppose this shy, silent man brimful of fun, and with a keen sense of humour? Yet such he was; and the friends circled round our hearth once in a while hailed his song or recitation with as hearty goodwill as the brotherhood did his " Rejoice brethren" on Sundays.

His wife, Mary Cuthbertson, was a fitting yoke-fellow to such a man. Calm, gentle, and yielding, when there was no principle involved, she was resolute, fearless, and outspoken when occasion required. Her character was seen to best advantage as reflected in the order and docility of the family, which was her chief care. Everything had its proper place, and every duty its appointed time; and in every duty light-hearted mirth and the cheerful hum of song resounded over all. But she required unquestioning obedience; indeed, it was a common adage with our female visitors that parents ought to be obeyed by the young as *principles*, in order that when they reached maturity they might obey principles as *parents*. Mary was the first woman I ever heard maintain that the only superiority of parent over child consists in his being wiser than the child, and that a parent's highest wisdom is manifested in his endeavour to initiate his children into the exercise of their own wisdom. These sturdy-minded dames committed sad havoc at times when they tried to square their creed with their own common sense.

Mary was a tallish woman, with a mass of dark-brown hair, clear, lovable gray eyes, and face slightly freckled, which gave her otherwise fine features a countrified look. Ah! and wee Mary their daughter; I shall not forget her till my memory withers. Our mothers and fathers never exchanged the kiss of love during the morning's worship with purer souls than Mary and me did in the intervals.

I have heard men of highly philosophic minds say that truth is *various*, according as it is viewed, but that goodness is *one*. In thinking of the goodness of the man I have just spoken of, and of him whom I next introduce to my readers, I would be disposed to alter the adage, and say, "if goodness *is one*, it differs very much in degree;" for while some men are unconsciously good, there are others of whose goodness we are unconscious—through whose rind the warmth never exudes, never reaches us.

L

Archibald M'Fee and his wife Margaret Cochrane verified
the old saying that "extremes meet." Archibald was a
reticent, well-informed man, with little tenderness of disposition, and whose manner being *stunkardy*, his kindest
acts were performed in a gruff, ungracious way, with little
or no regard to the feelings of others. His thoughts came
all direct from his brain, in hard, cold, clear, well-expressed
sentences, and all his emotions were kept in wonderful
subjection to the dictates of what he knew for a certainty
was *truth, all of which*, he said, was delivered long ago to
the saints, of which congregation he was an assured unit.
Believing grace to be irresistible, he denied the freedom
of the *will*, and all duty done (by Christians) he held to be
the result of grace.

His wife, on the other hand, although believing the same
tenets generally, had no assurance except of her own un-
worth, and of the infinite love. And on the subject of
freedom she maintained that we appear free, and therefore could enjoy all its benefits, and must sustain all its
responsibilities. With her duty done was the proximate
or procuring cause of grace. Her philosophy, in a word,
was that of the heart; and as it welled up from hers, it
sent a blush over her face before her warm loving words
were uttered.

Some natures receive truth—or what they conceive to be
truth—as apathetically as if it had no beauty or use; and
it is not till the Husbandman undertakes to do a little
top-dressing, or it may be subsoiling, that its inherent
worth is discovered, by the upturning of seeds whose
existence was unknown : when a *braird* begins to appear,
whose "fruit is good for food, and whose leaves are for

the healing of the nations." The wise Swedenborg says,— "The human mind is as ground which acquires a nature according to its cultivation;" and to that end there is, perhaps, no parts of human experience of greater value than the alternations of sorrow and solicitude for what we love. It is pleasant, indeed, to sail with the stream; but it is not when everything flows in the channel of our wishes that *we* advance with them. Such at least was the experience of Archibald M'Fee and his wife at the times when any of their children, several of whom had died, were ailing. On these occasions that couple changed places, and appeared to change natures, for then she became supreme. Calm, vigilant, sleepless, and imperious, she issued her orders with the air of a master, whom he felt constrained to obey. All she did was with seeming stoicism and a cool determination to win. What he did was with trembling hands; when he spoke, it was with quavering voice; and when their eyes met, his were beseeching for some word of hope. With the little one in arms he paced to and fro, emitting no words, but only grunts of a yearning love; or, sitting docilely as directed, applied such medicaments as she desired. And they continued thus till the child recovered or passed away. When, on the first occasion, the latter event took place, he put the little burden in her lap, stood for a moment with a hand on her shoulder, brought his lips to her cheek, and said soothingly, "Puir lass, it's a sair thud to thee." Then, straightening himself up, he drew a long breath and sighed. Excepting the double quantity of snuff he consumed, there was no evidence of his grief manifested; he waited, however, not without tenderness—for him—on

his "puir lass," whom the floods overwhelmed in a tearless
sorrow.

On the close of the short winter day when the remains
of the little one were put away, Archibald sat beside his
wife a while, and endured her moaning, but at length said
he would feel happier at his "duty" on his loom, to which
he went in the other end of the tenement; and as he thought
the familiar noise of the shuttles might distract her attention, he left the doors between his house and the weaving-
shop open. His 'prentices and other mates, with whom the
child had been a favourite, with a considerateness for the
parents' grief not uncommon in the class, occupied themselves at odd jobs about their looms, but did not weave.

Mrs. M'Fee, too, thought that work would be of use to
her, and turned to her wheel, the noise of which reached
the shop—the only evidence of life in the premises. By
and by every one was startled at discovering that the
whirr of the wheel was, as it were, drowned by the
louder, clearer notes of her voice, as if singing to a child.
Archibald returned to the kitchen, where he discovered
that she, forgetting her loss, had, through habit, put a
foot under the cradle that stood beyond her wheel, and
touching it, rocked it, and rocking it sung. She did not
know that he had returned, but, by means of that in-
explicable affinity that subsists between two hearts beating
near with a common sorrow, she recovered her memory,
and with a great cry said, "Lord, Lord, forgie me! I
forgat my bairn was awa," and fell back in convulsions
into her husband's arms.

The illness of the boy, who was large-brained and pre-
cocious, had continued for a short time only; but for weeks

and months the mother mourned the loss with an intensity
of grief such as only young mothers can feel at their first
heart-scud. Of denser material, absorbed in the evidences,
and rejoicing in assurance, Archibald, who was being sub-
soiled unconsciously, could not understand how the removal of a child could produce "in a believer" such grief
as hers, prostrating all the powers of mind and body.
After the sigh when the boy went home, he never willingly
recurred to the subject, so that his wife mourned alone,
secretly and in silence—his want of sympathy deepening
her sorrow, and causing both to experience feelings of
isolation.

Archibald, although unable to appreciate the state of his
wife's mind, felt, nevertheless, that the charm of their unity·
was broken; and as the double tie of creed and kinship
subsisted between her and her brother Andrew, he requested that deacon to pay her a visit. For the first time
since her bereavement there was a sparkle of the old life ·
in her eyes when he said, "I met An'rew in the toon this ·
forenoon, wha said he was gaun tae look oot an' see thee:
some day sune. I thocht it 'ud please thee tae ken."

When Andrew made his appearance, he was astonished·
and vexed to witness the ravages grief had wrought in his
sister's health and looks; unfortunately, he did not speak
from vexation, but from astonishment, and instead of con-
doling, he upbraided her with want of faith and submission
to the Divine will. He, too, was without the sympathy
she craved, and for the first time in all their life they parted
in coldness—she feeling that her last earthly prop was torn
away; he, that he had hardened and lost his old playmate and confidante, with his well-intentioned admonition.

Heaven pity those whom creeds harden, or cool to the sorrow of others.

This state of matters did not continue long, however. Within a week after the interview just referred to, Andrew lost one of *his* children, from the same complaint of which his sister's boy had died ; and on the day following the interment he visited Mrs. M'Fee again. Seating himself by her side, he took her hand and remained silent for a time— till both found an outlet for their tears. He then said meekly, " I cam' oot, Maggy, tae beg thy pardon for the heartless words I spak tae thee short syne. I didna ken what I was speakin' aboot; I kent naething aboot it. I ken noo, an' am vera sorry I e'er cam' on sic an erran'." How they conducted themselves during the remainder of that interview I never learned ; but I heard Mrs. M'Fee say, a long time after, that her " heart lap wi' perfect joy that Andrew un'erstud what ailed me, an' had sympathy for me."

When their eyes met, as he joined our " denner pairty," all our visitors could see in both a look of gladness such as whole-hearted people never experience.

CHAPTER X.

AS I have repeatedly introduced Andrew Cochran's name, it appears to me about time that I should present him personally to the notice of my readers. He suffered the fate of all eccentrics in small communities—of getting a nickname. In his youth, from his flighty, fidgety disposition, he was called "Mercury;" but as time and grief quieted his nature, that name gave place to "Sixty-two," as more appropriate to his changed state, and to his height, which was five feet two inches. His hair was light-coloured and sparse, his eyes blue and large, his nose of very extraordinary dimensions, and, in fact, his head and features were altogether large in proportion to his body. He kept a Bible, a few tracts, and a large pocket handkerchief in his chimney-pot hat, which bulged at the sides, and was apt to topple over when some streak of his old mercurial disposition came into play; to prevent which he pulled it well down over his brow. He had small, well-formed feet, of which he was somewhat vain; his shoes were usually of the slipper kind, and his stockings a bluish gray; he wore knee-breeches of black, and a long swallow-tailed coat, always buttoned up to his throat. He was a particularly earnest man, and easily provoked by irreverent opposition. He was near-sighted, and stood in disagreeable proximity to those he conversed with. A tailor to trade, he had ample opportunity for quiet meditation, a habit which became morbid, making him finical and fault-finding at times; yet he was of great simplicity of mind, and easily imposed upon by the wags of the neighbourhood. He had " connected" with the brotherhood in its early years; but when the member-roll increased to seventy-five he felt impelled to secede, and join one of twenty-five, as being more within his " knowledgeable grasp."

His new connection was the very purest of the purely democratic in the order of their worship, each male member being required to occupy the pulpit in turn. Andrew's day came round in due course, and the sermons he delivered were long spoken of as the very cream of the faith he ultimately renounced. To render himself less "kenspeckle" to strangers on that day, should any chance to be present, he provided a chunk of wood for his use as a pulpit stool, three or four inches thick, at which his adopted brothers were so incensed that, at a special meeting of the members, it was resolved that " such conduct being at variance with the equality of Christians, he, Andrew Cochran, be ' cut off' the connection;" and expelled he was, once and for ever.

The incident had results unlooked for by any one concerned. Till then everything in life, it may be said, had gone as smoothly as his heart could desire. Once in two years since the time of his marriage he had gratified his erratic disposition by going to sea, which service he had entered when young—improving his health thereby, as well as adding somewhat to the revenue of his house; but now, when well up in years, expelled the church which he loved so well, and in the same month " stricken " in his tenderest part by the loss of his child, he felt as if discarded alike by

God and man. It is impossible to say where he might have
drifted to had he not been caught by the quieting influence
of Henry Buchan's more elevating faith.

Into the particulars of *that* faith, however, it is not my
intention to enter here, further than to say that on one
point it was comforting to Andrew in no small degree.
Henry, it seems, had told him that he was more disposed
to sadness when a birth took place than when a child died.
At birth, he argued, the tree was only planted and its
future undetermined ; and the questions that disturbed his
mind were—" Will the little one grow up to be a blessing
cr a curse ? Will it become a virtuous father or mother, and
train *its* offspring in the fear of evil and the love of good; or
become a wreck on the waves of time, saturated with its
impurities, a heartbreak to its parents, and a loathsome
thing to strangers ? At death the case is reversed; for
the plant is then uprooted—is taken beyond the possibility
of evil, and transplanted to a more genial clime—into the
very atmosphere of the Divine love."

The events and the philosophy changed every current of
Andrew's mind and life. It did not occur to him, however,
that' there was any discrepancy between his old and new
faith, till he desired re-admission to his old connection ;
when, being refused, he began to generalise and compare,
and discovered that, however sincere the mutual esteem, so
long as technical teaching was the bond of union, they
could not coalesce as of old. He, in fact, had become the
henchman of Henry Buchan in all things relating to human
destiny; and although the latter had been tolerated when
standing alone in his belief, Andrew's adhesion to it made
them both objects of distrust. There was no persecution

resorted to or intended; yet the effect of being shunned in a small community, and every word they uttered weighed and twisted, was felt to be of a persecuting nature. It made the two fast friends, however; and it were difficult to say whether Henry, as teacher, or Andrew, as pupil, was most satisfied. If the latter hung, as it were, on the words of the former, the former was not less pleased with his friend's aptitude—an instance of which, and its effect upon others, I will here relate.

At one of our yearly gatherings, Mrs Henry and Sarah Troup had been discussing—amicably, for a wonder—the question of the loss of free will, and of God's image by the Fall; and having, as they thought, exhausted that subject —it is remarkable how soon a topic dries up without opposition—one of these theologians turned to Henry Buchan, who had sat an attentive but silent listener to their discourse, and asked abruptly if he "fell in wi' the view we hae ta'en o' that maitter?" Henry shook his head and replied in his slow, hesitative way, "I doot ye dinna un'erstan' properly what an eemage is or means. If ye luik yersel' i' the glass, your eemage is there—but it's a' reverst; its left is your richt, and its richt's your left. Sae it is wi' God's eemage in man. God is infinite fulness, an' man is finite empiness. God is infinitely able an' willin' tae gie; man has a constant craving tae get; for he was made 'very good'—as an eemage."

"Ye'll surely no say that the carnal min' has ony sic cravin' for it's enmity against God?" Sarah asked.

"That's true enouch tae," replied Henry, "for carnality is not an eemage of God, but o' what is really animal an' no human in man, an' wadna only tak', but keep, an' ca' its ain,

every gift an' grace that comes frae God's fulness; for it
canna rise aboon its origin, which is the yerth; but it's
itherwise wi' the real true human eemage o' God in man,
wha stan's wi's fit on the boddum rung o' the ladder o'
which Jacob's was the symbol, and luiks up till *his* origin,
which he never can rise up till, an' like an unweaned bairn
yawmors tae be filled. Whan the carnal min' uses the
ladder, it first o' a' whamls't head formaist into the booals o'
the yerth, an' stretchin' *doon* the ladder on's belly, cries oot,
' There is no God,' an' an echo rings through the cawverns,
' No God.' Yet we wadna be men without the carnal min';
for then we'd hae nae choice an' nae progress, but only gude
instincts, like the domestic brutes that perish. There's an
unco difference atween creatin' and makin', ye see : the ane
is the raw material, an' the ither is the article o' use. God
creates the oo', but we hae tae make it intil claeth. Sae, tae,
He created us, but wha amang us can say truly they are
made in a heevenly sense ? Had Adam no hearkent till the
carnal min', we micht a' hae had the open communion wi'
God he had, an' wi' angels, like Jacob an' ithers. An' if
we accep' the proffered gift frae His fulness, we will e'en
recovèr that preevelege, wi' mony ither anes that's maistly
lost us."

" Maistly lost? It's a'thegether lost lang syne," cried
Sarah.

" There's nae warrant for sayin' it's lost utterly," Henry
said. " The request o' the rich man tae sen' Lazarus, an'
the refusal o' Abraham, hauds oot the possibility o 't tae the
'hale race."

" Weel, ye may haud on tae that delusion, an' it please
you, Henry Buchan," said Mrs. Henry; " but it's a settled

thing in my min' that it belangt tae the shadowy dispensation, an' at the fulness o' time it ceas't for ever."

" Ceas't? said ye," cried Andrew Cochran from his corner, starting to his feet, a porringer of ale in one hand and
a biscuit in the other.   " Ceas't? ay, it has ceas't; sae has
the rule o' three amang the savages !   But wha's tae blame,
seein' that God waits tae be gracious?   The capacity that
was there then is here still; but an' we persist in oor
savagery, an' sae turn oor back on God and His providence, mair than that'll cease.   God's life i' the soul will
cease, as belief in Him has maistly ceas't already.

" Forty years syne Willie Hutcheson left hame because
he lost the lass he lo'ed—as fine a chiel as ye cud hae cast
een on—an' was awa', an' aye awa', till ten years syne.
When I took my last voyage to the Cape, I was tauld there
that a white man liv't far in the country wi' a tawny wife ;
an' as I kent an' liked Willie in oor young days, I thocht
it micht be him.   Sae I took fit-in-han', an' ran awa tae
mak' certain, for his mother's sake, wha mournt him sair.
Weel, after twa days' trampin', I forgathered wi' a lang
broon fallow an' a black woman, an' I kenna hoo mony
smouts o' bairns aboot them; an' it *was* Willie.   If ever
I thankit God for His guidance it was that day.   For awee
I couldna speak for gladness.   First ava I said, ' Willie
Hutcheson ;' but he didna seem to heed me; then I
spak' to him o' 'is mother, hoo she mournt for him, and
mentioned his twin sister's name, an' a' his brithers' names,
an' refert tae oor auld cronies, an' the splores we had
lang syne.   But Willie had forgotten everything, even his
mother and his mother-tongue; he didna ken a word I
said; he shewed no inklin' o' recognition; he hadna

even the tradition o' a Papist—*he was a savage.* An' if he, educate an' trained in a God-fearin' family till man- hood, fell sae far in therty year, may we no see hoo a race can degenerate in the coorse o' centuries that God an' heeven, an' angels an' divels' vesets may dwindle intil aul' wives fables? For my pairt, I hae nae doot o 't; we hae forgotten God, an' we wyte him o' forgettin' us. I canna see hoo we can gae farer."

"Tuts, Andrew," said Sarah, "that case is no tae the pint. I hae heard thee tell that story, word for word, owre an' owre, an' my min' o 't is that Willie was clean daft, or he wadna forgat his mother"

"Of coorse, he was daft," replied Andrew. "I ne'er had a doot o 't; an' if thou, Sarah, can lay thy han' on a man or woman that is cloathed an' in their richt min', and wha sits at the Maister's feet, learning the things that belangs tae the kingdom o' God, I'll admit the case is no tae the pint, but no itherwise. But they 're daftest wha beleeve themselves wise. I think personal assurance just anither severe form o' the malady."

The incidents of Andrew's African tramp were known in every family of his acquaintance; but never till the evening in question had I heard himself speak of it. The calm and silence that followed the rapid outburst and hard hit he dealt to Sarah was such, that others besides me were startled when the clock *warned* the hour it was about to strike. But the spell was broken quite as Kath- erine struck with the long-shanked hammer the coal in the grate; and then, as if to keep to the original issue, she, on resuming her seat, said—

"I ne'er concernt mysel' by-ord'nar' aboot sic things

being possible or no; but I hae af'en won'ert what puir
Lazarus' reception wad hae been had he been allooed tae
carry word tae the five chiels. I ne'er came tae ony
conclusion that satisfit me; but I hae imagint him dawn-
erin' awa aboot his aul' haunts, an' castin' up in his
min' the change frae times bygane. An' I hae seen him
open the door like ane in authority, an' naebody hinderin'
his ingangin', whar he used tae crave a morsel tae sus-
teen him; no ane speakin' or noticin' him, 'cept ane o'
the dougs gaed up snokin' at him, an' waggin' his tail,
in token o' auld freenship. An' whan he open'd the big-
room door, nae notice was taen o' him; ae lad was in a
corner coonten' siller, anither ane was lookin' owre papers,
speakin' tae himsel'; a third ane was smokin', an' a toom
jug afore him, balancin' a bane on a doug's snout, snap-
pin' his fingers tae gar't catch at it; another stood before
a glass admirin' the rings and chains he was array'd in;
an' the auldest lookin' ane had faun owre a-dozin', after
his heavy denner. An' then I saw Lazarus gang up tae
him, an' whusper sumthin' in his lug that made *him* start.
Glowerin' bewildered-like, he shook his heed, an' fell owre
again; an' again Lazarus whuspert; the heed turns, an'
a soun' sleep comes owre him, when the erran' is again
presst hame on him. At length he starts up, an' wi' some
ill-faur'd words struts awa oot o' doors. Whan nicht fa's
an' bedtime's come, he dovers an' dreams; an' aye the
same patient face hings owre him, an' the same message
is whuspert till him; an' for as af'en as he turns an' tumels
a' thro' the nicht, the same beseechin' een meets his. At
the mornin' meal he tells the family o' his dreams an' their
warnin'—an's laughed at for his pains. A' day lang the

sough o' that sweet voice bums in his lug sae, that e'er
he daur gang tae sleep again he behooves tae see his
Rabbi, an' tell him o' the maitter. But the Rabbi laughs
looder than the lave, an' tells him tae tak' some op'nin'
medicine, an' no fash his thoom wi' sic havers. For ye
see the Rabbis lang syne were like Kirst there; it was
a' settled in their min' that thae things had a' ccas't. An'
it's sae wi' maist folk; they think that God made a' things
at ance, and then left them for gude an' a', fashin' nae
mair wi' them—like as we do whan we row up the aught-
day clock."

As it was Katherine's specialty, when matters were
getting beyond ordinary wading depth to introduce, "for
peace sake," some novel aspect of the subject, these
imaginings were delivered very deliberately, amidst the
greatest hilarity of every one present, excepting Mrs.
Henry, who said she "cudna bide tae hear sawcred
subjects made fun o'." That little lady tried hard to bring
the company back to the Fall and the loss of free will, but
it was too late; and so she had to repress her philosophy,
and sail with the tide of social mirth that followed. She
did so ungraciously, however, and to avoid participation in
the light talk, she shortly after proposed to retire to the
dormitory upstairs. But she was reminded that as some of
the younger children were recovering from "kinkost," she
might forego the use of her tobacco pipe for one night—a
luxury she enjoyed when perplexed in any way. Father,
who indulged in that weed in another form, was more
considerate, and led her to the weaving shop, where she
"luntet" alone for a while, and I had liberty to laugh as
loud and as lcng as kindly Claud Wilson furnished material·

On her return thence, Claud told her it had been settled
in her absence that she was to sing a song or give a recitation, or find a substitute.   Not a word had passed on
that subject, but she believed there had, and amidst some
quiet laughter she requested " Samuel would officiate" for
her.   And of course he adjusted his glasses, and gave us
his inimitable rendering of the "Bashful Man," which was to
me worth more than all the free wills in the world.

CHAPTER XI.

THESE, then, were the most notable of our annual guests: there were others besides, good amiable people, but they did not contribute much, except by their presence, to the enjoyment of the gathering. One, indeed, could have enlivened by his humour or his wisdom any company he entered, had his modesty permitted. But his constitutional timidity kept him silent everywhere, excepting in church and at the bedside of the sick, where his worth was known and appreciated. That was Thomas Taylor: his wife Grizel, or Grace, who, from her peacemaking disposition, humour, and unobtrusive almsgivings, was lovingly named "Charity Taylor" by her friends—always accompanied him. They were childless.

There, too, was John Bulloch, with his deep, soft voice, to whom all children seemed to cling instinctively. John had only one topic of permanent interest beyond that of beed-lamb-lappet cording—a topic which gave him unspeakable concern. On the subject of man's immortality he had no doubt; but he could not, he said, find in the record any intimation that woman was destined to everlasting life. His wife was a tender, loving helpmate, of whose wisdom he had profound veneration, and he could not bring his mind to believe that *she* would perish like the beasts; and hence his head and heart parted company, and took different ways, as all heads and hearts will do at times on some matter or other.

M

Then there was Willie M'Hutchison, packman from our county town, where, from the number of men having the same name, it became necessary to distinguish each by a word that embodied some feature of mind or body, or manner of speech. His hands, neck, and face, from constant exposure, were bronzed, and mottled with freckles; and his voice was loud, confident, and cheerful, as befitted a man who believed that creation was a less laborious work than trudging over the country under a load of ginghams and napery; and who spoke of the Creator as only a packman with a larger business on hand. Our Willie was known as " Homo," for two reasons, it was said. In the first place, he contended that the interest of one man was the interest of all men, for all were brothers in spite of themselves. The other reason was of a more recondite nature. Henry Buchan's exposition of the " Eemage " was well calculated to rouse Willie, who was known to entertain very conclusive objections thereanent. And as Henry "demurred" at every opportunity to the tri-personality of God, Willie lifted up his voice in defence thereof; for he had solved *that* problem. Creation, he said, was *not* finished when Adam, man, Vir, was formed, but when man " Homo " was completed; which took place when Eve brought forth her first baby. Then there was a full image on earth of the Divine Three. As Henry did not attempt the refutation of that illustration, it was considered unanswerable, and Willie was jubilant over his victory; and the matter was so settled finally. I am not aware which of the Divine Persons he said was represented by the *female* line.

I never could comprehend how Andrew Cochran allied

himself by marriage with Lizzie Tannoch. I can understand why she accepted that jerky little man, as a forlorn hope; but that he, so kind and soft-hearted, fell in love with that long, gaunt, silent block of ice, has always remained one of Nature's mysteries to me. Yet so it was; and there she sat by his side with compressed lips and arched nostrils, taking no part in the sober talk or innocent mirth that passed around her.

Lizzie was not without good qualities, but she was very peculiar. She did not believe a word any one of our company said on theological matters; but though satisfied that they were one and all utterly wrong, she remained silent till a more convenient season. She was what I can designate only as a Jew-Christian or Christian-Jew, as any subject of Christian kind which did not include, and keep in the foreground, that wonderful branch of the human family had no interest whatever to her. Mrs. Henry's half-contemptuous epithet of " Shadowy Dispensation " was known to that vinegary little woman to be wormwood to Lizzy, as every view she took of revelation,. and every promise she read there, pointed, she affirmed,. " to Abraham and to his seed, whose restoration to. Pawlysteen all the Divine economy subserved. When the bride was ready that event would take place ; the bridegroom has been waiting for it these eighteen hundred. years, and the whole creation waits also, and groaneth. and travaileth in pain together until now."

Such was her language on one occasion when she encountered Henry Buchan accidentally at our house ; to which he replied—

" Whan ance the worshipping church is a'thegether

engulfed in forms and ceremonies, we may safely conclude
that the speeret o' God is amaist quenched i' the hert o'
the race. An' as He ne'er lea's Himsel' withoot a witness
on the earth, we may then expec' that a new order o'
things — in which Good is recogneest as mair valuable than
Truth — has begun; an' what is noo ca'd the church 'll
hae become a cuesten-off garment, as the Jewish ane has
been for lang."

The sensuous worship of Rome being more in harmony
with the gorgeous ceremonials of the Jews, and therefore
better adapted to usher in the consummation desired by
Lizzy, than the bald forms of Independency, in which
mannerism is considered of secondary importance, she
advocated the institution of an hierarchy of duly sub-
ordinated grades, each arrayed in distinctive garments.
Her organ of wonder must have been unhealthily large, as
her perceptions and reason never rose above the senses.
And except that she spoke sometimes of the Divine Being,
her language was that of a materialist; her creed was a
kind of baptised negation—the materialism of Christianity.
For, like the scientific men of the present day, in whom, it
would seem, the Son of Man has nowhere to lay his head,
Lizzy had no "*king* but Cæsar." Yet "Wee An'rew's wife"
was a favourite with our circle, for she was unobtrusive,
kind, and conciliatory—when the Jews were absent.

.   .   .   .

About noon of the feast day a woman might be seen
wending her way southwards, dressed in a gray duffle cloak
which nearly reached her heels, bare-headed (for the cloak-
hood is lying on her back), her long white tapering neck
bare to the "*hause*-bane," ringlets of glossy brown hair

falling down her fresh cheeks, her dark-blue eyes dancing
with mirth. She walks slowly along, resting at times to
ask a friend, "Are ye a' gaiylie?" and then resumes her
measured pace toward our .dear old home. She takes
the nearest chair when she enters, and as she spreads
out her cloak, mother takes away from her side two
delf pitchers, which till then were hid. Our visitor is
Peggy Downie; and the pitchers contain each a Scotch
pint of Lydia, or Leedy Lawson's famous home-brewed
ale. "Hurrah" from us youngsters, and "Hurrah"
from Peggy, who bestows kisses round. The sounds of
the shouts reach the weaving shop to the amusement of
father. Work is suspended for the day; the 'prentices
cover up their webs and leave; and father tidies up the
place, provides coals for the evening, trims a lamp to
be ready; while we—we that have wearied for and
talked and dreamed of this day and hour—run over with
delightful excitement.

By and by the first guest arrives. If a matron she is
ushered into the "ben-en'," where she doffs her cloak and
Leghorn bonnet, puts on a lace-bordered cap, replaces her
damp shoes with prunella slippers taken from her pocket;
and after undergoing a general titivation, gets a news-
paper with which to amuse herself till others come. If a
man, he speels the narrow stair leading to the dormitory
above. It seems to me now that Claud Wilson always
came first, and that *our* fun commenced in earnest when he
came up. He approached me with majestic salaam, and
in high English said—

"May I ask how your Royal Highness's health has been
since I last had the honour of seeing your Royal High-

ness;" and continuing to bow near to where I stood, he whispered, "Is 't tae be bonnety-blin' or Andrew Barry till the tawtaes are riven."

What fun we had then! What laughing and jumping, and such noise as brought a rebuke from mother in the kitchen, from whence we could hear father·say in the lull that followed—

"Let them romp, wife; Claud wadna miss that prelude for a' that follows."

Claud Wilson came to enjoy himself, and he gave enjoyment to all within his influence. He and Peggy were the youngest of all our guests.

I will here, in a short digression, leap twenty odd years. I went to the United States on business in 1840; and Lowel being the centre of American manufacturing industry, I paid it a visit. On alighting from the railway car, I went in search of a hotel where I might place my valise before presenting my letters of introduction. But I misunderstood the directions given me, and strayed into what I afterwards heard called the "Scotch block"—*i.e.*, dwellings occupied by Scotch people, which, as it had a rather retired appearance, caused me to suspect I had wandered. By and by I met a tidy middle-aged woman, having a home-like appearance, being dressed in a lilac printed wrapper and a blue and white checkered apron; the latter filled with vegetables, and grasped by her hand, on a finger of which I saw the old-fashioned, substantial gold marriage ring; in the other hand was a basket—her appearance was evidently that of a housewife returning from market. I inquired my way, but instead of answering me, she stood gazing in my face intently for a few moments, and then "Yes" came from her in a dreamy sort of way; " But you must retrace your steps," she added.

After walking a few yards she stood and took another steady look at me, saying in a cheerful, coaxing way, " Excuse me, sir, but your face is familiar to me. I know you. Don't tell me your name, I'll come to it in a jiffy;" and proceeding on our way, she again stopped, and at an open door hailed the inmates by saying, " Are you in, David?"

" Yes," came from two voices.

" What," she asked, " was the name of the shawlwasher I served with at home?"

Laughter from two inside followed, and then husband and wife appeared; the former—who by the way was paralytic—saying, " Hast thou lost thy memory?"

" No; but this young man has driven me stupid—tell me."

They told her; "and," she answered, "ye're their son, sir. Hotel? Na, na, nae bairn o' your mother's 'll bide in a hotel in Lowel as lang 's I 'm tae the fore; I 'm your hotel keeper." It was Peggy Downie!—Mrs. Wilson. She led me to her house, and despatched a messenger for Mr. Wilson, who I learnt was manager of the Lowel Carpet Factory. He came in a little while, and tried to address me in the high English of old days, but stammered, stuck fast, broke down, put his hands on his face and cried like a boy—Peggy and I accompanying him.

I remained two weeks under their roof. I did not require to present my letters, Mr. Wilson's influence was sufficient to open every door I wished to enter. His racy conversation and well-stored mind rendered my sojourn in Lowel by far the most pleasant time I spent in the States.

There was a grand tea-drinking night in Mr. Thomas Railton's during my stay, where I met with the sister and stepmother of Alexander Wilson, the American ornithologist. I knew them before they left Scotland. It was a really pleasant evening; to me it was particularly so, from a very simple incident. During tea-taking, Mr. Railton requested me to examine the fly-leaf of a book he handed me, which I discovered to be an old hymnal, and on the leaf referred to was written, in my mother's peculiar caligraphy:—"Presented to Thomas Railton, on his joining the church on the Pen Brae.   14th May, 1807."   (Signed.) The incident will be best appreciated by those who have been long and far from home, and anxious for the promised letters which they had almost lost hopes of coming; to me it was like the smell of pressed thyme.   But to resume.

It is not indispensable that I describe the prosaic process of masticating our Martinmas dinner; and it is well so, as I am not qualified therefor, for this reason:—The order of the day was this: When dinner was announced the guests trooped in, each taking the seat assigned them.   My father stood at one end of the table and my mother at the other, with us youngsters at her side.   Before taking his seat, father addressed the company with what he called an "observation or two," part of which I here give as a fair specimen of the language in use by both male and female in our church circle.

"Although we do not all see the Divine will to the same extent and in the same view, it does not rise from the word being yea and nay, but from causes in ourselves, and connected with our upbringing and knowledge, which prevents our being so perfectly joined together in the same mind and in the same judgment as would justify our having 'fellow-ship' in observing all things whatsoever Christ hath commanded; yet, ye are all baptised of the Holy Ghost, having your fellowship with the Father and with his Son Jesus Christ, in one body and one spirit, even as ye are called in one hope of your calling, having 'one Lord, one faith.' Ye will bear with me while I call your attention to the 'one baptism of the one God and Father of all, who is above all and through all.' The only way we are to make manifest the truth to each other is by consorting one with another, that we continue steadfast in the Apostles' doctrine and fellowship, and in breaking of bread, and in prayers. Christ has not called us to 'compass sea and land to make one proselyte,' neither are we called to strive or cry, far less to imitate the 'axe boasting itself against him that heweth therewith,'" and so on, and *so* on for ten or more minutes—till in fact mother's eyes warned him that the soup was cooling, and then he offered thanks in a few brief words.

We small folk then adjourned to the dormitory above, which Peggy had tidied-up and placed our trenchers in proper order, furnished with due regard to our several capacities. Nor will I attempt a description of our mimic feast in that upper room—of how father's observation or two was travestied, and the delinquent rebuked by Annie for that punishable offence, and the fun we got from her being nicknamed " Mrs. Henry " for her perjinkityness in trying to keep " ordinary order." There was no lack of enjoyment or noise till Peggy came to make the room comfortable for the younger children till tea time, after which she went and put them to their crib. Her husband came with or shortly after her; and I very well remember being present when he remained till the little ones were undressed, and that he knelt between them, an arm round each, and heard them invoke a blessing on every one related to us by natural or spiritual kinship. When Peggy had made everything and all tosh and comfortable, Claud took me under his arm and landed me in my corner beside father's chair.

Every appearance of the recent feast had been removed, but in my absence three new guests had made their advent. These were Sandy from the Craighead, Will from the Laird's Corner, and Archy from Carsegreen, come for their aumous:—Naturals they were called—the reason being, I suppose, that those having an average share of gumption are more or less artificial. Sandy was a harmless man, and had flashes of mother-wit at times, of which the others were destitute; although Will had perception enough to relish Sandy's pawky replies, and disturbed his neighbourhood in the night watches occasionally with roars of laughter at what Sandy had said on the day previous. Will was a terror to the young, for he had a vicious temper when annoyed, and after nightfall those having gardens required to watch them in the fruit season. My father on one occasion promised him sixpence if he would catch and bring the thief that robbed his apple-trees, which Will having told Sandy, that 'cute chiel watched, and claimed the sixpence by bringing Will on his back one night after we were in bed. Archy was a quiet, gentle creature, whose face became radiant with delight when any one tied a bit of bright-coloured yarn on his coat. He must have had a perception of the beautiful in a hazy way; for a child with curled hair or one exceptionally pretty caused him to linger for hours, gazing at them and scratching his head in ecstacies. The three were good friends, and on the evening referred to they went away happier than kings.

CHAPTER XII.

ON the last of these occasions, after the dinner, and when every one had ranged into their place for the evening, Mrs. Gillespie said, " I think, William, that we hae argued the maitter o' thy fore-denner speech sae af'en till little mair can be said anent it."

To which my father replied, " I spoke to every one present, as well as to thee, Sarah, so I hope thou speaks for thyself only."

" I think that is a proper remark," said Henry Buchan, "as others may be of a different min' from oor frien' Sarah."

" It maun be yoursel' than, Henry, for every ane except you an' me is o' ae min' on the maitter—except, it may be, Lizzy Tannoch; an' naebody kens what you an' her wud be at. What, may I speer, is *your* opinion on baptism, Henry?"

" I meant to say what I said only—not to argue on a subject of so little importance as that or ony ither form o' Jewish origin," answered Henry.

" I wuz sure ye despised that as weel as a' else o' a relegeous natur," Sarah said somewhat bitterly. " You wha rejec' the ordinances maun hae gude grun' for your conduct, onless ye despise the message a'thegether."

. " I wud require different grun' frae what I hae to rejec' the message; an' I despise no thing; but I'd like tae value a' things at their proper worth. I think we cud get topics o' deeper interest tae spen' the nicht than that or ony ither form."

"Maybe ye wad condescend tae gie us a sample o' what ye think o' mair importance," was Sarah's rejoinder.

"Weel," said Henry, "whan we obey the comman', 'Thou shalt not steal,' we become honest, an' through grace an' strivin' we. come tae love honesty; but what better are ye o' being bapteezed? Ane wad think, to hear you speak, that it saves you."

"Is 't no eneuch that we obey an ordinance?" asked Sarah.

"No," said Henry, "I think no; we maun get before we can gie a reason for the hope that 's in us. Forbye, I 'm no clear that it 's an ord'nance o' the Maister's ava. His is the baptism o' love an' truth, yours is but a washing o' the body—ye mauna lose sicht o' the difference."

"Ye may say sae o' a' ootward things, an' syne we may close the kirks an' bide at hame, like you, on Sabbath-days. But maybe ye hae something tae substitute," Sarah added with a sneer.

"Thou forgets, Sarah," Mrs. Henry said composedly, "that Henry Buchan disna gae in wi' the doctrine o' substitution."

"Then," cried Archibald M'Fee, "he maun deny the doctrine o' justification."

"Ye 'll disbelieve," asked Samuel Cameron mildly, as he adjusted his glasses, "the doctrine of personal assurance?"

Henry, who, as I have said, was a slow, precise man, did not answer immediately, and before doing so the company became silent but expectant.

" Your question, Sam'l, is the only ane I can answer with a yes. I consider that the want o' assurance is ane o' oor safeguards, for without it we are keepit vigilant an' humble. Its present possession ten's tae the undue exaltation o' oorsel's; an' tae assume that they wha have it not canna be Christian, is an unhealthy, unsafe state o' min'. Forbye it subverts the doctrine o' the perseverance o' the saints, whilk is the mair valuable o' the twa."

" It dis naething o' the kin'," Kirst said, " if ye cud un'erstan' the record."

" If I was assured o' my acceptance I wad hae nae need o' perseverance."

" Wad ye hae nae need o' perseverance in weel-doin'?"

" I micht avoid ill-doin'; but that's no what I un'erstan' b' perseverance. Perseverance, I opine, means gettin' a deeper an' deeper view o' the Lord's will, a clearer an' a clearer perception o' His truth, a steever love o' mercy an' peacemakin', an' risin' higher an' higher in heevenly mindetness. I dinna fin' thae graces shinin' encreesin'ly in ony wha say they hae assurance. I see them a' mair or less strong in folk I ken, but they dinna strengthen wi' conflic' an' years—just, as I think, because they hae, or say they hae assurance.

" An' noo, I maun recur to justification an' substitution. Ye do me but scant justice whan ye say that, 'cause I view thae maitters different frae you, I deny them a'thegether. In aul' heathen times, when a man, for some crime, was to be exicute, it wasna an oncommon thing for a freen' or kinsman tae offer tae stan' the verdic' in his stead; an' whan thru' favour the offer was taen, the law was satisfit, an' the criminal was held sackless. A Christian book I ance read

on this maitter instanced that heathen practice as a proof
o' your view o' substitution; an' dootless it had its origin
wi' the heathen.   But if it amaze us wi' its onjustice whan
applied tae ae heathen man, is 't less onrighteous whan re-
ferrin' tae millions?   The Romish mode hauds the sinner
sackless if he dree the prescribet penance—whilk is anither
kin' o' substitution, although a puir ane.   It wad gie me
vera sma' pleesure were a judge tae let bairn o' mine gang
unpunisht if he was guilty.   Freedom frae sin is o' first
import, for that, an' naething else, meets a' wants an' satis-
fies a' just requirements.   I 'll convince you o' that, if ye 'll
alloo me tae read you a passage o' Law on the pint."

"No, Henry Buchan," snapped Mrs. Henry, "we want
nane o' your law, we 're un'er Gospel grace, God be
thanket."

Henry smiled, as did the others, at that earnest little
woman's unconscious pun—to whom "law" in any sense
and old Henry's utterances were alike abhorrent.   Resuming his reply, he said—

"The true doctrine o' substitution consists in gettin' oor
nat'ral evil dispositions replaced by gude anes—no by im-
putation, as ye say, but in gettin' new anes *gien* us.   An'
the true doctrine o' justification is the result o' that process;
for as we strive against, say cruelty, we come tae be
mercifu', or against injustice, we get the spirit o' justice
imparted tae us, an' we are justifit by becomin' just.   An'
sae, if we are faithfu', there comes a time whan we love
justice an' mercy abune a'; whan the vera thocht o' injustice, un'er ony form, will mak' our flesh creep; whilk
will be a token that the Maister is wi' us, an' bapteesin'
us wi' His ain speerit."

"An' ca' ye that Gospel?" Sarah cried. " Ye ha'ena daured tae quote a sin'le verse o' Scriptur for 't. Div ye think tae turn the worl' upside doon wi' fushonless nonsense like *that*, Henry? Ye begin' b' rejec'in' ootward things, an' en' b' whamlin' the essentials o' revelation."

" Weel," answered Henry, " a' ootward things that comes frae the Jews I rejec'; but I rejec' naething, nor do I pervert onything, that perteens tae the Word. I dinna of'en quote frae Scriptur, for it 's like a fiddle—ye can play ony tune on 't b' quotin'. But I beleeve that the method I hae gien expression till, is the ane b' which the Lord builds the waste ceéties, the desolations o' former generations.

" If I dinna gang tae public worship, its 'cause nae worshippin' body 'll gie me the richt hawn o' fellowship. Belief an' worship are common tae a' religions, and sae I wish tae cultivate a devout speerit. I cud worship wi' earnest Jews, although their dispensation 's withered an' worn, for worship belangs tae the heart, an 's no confint tae ae creed. But its held by maist folk tae be unseemly tae hae fellowship wi' those haudin' different views o' the Word; an' than, I'll no say ' yea ' just because ithers say ' yea.'

" An' than, again, it's no in prayers, an' forms, an' ord'-nances, that the Maister delights—but in service. No that He needs or wants tae be sair'd, etherans, but that they only wha serve can hae peace—for service comes o' humility, the only soil on whilk peace can grow.

" I whiles think, Sarah, that if hauf was said anent honesty an' mercy that you Burgar-folk speak aboot the keepin' o' Sunday, there 'd be less evil-speakin' and general backslidin' in the toon we bide in."

It appeared that Lizzy Tannoch could not contain her

wrath any longer; for she hissed through her teeth—"It's an unco pity that evelspeakin' is a sin, Henry, for it seems the pleesantist o' pass times tae you, or ye wadna speak o' the Jews as withered or worn oot."

Fortunately for Lizzy, her bombshell missed the target in an unexpected way—in scientific phrase, it was not permitted, without rebuke, to " strike below the belt " in that fashion; besides, although Henry's " views " were held in detestation by many of those present, his conversation was proverbial for its want of personal detraction—just as she finished her biting remark, Peggie Downie announced, "Tea 's ready," and every one felt relieved that a hitch had been avoided.   And then, again, Mrs. Henry, who missed the point of Lizzy's words, and always alert to trip-up a heretic, " wud like tae know if that demure woman's principles allood her tae think ony sin pleesant ;" at which there was a general guffaw; and Claud Wilson, eager for fun, then wished Kirst to " name, were 't but ae sin, that wasna pleesant tae some o' us," which moderated the mirth.   By the time that pleasantest of all repasts—that is *not* sinful— was over, the threatened breach of goodfellowship was forgotten ; and by tacit arrangement the discussion of theology was postponed till some future time.

From the tea-table the males adjourned to the weaving-shop, which had been prepared for their comfort.   An oil lamp, with tall glass moderator and burnished tin reflector, shed a bright light over the place, where stools and " seat-trees" stood arranged round the large fire.   Smokers prepared to enjoy their pipe, and snuffers exchanged mulls. There was great antipathy on the part of our female friends to the discussion of political subjects, and now that *they*

were absent, several tongues began to wag against the
" olagarchies."

During the half-hour occupied there was one feature of
the discussion which I did not understand at the time. It
was this :—Henry Buchan and my father never agreed on
the subjects they debated throughout the year at our fireside ; but in the shop, when the condition of the country
and the doings of Government were the matters in hand,
they stood shoulder to shoulder against all the others.
Henry was a shrewd man, and had no faith in the undis-
ciplined forces of the people ; and I learned in after years
that my father got such a *glisk* for part he took in '93 as
sharpened his wits and rendered him more patient of evils
he could not cure. And although the times were ticklish,
or thought to be so, there were loud, bitter voices raised by
the others present ; and opinions expressed so hostile to
civil order, which so alarmed my mother that in a lull of
the storm of words she was constrained to join the fray and
appeal to their Christian profession to desist. "No that I
need care," she added, "everybody kens that my William
taks nae pairt i' the ploys afloat." And I feel certain she
spoke truly ; and yet the memory of '93, and his activity
in the movement of that time, rendered him an object of
suspicion up to the time I now speak of. For I very well
remember that in 1819 Campbell of Barnhill, then our
Sheriff-Depute, and four mounted soldiers, visited our house
with a search-warrant. It was an episode not likely to be
forgotten. Two soldiers rode through the entry, and, drawing swords, stood guard there ; two stood in front in similar
position, to prevent egress ; and Mr. Campbell came inside
and told his business, but he said he regretted the necessity

N

of the visit; and looking round from where he stood, he expressed a hope that his visit would prove bootless, as none of the houses he had searched presented the same apparent comfort. " Do your duty, shirra," mother said, " we 're sure that your hope will be gratifit'," and so saying, she unchained her house keys, which she put into their respective locks. My old brother, then recently returned from the army, came in with a " gang " of water, and said he was at Mr. Campbell's service if he wished.

Intimation of the sheriff's approach had been sent on, and my brother had deposited in one of the " stoups " all the seizable implements the 'prentices possessed, and dropped them into the open " hoose-en'-well." My father did not know of their existence till they were out of harm's way. They were recovered when the well was cleaned two years after; but my brother was then in the backwoods of Canada, from whence he never returned. Mother plaintively said, twenty years after, " Oh, thae weary colonies. Mony's the heart they 've broken forbye mine." But to resume my narrative.

Political discussion interrupted in the manner above stated was stopped altogether by an invitation to the kitchen. Each smoker lays aside his cutty-pipe and obeys; whilst Claud Wilson, to my great delight, slily appropriates the pipes. Now was the time of times! Now came the enjoyable hours! Never have three hours passed so rapidly in my life as did those evenings after tea. We had dinnered at two, took tea at six, now it was near eight, and " we maun a' be hame gin eleven."

On a table, standing between the " dresser " and eight-day clock, was the can of ale, surrounded by a kebbuck, bread-basket, and row of delf porringers, to which the guests were directed to " help yoursels without need o' mair ceremony." When all are seated, some with, some without ale, Claud Wilson is supposed to be absent, being planted in a corner of the fireplace on a low stool, and hid by the ample folds of my mother's dress. He is busy cleaning the tobacco pipes, which he fills with fine coal and covers over with clay. One by one the pipes are laid aside, till the whole is so dealt with ; he then inserts one of them into the fire, when lo ! to my amazement he applies a lighted paper, and it flames—*lowes!* As one pipe begins to wane, he prepares another and another, till the whole has emitted gaslight. During the process there appeared breakers ahead, on Henry Buchan saying, " They say there 's some toon lichtet wi' gas," and Sarah answering, " Tuts, nonsense. Can you, wha believe naething, believe *that* Henry ? "

" I 'm far intae years, Sarah, but I may leeve tae see oor ain toon lichtet up wi' gas yet," Henry replied.

" That 's the most sensible thing I ever heard you say, Henry," Claud said ; " an' if what ye believe on ither maitters be as certain as that is, it 's time we a' were lookin' into them."

" Now then ! " father said sharply, bringing his palm down on his chair-arm, adding in gentler tones to mother, " Noo, lass," whilst he placed before her a small round table, on which was a dulcimer, and then he points to me to go to her side—for to amuse me Claud was charging the pipes anew. " An' what is 't to be? " she asks. One shouts " Gloomy Winter," another " My Nannie, O ! " I whisper my choice, and looking round, with a smile she says, " The youngster's won the race." Then, purpose-like, striking the wires, she sings with accompaniment, " Loudon's Bonnie Woods and Braes."

After all the many years that have passed, when I recall the sweet tones of her clear, cheerful voice, as if daring fate, alternated with low, pitiful notes, plaintive as the cooing of the ring-dove, I declare my heart feels too large for its cavity; and often as I have heard the song since, in house or on the streets, I have always experienced a delight amounting to pain ; yet never have I heard such soul thrown into its words or music. One must be much older than I am to forget their mother's voice. It is something like the twenty-third Psalm, which every Scotch boy, young or old, is presumed to know by *heart*.

As the last notes of " Loudon's Woods and Braes " died away, father asked Mrs. Henry, who with others had named a song, which it was she wanted, and her reply was, " *That* youngster wha rules the roost may say what *he* desires." Claud Wilson, who had not left his corner, whispered across to where I stood, and I promptly requested James Gillespie to sing " Tam Glen "—not knowing that Mrs. Henry held the maiden of that ditty to be " a brazen-faced young gypsey without a spark o' modesty in her "—which words were expressed with unwonted *birr*. James sung it, however, and he did it in such admirable style that Sarah said the " pictur o' a love-sick lassie 'ud hae been complete had Jeems changed claes wi' me for a blink." James, whose ale was finished, said, as he went to replenish his porringer, "I micht hae cuesten thy goon owre my heed, Sarah, but it 's lang sin' thou foucht an' won the battle for the breeks ; a' body kens that, gudewife." That sally was followed by much goodnatured banter, in which Sarah joined heartily, and justified her domestic conduct by contending that "in every weel regulate hoose the wife is maister;" and pointing to Mrs. Cameron and Mrs. Thomson, she added, "Just luik at thae twa, ye 'd think butter wadna melt in their mooth, they 're aye sae mim an' fair spoken, an' yet they row their men aboot their wee fingers; but they 're gran' at hidin' the strings they draw, oh gran'." Mrs. Henry, who did not relish the subject, intensified the mirth by suggesting that "a topic o' a less personal natur' 'ud be mair eedifein'." She, too, had "fouchen for an' won the breeks." But she was everlastingly fault-finding with *something* or *somebody*.

The subject was not allowed to drop, however, for Henry Buchan, whose mind was most prolific of theory, and always intent to "improve the occasion," said that "in every case whar maistry was contended for, the idea o' marriage in its proper sense is excluded : marriage involving the acknowledgment on the part o' each that the ither had the richt to be consulted. 'I am thine' maun ever be the response o' every wife an' husband to their consort. A true wife will aye see her highest wisdom in her husband's, an' a true husband will always rejoice in his wife's love o' his wisdom. Mairfortoken that love o' his wisdom gi'es her a pow'r tae rule owre him an' his household, whilk a true wife will do, while, as the poet says, 'she seems to obey.'"

Willie M'Hutchison, between whose wife and himself the headship was still in an unsettled state, stoutly maintained that, "Whuther or no, a' the managing women o' my acquantance are disagreeable to deal wi'; smashin', snebin', owrebearin' hizzies, wha ane ne'er cud dae bizness wi', onless ye took them on their weak side, an' frazt them—what I canna thole daein'." And having made a fair start, he branched into a dissertation on the nature of mankind generally : of " men wha I hae led into the narrow path that aifter-hin' bocht my gudes an' never paid them ;" of " licht limmers wha gied me their ill-gotten siller an' ordered me tae tak' gudes for 't till poor-folk ;" of " ministers—as toom an' as useless as pea-shawps—wha expeckit, because they wur ministers, my gudes for a wanworth ;" of " weel-ta-dae elders wha cheated or try't tae cheat me," besides other instances more or less favourable than these. But, " on the whole, I fin' gude an' bad in a' classes, an' on the whole there's mair gude than bad, which is a gude thing, as, on the whole, trade cudna be conducet profitably if 'twerna."

When Packman Willie had settled the domestic and commercial aspect of matters, wee Andrew Cochran volunteered to sing ; and several faces grew pale, and lips quivered, whilst he sung " Tom Bowling," and which he supplemented by graphic touching tales of sea dangers and sea life. Then followed a request from my father that Samuel Cameron would " yoke into the ' Flowers o' the Forest,' or the ' Bashfu' Man ;' " and as the song was considered too saddening to follow Andrew's descriptions of wrecks at sea, the recitation was preferred. I close my eyes now, when upwards of half a century has passed, and I see that sainted man bending helplessly over the top rail of his chair, appealing pitifully for sympathy on account of the blunders he details — blunders that were identified in my mind for years as his blunders, so real did his delineation appear. The tide of emotion was fairly turned by Samuel's exhibition, and every one seemed disposed to dispense with douce subjects ; several were laughing quietly at some of the mishaps which the story contains, whilst others called for Claud Wilson's song, one of whom named the "Toom Meal Pock ;" others, knowing his leanings, would be pleased with his choice. Claud, who had risen, took from the fireside the long burnished poker, and said it would ill become him, or any one present, after such a repast "as we hae gotten to sing the dolefu' ditty o' the 'Toom Meal Pock.' I'll sing my favourite—ye a' ken 't." The song is an invocation to the spirit of freedom, the chorus of which was sung first, and again at the end of each verse ; and the reader may be sure that in a company where each was Republican at heart, there was a whole-heartedness of expression not common in our day with sedate church-going people on such subjects.

I am sorry I can give only portions of the song ; but what I do give may be deemed sufficient :—

> *Chorus.*—Come, Liberty, come,
> Thy blessings, Oh haste, let us see.
> Come, Liberty, come.
> All nations are waiting for thee.

Oppression's dominion is dying away—
The hind soon shall feel himself free ;
He'll stride down our glens and climb up our hills
Inspired by the spirit of thee.

The men of these isles in thy cause are aroused,
Resolved to establish thy sway.

. . . . . .

And sweep all thy en'mies away.

Oh, come thou in peace, midst the prayers of men,
On the throne of the earth sit thou queen;
Gratefully then shall our homage be paid
From cities and each village green.

The air to which the words were set was " Begone Dull
Care." When all the verses had been sung, the chorus
was repeated twice. Claud sang or said the first line solo
piano; he had less love for the music than of the senti-
ment; in the second line he was joined by one alto voice,
the third line the alto and tenor sang with him, and the
fourth line was sung by the bass only. Then there was
a pause, while Claud waved time with the poker; and as
he raised it with a jerk from the edge of the dulcimer,
which he touched, every voice burst forth *forte*. Whether
it was from the nature o' the tune, or the enthusiasm of
the singers, I cannot say, but I know it was the song of
the evening to me.

Drunken Rab Boyd, I remember, was heard once to
say, as he passed, to some neighbours who had gathered
outside to hear Claud's song, "Thae water-kelpie Radicals
are at it again. They 'll ne'er halt till they get auld William
intae trouble. I won'er she allows 't."

Claud's song begat the spirit of prophecy: " That the
steady advance of liberty could not be retarded, but was
destined to ingather all men and nations to love it, and
pray for its advent and establishment in our land." To
sing what was then considered a treasonable song might,
on occasion, be permitted, but to speak treason was out
of the question; and as extreme language was being
uttered, means had to be adopted to change the current
of thought and feeling. The hostess, therefore, hinted to

Mrs. Buchan that she might request Henry to sing—it being known that he never complied, except at her solicitation. Henry had a low, sweet voice, of no great compass; but he had exquisite taste—better than any of the others, excepting, perhaps, my mother, who, when not singing, accompanied all the singers with her dulcimer.

As Henry's ditty is peculiar and not generally known, I will here give it in full :—

> If you mean to set sail to the land of delight,
> And in wedlock's soft hammock you'd swing every night ;
> If you wish that successful your voyage may prove,
> Fill your sails with affection, your cabins with love.
>
> Let your hearts, like the mainmast, be always upright ;
> Let the vows you have taken, like your union, be tight;
> Of the shoals of indifference be sure you keep clear,
> And the quicksands of jealousy never come near.
>
> If vapours and whims like sea-sickness prevail,
> Then spread all your canvas to catch the fresh gale ;
> But if brisk blows the blast, and there comes a rough sea,
> Then lower your topsails and scud under lee.
>
> If, as husbands, you mean to live peaceable lives,
> Keep the reckoning yourselves—give the helm to your wives ;
> The nearer we steer, boys, the closer we sail,
> For on shipboard the head is still ruled by the tail.

Before the faint echoes of Henry's voice from the tin covers on the walls died away, there was heard a sharp "bark o' a horse" in the dormitory, at which mother compressed her lips, and her face grew pale ; Peggy Downie threw her hands over her ears, and several voices groaned audibly "croup." Somewhat of a turmoil ensued ; the fire was "broken up" to provide hot water; a tub was substituted for the table with its dulcimer; flannels were spread to harden and warm, while Peggy ran upstairs, where she was heard talking soothingly. Then we heard her coming down with the child in arms, who laughed and leaped as Peggy bargained with the universal "John Smith" about "shooing this horse o' mine." Willing hands were busily employed with such means as were considered necessary to ward off, or at least to moderate, the anticipated attack; and in a while the little one was in mother's lap, returning her caress, and in the fulness of delight closed her eyes as if to sleep, whilst mother crooned in her ears as mothers only know how to do. Holding the pet closer to her breast, and still singing, she rose and paced the floor. Then Peggy, as she followed, gave words to the tune; then another, and another, and another joined, till every one lent their aid in singing that beautiful secular hymn of Burns, beginning with—

> "Thou lingering star whose lessening ray
> Delights to greet the early morn."

The child was asleep before the song was finished, and Peggy, who knew "mistress'" ways, had prepared mother's bed in the "ben-en" for the child. Father, laying his hand on my head, said, "I'll be thy bedfellow for a nicht." Then came the benediction—but without the usual dismission hymn—and then the parting kiss of brotherly love; and our grand Martinmas company separated, some with moist eyes, in remembrance of little cribs that were empty from croup or other less distressing complaint.

CHAPTER XIII

THE little one did not die of croup till three years after the attack referred to in the preceding chapter; but "Thou lingering star," then sung with such despondency, was the dirge of our annual dinner parties, and of much pleasant intercourse on intervening occasions.

Twenty years after the child's death, I visited the mother one day, and found her enjoying herself weeping. When I asked the cause of her grief, she answered me, smiling pitifully—"There was a wee lassie-bairn looked in through the window short syne that mindet me o' my Jeanie that's awa'."

"Surely it is wrong," I said, "to nurse grief in that way for such a long time?"

"Maybe it is," she replied, smiling and sighing, "but thoo sees, the sluices o' my tears rustet up whan I was young, an' ay sin' syne I hae had unco little control owre them."

In order to lift her above herself for a time by a change of subject, I asked, "How was it that your social tea-meetings and Martinmas dinners were all broken off so abruptly?"

"Weel! there waur mae causes than ane; first o' a'—an' little as thoo wud think it—Hugh Hart cuist the first fire-brand amang us."

My experience of the Rev. Hugh Hart was not extensive;

but when I was a "growin' laddie," and could steal a visit
to hear some of his extraordinary utterances I did so,
and enjoyed them very much. His evening services were
attended by crowds of young people, who went to *make*
mirth.   I can recall only one evening sermon I heard from
him, which he delivered amidst much talking and laughing.
There was more decorum with his morning audiences. His
subject on that occasion was the seed falling where "it had
no depth of earth." He illustrated the conduct of those
who are religious by "fits and starts," in going from one
side to the other of the pulpit, and saying, "I'll away to
George Caldwell's, the bookseller, and buy a New Testament." As he returned to the desk, he took a book from
under his arm, and opening it read a passage or two; interrupting himself several times by pronouncing it "magnificent," "glorious," "very grand," "really very good," "very
good," "real good;" and yawning, as if wearied, finished
with "no amiss." Then after turning over the leaves in a
listless way and closing the book, he laid it down behind
him. Standing in silence a few moments, facing the audience and pointing a thumb to where it lay, he exclaimed in
stentorian voice, "And there it lies till you could write
damnation with the stour that has gathered on its boards.
There's plenty of damned dust, but no depth of earth."

A friend who heard the sermon in question says that Mr.
Hart modulated his voice to express the different degrees of
excellence conveyed by the words, but I cannot recall that
feature.

He was brightest on Communion days; and as I was not
trained to be unduly impressed with solemnity for such
occasions, this suited my mood better than ordinary preach-

ings. One morning when I was present he selected the
words, "Come unto me all ye that labour, are weary, and
heavy laden," &c., and his opening words were, "I am
going to fence the tables;" and he hoped that intending
communicants would proceed at once to their proper seats
while they sung a portion of a Psalm. After waiting a few
minutes, he repeated the text—the words "I will give you
rest" were said again and again. Then he proceeded by
saying, "That's the condition of fitness to sit down here,
and I dare not adopt any other standard. Some of you
may be an inch or inch-and-half too short for this standard,
and some of you too tall, and if I wanted uniformity I could
not get it. Let the tall come in their stocking-soles, and
the wee anes on their *tiptaes*, if they are wanting rest; but
come, come all such. Do you believe? come! Do you
doubt? come! Are any of you unbelievers? come!—in
God's name, come! if you want rest—*that's the ticket!*" I
had never before heard of "fencing the tables," and did not
understand the meaning of the words, but I felt sure at the
time that Mr. Hart had picked up "the ticket" from boys
on the street. I went out with those who had sat at the
first table, and was intensely amused at hearing him address
them as he leaned over the pulpit, the thumb of his left
hand introverted behind his ear. He said, "If any of you
need a refreshment, you can get it good and reasonable
over the way at Brother Whyte's."

"Brother Whyte," I may as well note, was Malcolm, or
Maycom Whyte, who kept a sma' public, that last resource of
the lazy and infirm—in a thatched house at bottom of New
Street. He had lost his position as church officer by "ad-
hering" to Hart's church, and much of his business as

"sawly" also.   Many may remember seeing the squat
little man, with his long white hair and splay feet, marching
in advance of genteel corpses to the graveyard.   He was
king and fugleman of the guild of sawlys; he whistled time
to them on the straight, and beat time to them with his
forefingers when rounding corners, whispering mildly the
while, "Steady, keep step, but keep dressed;" and when
the turn was performed to his satisfaction he drew a long,
long breath, and was wont to exclaim in low tones, "Ad-
mir-ably done, gentle-men."

"How," I asked, "did Hugh Hart affect you? he did not
belong to your circle."

"Thoo sees, he was toon-born, an', like the lave o' his
family, a weaver; but he had a won'erfu' gift o' ta'kin', an'
whan a laddie, he used to keep the neebors aff work at
meal times expoundin' the Word.   Than he listet during the
aul' war, an' got promoted tae be a kin' o' chaplin.   After
a while he cam' back, an' instead o' yokin' intil his wark, he
began preachin' on's ain han'; an' belyve he gathered aboot
him amaist a' the restless i' the different kirks, forbye
soberer, sedater folk, wha ye wud hae thocht naething cuda
liftet.   Amang the rest my aul', aul' freen' Sarah Troup
gaed; an' if she was lood whan un'er the Doctor, she gaed
clean wud after she joined Hughie.   Naething wad please
her till my gudeman consentet tae let Hughie pay us a
veeset, an' explain his principles.   She confesst lang aifter
that she was sure o' me.   But I kent him whan we were
young—it taks mair than ta'k tae mak' a gospel preacher;
an' he had nae boddom—naething but a jingle o' bonny
words; although, I'm free tae confess, he had a gude deal
o' cleverness.   Accordingly he cam'.   I had taul' Henry

Buchan an' my brither William tae step oot on the nicht
set apart. William taul' Claud Wilson, an' he took a pair
o' breeks tae jam tae An'rew Cochran, an' gied him a hint.
They a' cam', an' mae, for there wur a roon dizen a'thegither.
It was a lood, lood nicht; for Hughie had a perfect spate o'
words at his tongue-en', an' some o' the ithers werena far
short o' him. Hughie made nae progress wi' them though;
but ithers that werena present had gaen an' heard him preach
—which I fan' nae fau't wi', for I'd gie the liberty I took;
but than they introduct Hughie's views in their exhortations
at worship, an' that caused dispeace."

"What was he?—a Methodist?"

"Yes—whiles—he was a' things in coorse. He was
Wesley at ae time, an' John Calvin at anither. Whiles
he .praised the Pope sae, that ye'd think he was bun' for
Room, an' neist time ye met him he was haun'-and-glove
wi' Ralph Wardlaw. Hughie's was a fleeing bab. He
was ae thing in the pu'pit, an' anither thing oot o 't. An'
sae he lost respec' frae douce, weel-meanin' folk, wha gaed
back tae their aul' connection, bringin' wi' them mixy-
maxy notions that wur the cause o' unkent o' heart-burnin'.

"Than death came amang us, takin' the ripe ears an'
the green blades alike, lea'in' us sober-mindit an' sabbin',
whiles, for them that had gotten the battle owre.

"Than emegration tae the colonies set in', makin' us
wush that *we* wur gawn tae, or that they'd come back, an'
as time gaed by an' letters gat scarcer, some gat sourt at
things and wadna gie the preveledges they claimed; an'
frae less tae mair God-fearin' men, whas views had changt,
wur luiket doon on and keepet ootside; and ony word they
spak' was weight an' mezzurt, an' because they differt they

wur denyt fellowship. But there wur ithers whas views didna change—kin'ly folks they were, that cudna an' wudna think harshly o' gude men that differt frae them—an' *they* gat little rest or peace, because o' their charity. Them an' ithers, in anes an' twas, drapit frae amang us, till naething was left but the hard hools o' grain, an' a' the nourishment we gat on First Days was like the lees o' soor wine.

"Oh, dear, oh, dear; what a change it was frae bygane times, when ilka ane's duty an' pleesure was in geein' service tae the needfu', or takin' o'ersicht o' the errin'; whan the sorrow o' ane spread, like God's love, an' was the sorrow o' a'. Sae it was that oor circle brak' up, an' britherliness was displaced wi' wranglin's anent maitters that shud hae been borne wi'. An' till the hert is touched by the live coal frae the altar, an' the pride o' knowledge is whar love shud rule, sae, I fear me, it will be. For pride glories in the shortcomin' o' ithers, in word as weel as in deed, whan love 'ud raither wink at what it canna men'."

My wish had been to raise the mind of the gentle, old dame above her sorrow, and I now felt vexed that my question had failed of its mark. For if she dropped a tear or two in remembrance of her child, floods showered from her eyes for the dispersion of those with whom she took sweet counsel till the mid-day of her life. I had therefore to address another side of her mind, which I did in silence, simply by rising to take my leave; for I knew of old how unwilling she was that any one should leave her threshold without partaking of her hospitality. When she perceived the movement, her tears were soon dried up; and with her old imperative but kindly command she said—"Bide still awee, an' break bread wi' us 'or ye gang;"

and in an incredibly short time tea was provided. And as we lingered over that pleasant meal, and till "far on i' the nicht," as she remarked at parting, the stream of old stories flowed from her as naturally and as soft as dew falls in an autumn gloaming.

Grief for the "dispersion" did not affect me, nor any of the youngsters, who continued to hob-nob as if no dissension existed. Indeed life went on in our house in the old grooves ; and except on rare occasions, when one or two old friends met accidentally, and were pressed to wait tea, there was no manifestation of sorrow by our elders. But I was old enough to perceive there was something amiss, for, besides long-drawn sighs, there were fewer fervid inquiries after the health of the absent, and little quotation from the Bible, and corroborating passages were not forthcoming. No husbands came to bring their wives home ; the pleasant thee-thoo-ings were gone, and the visits, which were stiff and formal, of shorter duration ; and for a day or two after there was unwonted quiet, silence, and gloom. Sometimes mother shewed marks of recent weeping, which made us all unhappy till we saw her smile again. And so, I believe, it was in other homes.

Common, plain, uneventful lives, reader ? Yes, and, perhaps, interesting to one like me only, that loved them. Yet, of such-like lives and people, I think, the backbone of society properly so called is formed ; and measured by the silent influence they exercise over the communities in which they reside, are of more importance to the State than lives that obtrude themselves in high places to the national gaze. Be that as it may, however, as I ripened in years I renewed our friendship on more equal grounds, which

o

continued till they died or left the country, and with several
of the latter I corresponded.

I can recollect only once that anything approaching the
old freedom and harmony became apparent. It was when
a letter from James M'Lean, in Nova Scotia, had been
received. Some of the "dispersed" were known to be
interested in James's Christian labours in that province,
and were invited to hear his report; but in order to secure
harmony, and if possible cement broken friendship, there
was a selection of the kindliest natures from both camps.

We are apt to consider all those who entertain narrow
or exclusive opinions—particularly on religious subjects—
to be narrow-minded and bigoted, and those holding
liberal views as liberal and broad. Such was not the
opinion of the authority I follow, whose words were,
"Thoo sees there's creeds that are sae worm-eaten they
winna haud thegether, that's hel' on tae by men o' mercifu'
min' an' o' great liberality; an' there's great truths that's
everlastin', mainteent by men whas min's are nae braider
than a thoom-naiL."

The company on the occasion referred to had much of
the old spirit and verve till they were about to separate.
What caused the change I never could ascertain. When
the usual parting hour struck, my father opened the hymn-
book and read over the dismissal hymn. There was a
faltering of voices noticeable during the singing of the
first line, but more so on the second, and which increased
on the third. No one attempted the fourth lin: all were
in tears. Father laid down the book, and, having taken
a pinch of snuff, and beginning the benediction, sobbed
out, "The Lord bless us, and "——— and, stopping, put

his hands on his face. Thomas Taylor added, with a deep sigh—"and pity us." "Awmen" and "Amen" followed from others. And so they separated almost in silence.

"Oh dear, oh dear, what a change it was frae bygane times!"

I was too young to remember James M'Lean when he left this country, early in the century; and he somehow assumed a position in my mind akin to that of Paul and other mythical characters named in Holy Writ. He was a thorn in my side now and then, nevertheless; for on the Sundays following the receipt of his letters, it was the custom for every one to remain and hear them read, which was done amidst the grunted approval of the old, but which deprived me of my interval.

In looking over his lucubrations, I find them to consist chiefly of strings of passages from Scripture, as if in imitation of the Epistle to the Hebrews. Perhaps it was on account of that feature in his letters that he was esteemed an apostle, and his long, rambling repetitions as of equal value and importance to the writings of the Apostle to the Gentiles. It was looked upon as a sort of high treason in us youngsters to shew dislike or impatience to his hair-splitting definitions; and many long years had to elapse before I dared to ask for the particulars of his character; certain parodies of his style which I had produced having made me suspected of wishing to make sport of him. Once, when I brought my authority into the proper mood, and inquired: "I'll tell thee," was the reply; and having taken "a note of it" at the time, I am enabled to repeat the information I received in the exact words. But I will withhold a few "thoo sees" and "accordinglys," with which my informant's narrative was interlarded.

"Thoo sees, James M'Lean was a stranger to the place,
an' at first was luiket doon on as an incomer; an' as the
sough was against oor connection i' thae days, he cam'
whiles tae the meetings. An' belyve he connecket himself;
an' aifter a wee he took up wi' and mairret a dochter o'
Andrew Tennant an' Jean Lock, a young wutless gypsey,
that wadna bide in-doors, but ran awa wi' her aul' onmarret
cronies i' the simmer's gloamin's, skelpin' thro Craigielee wuds; and slidin' amang the curlers on Mucklerigg's
dam, whan the frost hel'; lea'in' Jamie tae manage the
hoose an' bairn as he best cud. Thoo kens that cudna
last lang; an' it was thocht an' said that if a change didna
come, there wad hae tae be interference, an' a seperation,
maybe; for baith o' them were members. We a' liket an'
pitied Jamie, the mair sae that he ne'er compleent. Mae
bairns cam' in coorse, and still she neglecket her duty. An'
than Jamie was Hielan', an' Hielan' fingars are a' thooms
amang fine yarn; an' he cudna speed his wark tae mak' the
twa ens meet, an' the connection had tae len' help. Nae
thochty man cud pit up wi' sic neglegence in the midst o'
poverty, the mair sae when twa or three young bairns were
cuisten on's care. But he bore lang wi' her, for he was a
douce, discreet chiel, and wyss for his years. But he took
the sturdies at length, and locket the door, tryin' tae keep
her in; an', failin' in that, he locket her oot. Nae doot he
remonstrated wi' her lang afore that, but that pit the cap-
stane on 't, for Jean wi' her lang tongue spread the scandal,
to the sair grief o' the connection. She wasna content to
rule her ain hoose, but insisted on managin' James; an' sae
her temper was roos't when her dochter gaed hame wantin'
a nicht's lo'gins; and sae she jumpit awa, hauf-naket, wi'

Mrs. M'Lean, an' fell foul o' Jamie on's ain floor heid. But my certie she didna bide lang there; Jamie wasna, like Andrew Tennant, tae be coo't wi' a word. His temper was as het as Jean's, and frae lood words cam' a dunt frae her on his back. Flesh an' bluid cudna stan' that, at least Jamie thocht sae, for he whamlt her across his knee and brocht the tawse owre her, and than he led her outside the door, daurin' her ever tae darken his hallan again. Than he shook the strap in his gypsey's face, wha was the cause o' a' the shangy, and taul' her in his broken English what waited her gif she didna behave. It did *her* gude; an' if Jean had been prudent, Jamie micht hae been amang us yet; but she behooved tae bring the maitter before the church. But they wyssly taul' her it was a domestic affair that concernt James an' his wife, an' till they compleent the church wadna interfere. After twa three rippets Jean cam' the length o' sayin' she 'ud be content if Jamie wud own a faut; an' Jamie, kenin' he had the sympathy o' a' the brethren, raise in his seat, an', takin' his wife's hawn in his, said he was vext—vext that he hadna doon't langsyne, for that noo he had as gude a wife as e'er trod heather—which was a gae big word. I was sittin' aff an' on wi' Jean that day, an' when Jamie raise I touch't her airm to devert her attention, for I thocht he wadna be sorry tae see her dementet; an' I taul' her I wantit tae speak wi' her ootside. But na, she shook me aff wi' a gowl, an' wi' an onscriptural tongue mad' sic a din that ane an' a' gied awa', lea'in' her flytin' like a fishwife. 'Mids the meantime Jamie cudna keep his heed aboon the water, an' had tae be helpit; an' week aifter week Jean brocht foret the family fash. Had it no been that wyss coonsels rull't she wad hae broken the

connection a'thegither.   Hoosomever, Jamie an' his wife
aye gree't aifter he sortet her mother.   The young hizzy
wasna withoot wut, for she was the first tae see that his duty
wasna cast amang silk yarn, an' advised him tae lea' the
loom; she had been a weaver afore marriage, an' was a
judge o' what cud be done.   Like the lave o' the connection, Jamie was a reformer, an' was aye craikin' aboot the
kintry being dune, an' aboot new lan's lyin' waste for want
o' tillage; it's been a weary cry tae me, first an' last.
Accordingly, whan my gudeman gat wittins o' him seekin'
for laborer wark, he proposed that he micht dae better tae
emigrate, at which Jamie jumpit.   Sae, instead o' a weekly
help, he gat as muckle an' mair than tak' them a' ayont the
sea.   But the best o't a' was, that he pay't every plack the
kirk had gien him.   First cam' promises an' then the siller;
but it took him years.

"Jamie was a real gude, quait, weel-inform't man; 'deed
an' 'twerna that he was a wee narrow an' positive, I ne'er
kent a better.   It's a gude thing that sic like as him haena
the keys o' the kingdom in their keepin'."

CHAPTER XIV.

I HAVE already spoken of my friendship with these old worthies, some of whom I loved better than I did others, and valued for various reasons. Claud Wilson, for example, and his wife, to whom I have so often referred, I loved because they were so truly human —they appeared to have been good at starting—being of that righteous class "who need no repentance."

Henry Buchan, again, was good by self-denial and consequent spiritual acquirement. His *aim* was to *become* better. Unobtrusive and singularly humble, he was the finest example of what a man may become by self-compulsion I have ever met with.

There was another for whom my affection, not unmixed with pity, was accidentally renewed in after years, to whom I will devote a few words before alluding to Buchan, whose company I frequently enjoyed till his "last day."

I had occasion to visit several towns and villages round our locality, in 1847, seeking tambour-workers; and one day I went to Dumbarton, where I had learned some such resided. After making a few fruitless calls, I tapped twice at a door to which I had been directed, and, not getting a response, took the liberty to lift the latch and go in. The passage and surroundings, I had observed, were much out of repair, and in miserable condition in regard to cleanliness; so much so, indeed, that I was astonished to find the house and its inmates, not clean only and comfortable-looking, but with an air of respectability and elegance even. The floor was carpeted, and every piece of furniture, from the fire-irons to the eight-day clock, appeared is if newly cleaned, they shone so brightly. At each end of the tambour-frame a woman sat at work. At the opposite side of the apartment was a small round table, on which lay an open Bible, which an old man was reading; only one of the women looked up; but the old man rose, and politely beckoned me to a chair. I forgot my business for a few moments, so surprised was I to find he was my old Bible preceptor, Thomas Jardine. After arranging what I had gone for—during which he stood in silence—I arose to take my leave, and turning to him, said—

"You have forgotten me, I think."

"Forgot you? Yes, sir. Who are you?"

I told him.

"Why—no, sir; I don't remember you."

"I was a drawboy to Sandy Reid, long ago."

"Sandy Reid—Sandy Reid. Oh, demit! *you* are not the bridler, and—and—the reader, you know?"

"I was both at one time."

"Oh, bless my soul! Kate, my dear, bring my bottle;" and patting me on the back while that old dame rearranged the round table, he whispered—"You will read me just a little bit of the Book? Kate there and Grace know all about you and your readings. Never thought of seeing you again, and I am proud to take your hand;" and dashing away a tear that fell on his cheek, he added, "Oh, demit!"

The sister called Grace, who was very deaf, did not partake of the venerable old Scottish repast of theology, whisky, and love that followed ; but Kate sat down beside us, and was pleased, I thought, to assist Thomas to tell the story of their early love—a subject on which I could see they were fond to dwell, and which I may repeat in a very few words.

They had plighted troth early in life ; but one was wise because one was foolish ; for Kate declined to ratify her vow till Thomas gave evidence of amendment ; and he, failing to do so, felt disgraced in the small community, and enlisted in the King's service. With the old canker gnawing at him, he paid her suit on his discharge, and being again refused, he could not remain where she lived, but came to our locality, where he remained till time and wisdom taught him she was right from the first. "It took forty years to teach me how wise Kate is," he said. When he was approaching threescore and ten he returned to his native lair, and laid in her lap the savings of his life—his pension being more than sufficient for all his wants.

" He disna drink noo, only on pension day," Kate said, " an' on times whan he meets aul' freens."

" I drink in this house only, and am never tipsy—keep my bottle here—gives me a reason for calling on Kate, you know."

" He was a braw, strappin' young man," she said, " afore he gaed a-sodgerin' ; an' had he keepit frae that fearfu' drink, I wad hae been happy wi' him."

When we rose to leave she turned up her withered cheek, and he kissed her like a child.

One fine trait of her character he mentioned on our way

down the street. The money he gave her she would accept on one condition—namely, that he would place it at bank in both their names.

" She 's an angel, sir," were his last words to me.

Thomas outlived her two years, so that there was wisdom shewn in the condition she insisted on in regard to the money he had saved.

Henry Buchan remained at home, as I have indicated, sneered at by those who did not understand him, and snubbed by that select class who never die out, that have sounded the deepest depth of the unfathomable and know all the truth of God. What other treatment could he expect? *He* only desired knowledge and wisdom; his highest aim was to grow in goodness ; he did not believe that any final goal in these was attainable in this or the other world. But he heeded not the taunts and doubts of his sanity, but pursued the path he saw ; and " when reviled he answered not again." He ripened as fruit ripens, becoming softer, mellower, and sweeter as he drew near the gathering-time.

When I heard of Henry's illness, I went to learn its nature and extent, and found Mrs. Buchan in the passage outside the door, speaking sharply to a visitor—one of the old exclusives. I heard only part of her words ; but the attitude she had assumed, and the scorn she threw into her voice, were recalled to my mind afterwards at such times as I saw Lady Macbeth personated.

" Na, na," were the words I first heard. " He 's ayont, as he 's aye been, onything ye cud say : he 's died tae a' on this side. What 's the use o' prayers whan the books are clos't an' claspit ? Div ye think *ye* can change the will an' ways o' God ? Gae wa', and pay mair heed tae His preceps an' less tae His decrees, an' it 'll fare better wi' you whan *your* 'oor comes."

"Then Henry is dead," I thought, and was moving away when she signed for me to enter; which I did, she following. I found the old man recovered from a "dwaum," which she had, perhaps, mistaken for the approach of the last summons. He stretched forth a hand, which she took tenderly in hers, and said, "O Lily, Lily, there's nae sic temper i' the kingdom as thoo spak' wi' enoo; an' we'se ne'er meet an' thoo dinna cast it frae thee. It's a' true thoo said; but oh! what's the yuse o' truth if it disna bring sweetness wi't. It wasna like thysel'." And turning his eyes to where I stood, he said, "Come back i' the afternoon or the morn's mornin'; I want tae say a word tae thee. I 'll be tae the fore here for a day or twa yet."

I called towards evening as desired, but as he was asleep I did not enter. Next day I found him propped up in bed, the Book on his knees, surrounded by other books he loved. He asked how I was? how I was getting on? and what my prospects were? To me, as to the young generally, the world appeared rose-coloured, and I answered like one full of hope and of thankfulness. His calm, slow reply brought me up somewhat sharply, however—

"It wud be an ill hert, indeed, 'at wadna be thankfu' whan a' things gang smoothly in the stream o' its likin'. But it's different whan the tide turns, an' we're tosst in a gait we dinna want, un'er a mirk lift, whan a' oor fair-wather freens turn their back on us. It's than, I trow, we learn hoo brittle oor faith is. We think, mayna God himsel' hae left us, seeing that God's folk gi'e us the caul' shuther! Eh! it's a tryin' 'oor—an 'oor that comes tae ane an' a' that's faithfu' tae God an' themsel's; whan, for dear life, we maun stan' an' fecht for the richt against the wrang—an 'oor, if it needs come a secont time, fin's us less able, 'cause less willin' tae thole the brunt o' conflic'. Blessed for evermore are they wha hae pairt i' the first resurrection frae the deth o' sin.

> When raised by Him, how changed thy state !
> A garden rich in fruit and flower,
> Thy mind the Lord's beloved retreat ;
> The wonder of redeeming power.

" I want thee tae accep' twa books frae me; an' I wuss thee tae lay them by till trouble comes—they're no' just fittin' folk that's happy an' prosperous; but if e'er thoo gets a backset in worl'ly things, or hae ony misgi'ein's anent God's truth or his dealin's wi' thee, thoo will fin' that there's comfort tae be had frae them that's no' i' the boon's o' ony creed." He then handed to me, as tenderly as if they were little children, *Law's Appeal*—a rare book and of rare value—and *Swedenborg's Doctrine of Life*, less rare yet far more valuable—both well thumbed and annotated.

Of his gentle, yet courageous honesty I had repeated examples before the end. When it became generally known that he was laid down in his last lassitude, as was supposed—he had been subject to attacks of painless lassitude for nearly a year—one of his old religious antagonists, prompted, I do believe, with a sincere desire to do him good, called on him when I was present, and inquired after his health; and Henry having told him he was getting " near the close," he said—

" I houp thoo has gotten a' things settled to thy satisfaction ?"

"Ou ay; I think I hae. I hae left a' oor gatherin's tae Lily there, wha had mair fash in hainin' against this time than I had; an' I know she'll deal richteously wi' the bairns an' their families."

"It wasna aboot what thoo's lea'in I was ettlin' at, but what thoo's gawn ayont tae. Has thoo settled thy peace wi' God, Henry?"

"No, Archy, no; it comes an' gangs wi' me; there can be nae settled peace till the battle's owre. The Lord'll fin' mine a ravelt hasp; it was sairly disordered, I whiles think, or it cam' my length; but he has the hank in 's ain haun, an' maun dae wi' me as it pleases himsel'. I'll be content wi' 'is verdic'."

"Archy" did not make any headway with him, and after one or two failures on other points he went his way. Henry then beckoned on Lily, to whom he said, "In ony deefeculty thoo has, Archy will be ready tae help; we hae differ'd a' ooi days, him an' me, but he's a good man, an' means weel."

On another visit I paid him about the same time, there was one of the leading men belonging to the church popularly known as the "Royals" went in with me, to whom Henry held out his hand, and with a smile and meek earnestness said—"We maun say gude-bye for awee, for my time's lapsin'. If thoo has anything thoo wud like me tae say tae thy Mirren, that's gane afore, I'll be glad to be the bearer o't. I think we'll meet; we were lang neebors, an' aye gree't." It appeared that theretofore the visitor had thought this, that, and other things about the bearings of the future, but never till that day really *believed* what he professed. Under the smooth surface of his easy life and dilapidated creed, there ran a strong current of negation, which till then had never been disturbed; and when his lost wife was spoken of so confidently, yet so earnestly, as living, he stood awe-struck, mute, as if petrified. The silence that followed, and the peculiar sacredness of his position, became so painful to me, that I rose and left the two friends together.

Shortly after I emerged from Henry's entry I met Mrs. Thomson on her way to relieve Lily during the night-watch. When she learned who was with him, the afternoon being mild, she proposed walking into the country for an hour; and as I always enjoyed her talk, we passed into the fields, and towards the hills in silence, till we came to a fallen tree that had served travellers as a seat for years, where we sat down. Taking the knitting-wires from her pocket, she said, "So ye veesit Henry whiles?" and she was pleased to hear he had given me two of his favourite books.

"Do ye ken that every door but mine and Margaret Cochran's hae been closed against him for years by-past?"

"I knew he had been avoided; but I was not aware he was so cruelly treated. I think he is a quiet, good man."

"Gude! had ye kent him as weel as I dae, ae word wudna sair'd your turn. He's ripe! ripe for the change. Nane e'er heard him compleen o' ill usage; but I hae heard him persist that they wha use him warst are gude men—better than himsel'. God forgie them! they dinna shew him muckle gudeness; but it's no richt o' me tae nurse ill-will tae them, and it's no for me tae judge."

"I am glad to hear," I said, "that your door has been

open to Henry, for I heard that your husband had been somewhat severe on him short since."

"My William? He can say hard words, I ken, but he ne'er did a cruel thing. He's a saft-herted simpleton. If Henry mean that he's a gude man, I daur say he's richt."

"Come now, Mrs. Thomson, judge the other as you judge William. Margaret Cochran will say as much for Archy."

"Weel-a-weel. We'se say nae mair aboot them."

"I sat the feck o' a nicht at Henry's bedside a week syne, an' really it whiles seemt as if the gate o' the kingdom wur open tae me; he spak' in his gran', certain way anent the worl' tae come, sae that I cud hae listent tae him for lang. It was just sic anither gloamin' as this is, an' whan he took my hawn in his, an' luiket oot on the redent sky, an' said, ' In a quait 'oor like this, atween the nicht an' the day, whan the noise o' earth subsides, an' oor worl'ly thochts recede, oor better self whiles opens the windows o' the saul an' shines doon on us like the silent stars ; an' the half-for-gotten faces o' the past troup in tae renew their freen'ship, an' we gang oot o' oor present cares an' gie them welcome wi' oor young ten'erness. It's no i' the glim'ering o' memory, Kathrine, that we see them, but frae shinkles o' the gates o' pearl; an' we ken they're no deed. The promises o' the Father, the revelation o' His Word, the intuitions o' immortality, the aspirations o' oor faith, and the anthems o' hope, a' testifie that they live an' love ; an' love tae sair ; an' sair mair perfectly in that lan' wherein no nicht is, than sic like as we can do.'

"An' keepin' haud o' my hawn, he luiket oot on the gathering dark; an' turning his sweet een on me, he said wi' a smile, 'An' we, bereaved, yet no bereaved, stan' on the vera edge o' time, gazing through the rays the sun has pencilled on the sky, oor herts speerin' the auld eager questions o' oor young years, whilst imagination weaves her story of clearer licht, an' intenser beauty, an' fulness o' purer joy beyond. An' whiles, Kathrine, I dinna won'er at the stupifit seer o' Patmos fa'in doon on his face like ane deed, when the licht an' glory o' the mornin' lan' shin'd in on him.'

"Wi' ta'k like that, but in far gran'er words, he spak noo an' than a' thro' the nicht; whiles I felt sae, that though John or some ither o' the auld saunts had stepit in on us, I wadna been greatly astonished, I think."

"You ought to write," I said, "or cause William to write down some of Henry's words; they are worth preserving."

"William thinks them havers! an' my duty lies here," she answered, as she stuck her wires through the stocking; adding, "Lilly'll be expectin' me; we'se gae toonward, an' ye lik."

And we went slowly townward, Mrs. Thomson talking cheerfully the while about the "incomin' o' better times, whan good men o' differin' views wud gie owre contendin' anent niceties, an' wud see that nae ae man or body o' men cud ken everything. An' thoo may rest assur't that whan they come that length, there will be mair unity, an' maybe less uniformity; an' bearin' an' forbearin'll be mair general than ony ane can hae wittens o' at this present." When we reached the crest of the hill nearest the town, she stood, and shading her eyes from the red rays of the sun, then far in the west, she exclaimed with deep emotion, " Is'nt a pity that sic a worl' is marr't wi' contentions, an' oor lives made bitter wi' tryin' tae weave us a' tae ae pattern? Stars an' suns differ in glory, an' sae does men; an' that can never be. In my father's house are many mansions."

Then, turning to me, her eyes dancing with mirth, she said, " I whiles think that the Lord's family is like a big schule, whare every class is at a different stage o' progress."

" You think, then, every class has not reached the New Testament ? "

" Just sae; yet every ane believes that nane but himsel' an' his class has reached it. That will men' itsel' belyve tae, whan ance the love o' God tak's the place o' His truth."

" I never can divest my mind of the feeling," I said, "when you or Henry speak on these subjects, that you imply the idea of merit, or self-righteousness? "

" If thoo wud only think, thoo wudna be perplext wi' that. Luik roon thee—a' the beauty thoo sees i' the worl' come intae thy een—the e'esicht ne'er gangs oot o' the een; sae is it wi' a' oor thochts, they come intae the min frae the worl' within an' aboon us; hoo than can we lay claim tae miret? The worl' withoot an' the worl' within us baith belang to Him wha made them; an' oor vision o' min' as weel as o' body are His gifts gien us in life-rent. They seem oor ain, just as we appear tae be oor ain; but we're His nae the less, an' oor wisdom lies in confessin' sae. It's true Henry or me dinna yaumor aboot being great sinners, for we think that sichin' and sighin' aboot what we canna men' itherwise than byddin' a' back frae sin is unprofitable, an' a waste o' time." With such like talk we reached Henry's door, where we parted.

P

CHAPTER XV.

IN gossiping as I have done about the friends with whom
I was associated in early life, it must not be inferred
that I think they, or the times in which they lived, were
superior to those of the present. My aim has been simply
to chronicle certain phases and forms of thought and idiosyncracies of character that influenced, without controlling,
mine, but which have been driven to the background with
our waning industry—which developed them. Each present
is better than any past; but as everything is, from various
causes, subject to the law of growth, and society in a state
of transition always, men and things may appear better or
worse than they really are.

And judging from things as they appear, I think that
possessing, as we do, the civil rights for which our fathers
fought with tongue and pen, we exercise them with unseemly frivolity, and value them at less than their importance deserves. We have less avoidable destitution, and
deeper sympathy with the poor; but instead of giving
personal service, as of old, we give money. We have more
talent and less mind. Our manners have markedly im-
proved; whilst with increased facilities, there is less thought,
and less desire for solid information. We are more anxious
to obtain riches, yet we give more generously of what is
acquired. We have more frequently periods of religious
excitement and public devotion; but it is questionable if

our convictions are deeper or our sense of justice keener.
If the past generation did not carry their religion more into
their business life, they did not bring their worldly affairs
quite so much into the place of worship as we do. We
have indeed a marvellous increase of public piety; but there
is a widespread belief, which deepens with time, that pious
sinners and godless saints are also increasing within the
precincts of the Church, and that the shepherds display
more anxiety to gather wool than to " wear the lambs " of
the flock. Such can never be more than a large minority,
however; those earnest souls who form the majority, who
are being perfected through suffering, are not organised like
the others, but are scattered in all the Churches, from Pio
Nono to Dr. Channing, and beyond ; whose lives are a
daily sacrifice, yet who feel too unworthy and are too
humble ever to raise their voice to ask more than for-
giveness for the past, and grace for the present. Were
it not that the leading men of the minority are, in many
cases, better than they appear—better than their profession
and their creed even—one would be shocked at their outcome as it falls under observation at times.

I had long the curiosity to visit some fashionable church,
in order to compare its general aspect with what I remember
of the meeting-house of old times, and also to judge of the
pasture provided. So I made up my mind one Sunday to
go somewhere with that end in view. I managed the first
part, but not the second, which was really the more important of the two; and this is how I failed.

While walking down the street leisurely, uncertain where
to go, I was met by two gentlemen on their way to church,
and just as we passed each other, one of them said to

his friend, in a loud, surprised whisper, "Ten per cent., eh?" After walking a few paces I paused, and then I turned, and then I followed in their wake, murmuring "Ten per cent." as I went.

John, the second in command at the church I entered, knows and is known by every one; and Sunday being a field-day, he is everywhere, serving in some way all who require his attention; and so he led me to a seat, "whar ye'll see aboot yaw," he said, as if he knew my purpose in coming.

I will not attempt more than a mere cursory description of the decorations in the church, which pleased without arresting the eye at any particular point. The pews were varnished; the seats that I saw were cushioned; there were bronze gas brackets, having tastefully cut-glass globes at regular distances along the chastely-coloured walls; the large windows were rimmed with tinted glass; here and there delicately-carved pillars, having contrasting colours with touches of gilding interspersed, and upon the top of the pillars there was lily-work,—all producing an effect which is expressed by the word "harmony." And then there came from hidden recesses bright-coloured or gold-edged Bibles to almost every pew within the range of my vision. The building was altogether religious looking, and contrasted very well indeed with the purple and fine linen of the congregation, which appeared to be on exhibition for the day. But with all their gorgeousness, there was awanting the glorious smell of the bleaching-green that surrounded the women of my youth, and for which various cosmetics are bad substitutes.

How different was our old barn-like church, with its

clay floor, rough-plastered walls, patched, and grim with
dust; small windows, ornamented here and there with
deserted spider-webs, through which the sunlight could but
faintly illuminate the loving faces of the quiet, sedate
worshippers; hard, bare, narrow seats; book-boards decorated with whittlings and initials; slender tin sconces
projecting like drawn swords from the pew corners: the
contrast and improvement was very remarkable indeed.

I do not know how the two gentlemen were pleased with
the service, or if they suffered, like me, during the incarcera-
tion. I felt very much like two strangers I met lately at a
friend's house, who began talking about railways, and the
value of their respective stocks; each cried up his own
favourite line, discussing warmly and loudly in defence of
their merits. They continued the argument till we sat
down at the tea-table. Our host with difficulty obtained
silence to say grace; and the " Amen " was hardly pronounced when both were rattling away on their main
lines again. Their steam was up all the while—they had
only shunted; and during the service I was deep in the
question of " ten per cents.," and distracted with thoughts
of fortunes made and fortunes lost by reckless speculation,
and the effects on the *morale* of society by our anxiety to
" gather gear by every wile," whether justified by honesty
or not.

As regards the service, it was neither worse nor better
than such services usually are. In the short intervals I
paid attention, I noticed that a considerable change had
taken place in both sermon and prayers. In the former the
words *duty* and *service* did not occur once; and the latter
were addressed more to the audience than to God. From

the apparent absence of vital Christian *soul* in both, one might designate them *bodies* of divinity only. Throughout the whole service, so far as I could discern, the attitude of the people was one of *reception*, a seeking to be blessed—a thing altogether impossible unless there is a desire to bless, and only possible in proportion therewith. But the music was splendid.

There was one thing I noticed that did not appear a happy change. In old times the simple form of benediction began with " The Lord bless us ;" now it runs, " The Lord bless *you* "—as if saying, " All *ye* are brethren, but one is your master." The chunk of wood Andrew Cochran took to the pulpit seems to have been symbolical.

But that or any other change in mere form is less to be deplored, because of less importance, than the degeneracy visible everywhere in all churches from simplicity and earnestness. One is constantly reminded of the fraudulent bankrupt who, when passing his chief creditor on their way to church, lifted his hat, and with bland smile made a respectful bow. The creditor, it is said, was so exasperated at the audacity that he rushed up to him one day and said—

" I will rather forgive you all you owe me than be insulted week after week with your mock civility. Will you desist?"

" Sir," replied the scamp, " I would not give up the courtesies of life for ten times the amount of your claim !" and raising his hat again passed on his way.

Much of our worship is near akin to the bankrupt's civility. Were it otherwise, many things that disgrace society could not exist. But we are so persistent in our desire to be blessed, so gluttonous of so-called " divine

things," so dropsical, gouty, and debilitated in the perform-
ance of our human duties, and so oblivious to our own defects ; we act as if we were unconscious that the very air we
breathe is pestilent with the fumes of vice, and the streets
of our cities hideous with the screamings of harlots. These,
we are told, are the results of "original depravity;" they
are, I believe, the consequence of the thorough rottenness
of our mock homage to God, and of our destitution of
Christian love of the neighbour. And were churches, or
even a minority of their front-rank members, doing their
duty, we never would hear of rich Christian parents standing by smiling when their daughters are being *sold*—sold as
veritably as slaves are sold—to men steeped all over in the
infidelity of the heart, because, forsooth, they are wealthy
and stand well on 'Change ! Nothing can be more saddening than to hear of a Christian pastor mumbling his "Lord
bless you" over the head of the innocent victim, and
calling the mock ceremony "marriage."

It cannot be that such men as we are God's end in
creation ; and yet, blind to the profanity as well as to the
hollowness of our lives, we presume to feel that He stands
well-affected toward us, because we insult Him with our
mock courtesy, while neglecting the weightier matters of
justice and mercy ! It cannot be that He turns away His
face from all such—however honest and upright and loving
—as do not pay Him the weekly civility !

Would we speak truth to Him for once, confessing our
hypocrisy and utter and irretrievable bankruptcy in honesty,
He would receive us with open arms, forgive freely all we
owe Him, and thenceforward dispense with all worship,
excepting such as we give in sincerity, and which therefore

would be beneficial to us.   Without *honesty* we may, indeed,
" buy at the cheapest," but we will—in a sense we do not
think of—" sell at the dearest."   He who cheats his neighbour *hates him*, whilst he who deals justly loves his neighbour as himself.   And what is true as regards our conduct
to each other is not less so of our relations to God.

But though the heathen rage and imagine vain things, it
cannot be too often repeated that, because God rules
supreme, honesty and goodness form the majority.   And
when in unexpected nooks we meet with " God's folk," we
get glimpses behind the veil, and whiffs of true humanity.
What is, if possible, more pleasing still, such people are
quite unconscious of the goodness of which they are the
temples.   It is to be regretted that although they are the
soul and life of every church, their worth is not appreciated,
unless, as David Wilson said, they can " haun in a gowpen
o' siller."

I will here relate one of their " works " that came under
my notice some time ago, such as I believe is more gratify-
ing to God, because more useful to man, than any amount of
ostentatious, or, indeed, any merely formal piety whatever :—

I was standing at a gable, where two roads meet, reading
a gaudy, obtrusive poster, when behind me there came two
quavering female voices, asking earnestly for each other's
health and prosperity.   Both were in good health, they
said, but one of them complained of want of work; and
then she detailed the cause of her condition.   It appeared
that the firm to whom both the women worked as winders
had recently changed their foreman, and that since the
change she never had gotten a moderate share of work.
The other had had more than she got during the previous

man's reign. In proof of this I saw that under one arm she carried a whole bundle of yarn, and a bagful of bobbins under the other. These burdens were placed at her side whilst she gossiped with her friend, during which I heard—

"I'll gie you a pickle o' mine the day, if ye like?"

"Are ye shure you can spare 't: ye may no get ony the morn's mornin', ye ken?"

"Weel," was the reply, as she stopped to untie the bundle, "an' I shudna, I'll can want it. Woman! I gat a poun' note twa months syne frae my An'rew in Canawda, an' it's no broken yet; sae I can spare you a pickle, seein' I get a gude share. An'rew promises tae sen' some mair siller in twa or three months. He's been a rail comfort tae me since his faither dee't."

"My Tam in Norwitch," said the other, "sent me something tae paye my rent short syne, an' as I didna ken hoo tae gang aboot gettin't frae the bank, I speert at the laird if he'd gae wi' me. I haena had as sair a hert sin' my gudeman dee't. I hadna thocht but to gie him the siller, for it was due; but I took it unco ill that he dootet my word, an' grabit the notes on the bank counter, as gin I werena lan'-biddin'. I wud amaist raither been in debt as ta'en the affront."

By this time the yarn was divided, and the two women were on their "hunkers" counting the bobbins; and as bobbins, like boys, will go astray if not taken care of, two or three of them made their way about my feet. Of course I lent assistance for their recovery, which gave the opportunity of "improving the occasion" by examining more closely what the pair were like. They were thin, and thinly clad, poor and old, but clean; and both had that subdued look peculiar to those that have had much sorrow, yet cheerful, as those whose love has no fear.

I walked by their side with a feeling of reverence for the single-minded, unselfish woman, who was so elated that her "note wasna broken," that of her scanty, uncertain means she contributed to the need of her less fortunate sister. It was a matter of indifference to me whether the two hailed from Rome or Geneva ; they reminded me of other women I knew and loved long ago—nobodies on earth; but " of such is the kingdom of heaven."

My pleasure was marred somewhat, I confess, by the abounding charity of her who "wud amaist raither been in debt as ta'en the affront" from the "laird," who she maintained " is a vera good man—an elder !"

But charity thinketh no evil.

I must bring these old memories to a close. The "ripe ears" of the old generation have all gone home. James M'Lean and Claud Wilson were the last ; few even of the then "green blades" remain on the hither side.

If I had an artist's power I would paint the old groups, in social meeting assembled, in the moods most familiar to me—each in their own corner, each man at his natural byeplay, exchanging snuff-mulls, whispering some political grievance with knitted brows, or agreeing with mutual smiles on some knotty spiritual or ecclesiastical nicety. The women would be employed knitting and sewing, and "glancing" at the *Glasgow Chronicle;* whilst the hostess and her henchwoman Peggy—that grand type of old Scotch fidelity—are busy with some required arrangement. The sweet old dulcimer and Claud with his poker would occupy the foreground, and in the near distance would be my row of gas-retorts safely on the hob, charged and ready. That mysterious sea-chest would peep from under old Henry and his books, and the ghost-like hammer would not be wanting. I see them all now—refracted, it is true, as seen through the bars of my chair in the long ago.

And methinks I hear the sad tones of the "lingering star," which is overborne by the martial air of "Come, liberty, come;" and again it mingles pleasantly with the softer cadence of the "Land of delight." And so I will leave them in the position I love best to think of them.

The friends have settled all their differences by this time, and at last are agreed. They fret not because of heresy, and argue not because they *know.*

I confess to a difficulty, however. My old friend Sarah Troup lived on argument in this world, and I do not see how she can be happy in the kingdom without it. But then, again, how will merchants get along in the city wherein is no price list, or stockjobbers without stocks? I really do not know. But we may rest assured that whoever lived then, lives now; for life knoweth no death, and never dies. Do not let us fret or sigh, therefore, that our "dishes are small," but bend meekly and thankfully to the inevitable that awaits us also, and in the meantime strive and learn to live as beseemeth our noble destiny. And—

> " There are left behind
> Living beloveds, tender looks to bring
> And make the daylight still a happy thing,
> And tender voices to make soft the wind.
> But if it were not so—if I could find
> No love in all the world for comforting,
> Nor any path but hollowly did ring,
> Where ' dust to dust' the love from life disjoined;

And if, before these sepulchres unmoving,
I stood alone—as some forsaken lamb
Goes bleating up the moors in weary dearth,
Crying, 'Where are ye, oh my loved and loving?'
I know a voice would sound, 'I am!
Can I suffice for heaven, and not for earth?'"

I conclude in the words of an old Hebrew writer:—
"If I have done well, and as is fitting the story, it is that
which I intended; if slenderly and meanly, it is that which
I could attain unto."

JAMES' SECOND COURTSHIP.

JAMES Gillespie outlived Sarah; the following describes his second courtship, which, with slight alterations, is given in the words of his " Blackfoot."

It was on a day in August, 1834, about noon, as a grocer, then busily engaged measuring potatoes to his customers, was accosted by a voice, saying—

" Can I get a word wi' ye ?"

The grocer, recognising the voice as that of an old friend, answered promptly, but without withdrawing his head from the sack—

" Twa o' them, Jeems. This is a fine morning."

" I 'll step roun' by the Wood Road till the thrang 's owre; I 'm in nae hurry ;" and so the two parted for a time, the one remaining with his head rising and falling with full or empty wooden measure, the other sauntered towards Wood Road, his hands, burgess-like, folded behind him, and gazing vacuously. The grocer, who followed him shortly after, had the laugh-provoking faculty of looking at every subject first from its ludicrous side ; and therefore James made a mistake in seeking " a word " with him on the subject of his present visit. When they met again it was at the Wood Road well, where James was sitting taking little note, let us hope, of the young damsels that came to draw water.

And when he inquired if the grocer could recommend a God-fearing woman to fill Sarah's place, an onlooker might have seen the laugh in the grocer's dancing eyes, and heard its suppressed gurgle in his throat. James, however, was too earnest to understand anything but his own pressing need.

"I heard," said his friend, gathering his wisdom with his wind,—"I heard of Sarah's death; hoo lang is 't since she gaed tae her rest?" his aspect becoming solemn.

"It's three months syne, an' it has seemed as mony years tae me. She managed me, an' a' else for me, for many years; an' noo, at the cool o' the day, I fin' I can manage naething withoot a wife."

"I canna recommend a wife tae ye, Jeems; it's no in my line, man. I hae had nae experience, thou kens, an' no likely tae hae, for my wife's family dees only ance in a century. But (and here the laugh broke fairly out) I 'll tell thee what tae dae : gae awa' doon an' see my twin sister; tak' my love tae her, an' say I sent thee; an' if there 's a woman tae suit thee within the ring o' the bell, sis' will ken whaur she bides, an' a' aboot her."

"I had clean forgotten her," James replied with a sigh. "Whaur 's this she bides?"

"Gordon's Loan."

"Can thou tell me her nummer?"

"Nummer! there 's nae nummering o' doors in the Loan, an' nae need; naebody ever flits there,—an incomer can get a hoose there only when a family dees oot; they are a queer, dour lot that came there, it's said, before the Conquest. Gang in at the wast en', an' speer at the first ye meet; an' if he 's native-born, he 'll lead thee tae her door.

An' min' this, Jeems," taking his hand at the road-end, " I
expect tae drink the bride's health on the bottlin' nicht.
Ta, ta ;" and before sundown, the grocer had enjoyed his
laugh whilst he spread the report of Jeems's approaching
marriage,—the name of the bride, for her sake, he said, he
withheld for the time being.

When James entered the Loan by the time the sun
slanted westerly, he found his old friend, who had not seen
him since Sarah's death ; and not having heard particulars
of her illness, she was prepared for a gossip of sympathy
and condolence. James, however, had recovered from his
grief, and instead of recurring to the past, he entered at
once on the matter on hand, by detailing with provoking
accuracy the interview he had had with her brother. She felt
scandalised, indignant, and contemptuous for a moment,
and remained silent. She, like her brother, had a share of
humour ; but, unlike him, never saw things ludicrous till
after the humane or human view of them was exhausted ;
and though feeling hurt that her brother would make mirth
of his friend's confidence, she by and by indulged in a quiet
laugh at James's simplicity, which laugh made her better
disposed to lend a helping hand as " blackfoot." (To avoid
offence, I will so designate her in what follows.) So,
saying to him, " Tak' a seat for a blink, till I hae time to
consider awee," she without ceremony turned to her wheel
to work and meditate; whilst James slid into a chair, and
entered at once on his afternoon nap. " Blackfoot " had
been " best maid " to Sarah many long years before,—a
circumstance which "Jeems, honest man, had tint wittens o',"
she said to herself, as she sat a prey to indignation at the
thought of her old friend being so soon forgotten. Yet there

was a feeling of pride mixed with her grief, that she was honoured in selecting a substitute; for, to the well-ordered female mind, the honour of "blackfooting" is as great as the responsibility involved thereby. By and by the lengthening shadows of passers outside attracted her attention now and then. One slow moving figure appeared, and instantly the wheel hand was raised, and its forefinger bent; "Blackfoot" exclaiming, under her breath, "A Providence,"—a phrase, by the way, quite unknown to "blackfoots" of first marriages. Then followed in the entry a low-voiced whispering, varied with a louder expostulation, and a cheery "Hout-tout; at six o'clock, min'."

There was a blithe look on "Blackfoot's" face as she laid her hand gently on James's shoulder, and said—

"I hae inveetit a freen' tae drink tea wi' me this afternoon, wha I think will suit you. She ne'er was married; a kindly woman, an' weel gathered forbye. I kenna that she has gotten what thou ca's God's grace, but she is gentle and sweet-tempered, which is whiles mista'en for grace, they look sae like ither. She's weel on for five-an'-forty; sae keep your min' easy. I think I hae sortit ye bravely."

Then there were questionings about her "forbears," her principles, and her kirk connections,—things unthought of in exuberant youth, into which I need not enter farther than to say that all were highly satisfactory. "Blackfoot," after trimming the fire, making certain preparations, and redding-up generally, turned to her wheel, chatting cheerily the while. James, on whose mind began to dawn the importance of the coming ordeal, which mingled uncomfortably with his early experience and buried hopes, paced round the apartment with irregular motions, after the manner of a caged redbreast. "Blackfoot" enjoyed his perturbation, and coined jokes for future use, as her custom was.

As the orthodox tea-hour of six tolled sonorously from the High Church bell, Miss Nancy Watson put in her appearance,—shyly, as became an unsought and somewhat hopeless spinster; for, let people say what they please, when one reaches "five-and-forty," and oils are used to conceal the silver of the hair, there is a fearful predominance of blanks in the marriage-lottery, and "hope's blest dominion" narrows amazingly. Nanny's one pleasant memory on the subject of marriage, of which in her innocence she spoke proudly, was this:—her twin-sister, many, many years before, was engaged to be married, and her betrothed, on one occasion, had bestowed a kiss on Nanny in mistake. It was the day of days in her life's calendar. She, therefore, like "Blackfoot," regarded the present opening as "a providence."

Being a memorable occasion, the best china were forthcoming at tea-time, which did not assist to allay the constraint experienced by the two guests; but "Blackfoot" had gone through the same mill in olden times, and knew when to mix in the chat she guided; never intrusive, she made them feel at home with each other. Conversation, or, more properly speaking, talk, depended almost wholly on "Blackfoot" during tea-time; and what with Nanny's maidenly reserve, James's eagerness to please, and his dread of failure, she felt in a rather awkward position. Even after that social repast was over, James sat innocently, but silently, balancing his teaspoon on his empty cup, till she told him to "lowse the table," which he did by canting his

Q

grace (end for end) into a thanksgiving. "Blackfoot" having swept the hearth anew, the young wanters turned fireward, placed their feet on the fender, and entered on the business of the evening by discussing the principles of the Associate body. "Blackfoot," not belonging to that communion, felt less interest in that subject than in wiping and stowing away her china; besides, she had had her innings, and to avoid being a mar-joy absented herself to the cupboard in the ben-end oftener than was absolutely necessary. Meanwhile, she watched and noted the progress of matters observantly; and it was with feelings somewhat mixed with pleasure and gruesomeness that on one of her return voyages she saw James lift Nanny's right hand from her lap and place it on his own knee. She managed, by drawing a long breath, which was half-laugh, half-sob, to control her voice till she was beyond earshot, when she nodded to her image in the mirror, and said—

"If Sarah could look in on the pair, I'd rather no be in Nanny's shoon."

By and by she absented herself occasionally to speak a word to a passing friend, or to gather vegetables for the morrow's broth, so that time passed pleasantly for some hours. Gas, which had reached the Loan for a wonder, was lit; which being observed by James as an excellent improvement, Nanny hinted her wish to go home, whereupon gallant James, aged sixty-seven, offered her his convoy, which was accepted, "Blackfoot" smiling approvingly. And so the kidgy pair passed out, hand in hand, lovingly,— so lovingly, indeed, did they appear to "Blackfoot," that she "turned the key i' the door," and followed in the shade, at a distance. She nearly lost breath, however,

when she saw them pass Nanny's door; and concluded
that they meant more than they wished her to know. They
went on till they reached Canal Street, and having passed
" Timmer-taes' " public, and keeping the north side, she
knew that Lucky Barr's was their destined houf. Mrs.
Barr kept a sma' public in the bottom tenement of Storie
Street; and there they entered. In the meantime, " Blackfoot" had planted herself at the opposite corner in the
shade, and the question arose in her mind, " What must
be my next step to make certainty more sure?" Drawing
breath for a minute, while she walked slowly up, the shim-
mer of Lucky Barr's fire shining in the entry offered her
what she wanted. Crossing over the street, she looked in,
saying,—

" Hoo's a' the nicht, Catherine?"

" Is that thee? Come ben, an' lean down a wee."

" Na, I maunna bide, I'm gaun up tae speir for Peggy
Minto's bairn."

"Thou maunna gang up, it's fa'en asleep, and a' depends
on rest; come ben."

" Na, I maun gae. Has thou company?"

Going into the large cozy kitchen, without answering in
words, Mrs. Barr pointed to a wood hole in her room door,
whereunto " Blackfoot," nothing loth, applied an eye; but
starting back, instantly she exclaimed,—

" Wha's that, Catherine, sae loving-like, shaking hauns?"

" Shaking hauns! said ye, an' the dram no in?"

" I dinna ken ; dram or no dram, that's a bargain, I'se
warrant thee." Taking another peep, " Eh ! it *is* a bargain,
they are nifferin' slippers. It's a gude auld custom, as may
be seen in Ruth iv. 7. Gude nicht." Mrs. Barr stood

dumfoundered with the big-bellied bottle and pewter measure in her hands.

And so after three Sundays, when the cries were out, our friend Nanny Watson closed her spinster life, and became Mrs. James Gillespie.

As a hint to such as, in their old age, are in quest of a second helpmeet, and as an encouragement to those having the honour of being "blackfoot," I may add that, when a year and a day of James and Nanny's married life had passed, that pair of old turtle-doves wended their way to the domicile of their "blackfoot" with a thank-offering for the wonderful amount of discrimination and knowledge o' human nature she had displayed in terminating their isolation.   James said he was "dreadfully pleased," as was also Nanny.   And so James Gillespie and Nanny his wife pass away from history.

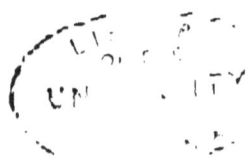